AFTERWORLD
WHEN GHOSTS DISAPPEAR

BY
CLAUDE LIMBERGER

A book by Pug Enterprises Inc.

Afterworld – When Ghosts Disappear

Published by Pug Enterprises Inc.
1060 Stacey Crt. Mississauga, Ontario Canada L4W 2X8

ISBN 0-9681387-0-5

First Edition December 1996

Printed for Pug Enterprises Inc. by Best Book Manufacturers

Cover Design by Frank Gal

Cover Illustration by Chris Stevenson

Author Photograph by Afsaneh Forghanian-Arani

Final Editing by Dawn Martin

Printed in Canada

Triz 012345678

To my lovely wife, _ _ _ _,
who wishes to remain anonymous.
And to my beautiful children,
without whose help
this book would not have been written.
With special thanks to Judy, Susan
and to Mike.

FAMILY TREE

```
Grandfather (Claude) (Nexus) ----- Grandmother
                                  |
                                  |
                  --------------------------------
                  |                              |
Kurt ----- Daughter                           Son --- Lisa
      |                                              |
------------------------------------------           |
|      |             |                  |            |
Bobby Daniel  Paul - Melissa - Peter  Mary   Rose - Peter
                 |           |                      |
              Lolita        Mary                  Claude
```

0

BEFORE

"Grandfather! Grandfather!"

I turned to see Rose, my youngest grandchild, running breathlessly towards me.

"Grandfather come quickly!"

"What is it Rose?" I asked, concerned that something tragic had happened. Rose had such a serious look on her face.

"It's Melissa!" she gasped raggedly.

"What? She's not? ..."

"Yes. She needs you."

"But she's not due for weeks yet."

"She's been in labor for at least half a day. I fear she may need some of your medicine Grandfather. I've been searching for you since the morning."

Rose looked so worried. It was hard for me to judge how urgently I really was needed. Rose had a tendency to overreact when it came to illness, and since she had never witnessed a birth, I judged that she was overreacting here as well. It was hard to tell how much weight to put to the message from my granddaughter. However, I still felt the need to make some quick decisions.

"Who's with her?" I asked.

"Mary and Paul." Rose's breathing had begun to slow. Her answers were no longer coming out in gasps.

I felt better. Paul had some experience helping in childbirth, and would do anything to ensure the safe birth of his child. He was very level headed.

Mary could assist Paul if she followed her instincts. Mary would do anything to help her older sister.

Still, I wished that Rose had stayed to help her cousin Melissa. I'm old. It would take me many hours to get back to camp. Everything might be over before I could get there.

I stared at my granddaughter. She waited for me to speak. She knew I was making plans, and waited for me to tell her what they were.

I made my decision.

"Rose, the hunters are down by the river. Fetch them. Tell them to get back to camp as quickly as possible."

Rose was obviously disappointed.

"What good will that do?' she asked.

I couldn't really give her a good answer to that question, except that I felt it was important we were all together.

"I'm not sure ... do as I say and let an old man have his way."

Rose pouted like a little girl, not as a grown woman in her twenties.

"But I should go with you," she said with a small voice..

"If you had stayed to help deliver the baby, you then could have taken your time in finding me.

"Bobby, Michael and Peter are no more than ten minutes away. They are hunting down by the beaver dam. We should all be together for the big event," I said.

"Can't Daniel go and get them?"

Rose knew that Daniel had accompanied me into the woods to gather plants.

"I sent Daniel to the clearing to gather some herbs."

I knew what my granddaughter was thinking. She wanted to help me back to camp.

"Daniel will help me back to camp. We'll take the deer trail through the forest. If you hurry, you can catch us before we get back," I said.

"Now Grandfather, do not strain yourself."

I laughed.

"Nothing will keep me from seeing my first great-grandchild. Now go, and be swift."

I watched Rose run off.

I jogged through the forest to the edge of the clearing.

Daniel saw me, ran across the clearing and asked, "What is it Grandfather?"

"Melissa is giving birth. Quickly! Put all the plants we have gathered into your pack. You will have to carry all of it, I'm afraid. I have need for speed today."

Daniel groaned. Roots and plants look light, but if you put enough of them together, they can be quite heavy.

I helped Daniel tie the plants in a tight bundle, and put the pack on his back.

We hurried through the woods as fast as my legs could go. Such was my excitement.

I was over ninety, but I could still muster up some speed when it was necessary. I heard the heavy breathing of Daniel behind me, as he kept pace with me.

I had witnessed the birth of all of my grandchildren and now my first great-grandchild would soon be born. I had lived for this moment. All my later life I had devoted to the survival of my grandchildren. Now the first of the next generation was about to be born ... and with this birth a new hope.

I knew that we had been better off than most who survived the dark times. In my youth I learned how to be able to survive anywhere and any place. And we had done just that. My children and I went into the woods of northern Canada many years ago and we did better than I could have expected.

We grew as a family. Others joined us. My children had children ...

Yet my biggest regret was the refusal of my wife to come into the woods with us. I wished she could have been here on this day. I knew she would have been proud.

I fought off tears as we neared our summer camp. Melissa had stayed close to the camp in the past months because she found it hard to walk about. She prepared the bulk of our meals. Everyone shared the work equally in our group.

Just before Daniel and I entered the clearing where our camp was, my ears were met with a wondrous sound.

The clear cry of an infant came from Melissa and Paul's hut. The wind carried the cry to trees which seemed to amplify the sound. We emerged from the forest to see a very tired looking Mary sitting in front of the cooking fire. She was slowly stirring something in a bowl, probably stew. Melissa, Paul and Mary were most likely famished after the birth.

Mary jumped to her feet when she saw us. Most of her weariness left her as she ran to us.

"Grandfather! Daniel! It's a girl!" Mary yelled excitedly.

We all hugged for a moment. When I drew back, I saw the fatigue in her eyes.

"Melissa?" I asked.

"It was hard on her, but she is okay. She fell asleep. Paul is trying to calm the baby. I'm afraid he's not much good at it though."

I laughed. I remembered how 'good' I was at comforting my first child. My first was a girl. My daughter wouldn't let me come near her for a year after she was born, without complaining that I wasn't her mother. But I eventually learned how to do it. I was sure that Paul would be a faster learner than I was.

"Good, all is well. But I think that you too should get some rest Mary."

Mary ignored my comment.

I turned to Daniel, who was letting down his burden. He was sweating profusely.

I suggested, "Daniel, finish preparing the meal, and boil me some water. I think that I shall brew some medicinal tea."

Daniel groaned again and said, "Yes, Grandfather."

"I'll help," volunteered Mary.

Mary always did things her own way and refused to show any weakness. She would never admit to being tired.

When they had left, I approached Paul and Melissa's hut. I knocked lightly, then entered.

I saw Melissa asleep in some furs. Even though it was warm, Melissa was shivering. She had used up a lot of energy. Her sweat had dried on her body, and left her cold. I placed another fur on her and turned to Paul.

Paul was cradling the baby in his arms. She had calmed somewhat, and was no longer crying. She was now merely complaining about having been born.

Paul looked up at me. His face showed his extreme pride. He was tired, however. He appeared barely able to keep his eyes open.

I looked at the child. She was healthy looking. Her nose was all scrunched up. Her head was elongated and she still had a tinge of blue in her skin color, but she was still one of the most beautiful babies I had ever seen.

Paul must have been reading my thoughts.

"Grandfather, isn't she beautiful?" Paul said.

Even though I was not Paul's grandfather, he called me that, as did everyone in our group. They were all so much younger than myself that it felt natural for them to do so.

"Yes," I agreed.

Paul was beaming.

I looked at my great-granddaughter for a little while longer, then said, "I will make you and Melissa some tea."

I left the proud father and the sleeping mother with their child.

When I emerged from the hut, I saw Bobby running into the camp. He must have run the entire distance from the river to the camp. The others would be far behind. None could run as fast or as far as Bobby. It must have taken Rose somewhat longer than expected to find them, because I had expected Bobby to have caught up to me on the way to the camp.

"What news, Grandfather?" Bobby said.

"A healthy girl. Congratulations. You're an uncle."

Bobby broke out into a large smile. He grabbed me in a large bear hug. He knew what this day meant for me. I had waited long, but it was now here.

"Can I see her?" he said.

"Wait a while. Your sister sleeps. Paul is tired as well. He looks like he spent quite a while getting his daughter to quiet down. Let them be. We will have plenty of time to see her later. We must have a celebration. But go now, and help your brother Daniel with the fire, and help cook up some food. "

Bobby's eyes lit up at the mere mention of food, and he gladly ran off.

I went to my hut and got out some carefully preserved herbs. I felt tired. My jog through the forest took more out of me than I had expected.

I decided to lie down for a bit before I brewed the tea.

I listened to the arrival of the others through my hut wall. I especially could hear Rose shout with joy. I knew she was unhappy about missing the birth, but she would be most pleased with the performance of her cousin.

I lay in my straw bed thinking about my grandchildren. I was extremely proud. We prepared well for this event. All had gone smoothly. I felt like that we could rebuild the world. So much evil had been done to the earth, but we had survived. Now there would be a new generation.

I fell asleep thinking these thoughts. I was happy.

I didn't even notice the moment when I stopped breathing.

1

FRIEND

It was strange seeing myself dead.

It was strange that I could feel strange.

My mind was in total disorder and my thoughts reflected that.

I was standing in front of my still body.

I looked at my body lying on the ground and then to my hand which was attached to what I can only call my second body.

I experienced severe disorientation.

I did feel different, but the only reason I knew I was dead was that my grandchildren were weeping beside my body. Rose was lamenting openly that they were doomed without me, that their deaths would soon follow. I saw them differently. What had started as such a happy day now felt without hope.

I saw now how everything was in vain. I felt with a new awareness the earth beneath my feet … my feet that felt so young on the surface of a planet so old. The earth was dying. I saw the damage that man had done to the earth. I felt the damage that man had done to the atmosphere. I looked at the ever present sun through the window of my hut. Its light was penetrating. It filled me with a flame, a flame that flickered to the very depths of my soul; but it did not burn. I saw now that the sun was contributing to the death of life on earth.

I felt the trees and the grass and the damage done to them by the sun. I felt the oceans and how the abundant life in them was sinking deeper … away from the life-giving and death-bringing sun. I knew that with the death of the plants there would be no new oxygen and the struggles of my grandchildren to maintain life was in vain. These thoughts flashed in front of my eyes in a mere instant … and I began to wail. With my new awareness I felt that all around me were wailing in unison … the rocks, the trees, even the smallest insect … all were wailing with me. It was more than I could stand and I begged for it to stop.

Suddenly I felt a touch on my shoulder, and the wailing did stop.

"It's really not that bad," said a voice.

I spun around to see a small man.

"Who are you ?" I asked.

"Don't you recognize me?"

I looked hard, trying to remember everyone I had ever met in my life who might match this peculiar apparition that was standing in front of me. He was plain of face, had dark hair, with a slightly dark or well tanned complexion. He appeared to be wearing only a loin cloth, like one out of a bad Hercules movie. It was held up by a thin piece of cloth going over his shoulder. Now the odd thing was that if I tried to focus my attention on this scant piece of clothing it seemed to disappear. Stranger still though was the fact that I then expected to see a naked man standing in front of me, what I saw instead was … nothing. Nothing! It was as if the man was not there. Yet if I concentrated on his face, the man appeared whole … loin cloth and all.

I started to lose it.

The man seemed to notice my distress and calmly spoke, “Do not be distracted. I asked you a question, do you recognize me?”

I stared at that warm face and saw that there was a glow all about the man. I knew instinctively that that glow had once been larger … so large that it would have rivaled that of the sun. As I looked at that glow, a faint warmth grew inside me. But as quickly as it grew, an overwhelming darkness leapt from within my depths and smothered any memory of any warmth.

“No I don’t know who you are,” I stubbornly replied.

“You always were a bit stupid,” retorted the man.

I tried to look indignant, but instead I broke out into a big stupid smile. I knew I liked this person.

“Well don’t keep me in suspense, who are you?”

“No, no. Things here are not to be freely given. Especially something that you already know.”

“Well can I have a name at least, or do you want me to play twenty questions?”

The little man looked at me and said, “Well since I once was and still am your friend, you can call me Friend."

“Friend?”

“Well at least until you remember who I am. I see dying hasn’t improved your perception much.”

I wanted to argue that being dead had opened my awareness to almost epic proportions; but the tone of Friend's last statement made me feel a bit sheepish.

“Look Claude, you're dead now … let the people that were in your life go and get on with it.”

It had been a long time since anyone had used my name. I had to get used to the sound of it again. I had been called Grandfather for so long, living among young people for almost thirty years. Even my own children had been gone for many years.

Now my emotion changed and I felt anger.

"Okay Friend, I'm dead. What am I supposed to get on with? Aren't you going to show me some white light and take me to some heavenly place? Aren't you my guide or something?"

He shook his head slowly and calmly replied, "No."

I waited for him to say more but time didn't seem to be operating in the same manner I was accustomed to. I honestly could not tell how much time was passing.

"As for what you are to do, you already know. And by the way I would stop wasting energy by being angry, you only have a finite amount now that you are dead."

As quickly as I was angry I became calm and asked, "What do you mean by a finite amount of energy?"

"Well," he continued, as he sat down, "The purpose of having life is to accumulate energy so you can have energy when you are not alive."

I sat down opposite him, "What does that mean?"

"What did you do all your life? You survived and then thrived when all around you was destroyed. How many of your peers survived into their nineties with all that has happened to the planet?

"The one thing that you were good at was finding power spots, attuning your energy to these spots, and using this energy to prolong your life and the lives of those around you.

"Just what did you *think* you were doing?"

"I don't know what I did. I just knew that it worked."

"Precisely. You didn't know what you were doing. If you had just wondered a little more about other things besides your own survival, you just might have come to an understanding."

I shrugged indifferently.

"There is a cycle to life and death. You live, gain energy, die, use that energy, and if you are lucky you move on. If not, you have to choose life again and build up your energy to try all over again."

These words hit me like bricks … one brick per word. Suddenly I saw my lives and how each time, just before I was reborn I had felt my energy waning. I cried at the pain of each life, and chose to forget, or else be overwhelmed. The thought that bothered me was what I was doing in between all my lives? I could only stare blankly at the floor.

"Don't give me that blank look. You know what you're supposed to do."

The feeling that Friend was right wouldn't go away. But what was it that one has to do when one dies? I always thought that this was something that was an unknown, when alive, and a definite known, when dead.

I was feeling frustrated, and without the physical feedback I normally had when alive … was more a bodiless frustration, one of spirit. Instinct told me that I should know everything that I remembered in life, but something was preventing me from remembering.

Friend looked hard at me and appeared to be reading my mind, "You are your own worst enemy, you are preventing yourself from remembering who I am and what you are supposed to be doing."

"Why would I be doing that?" I asked.

"I don't know, I don't know everything. I can only guess."

"Well what's your guess?"

"Sorry … no freebies."

I started to get angry again, "You say you're my friend but up until now you've been nothing but a source of frustration."

"Sometimes friends have to know when to shut up."

I paused a bit then said, "Just how long have you been my friend?"

"A long time."

"You really aren't much help, are you?"

A large smile grew on Friend's face. "You never used to say that."

With that smile staring at me, I lost all my anger. And I even began to laugh. After I stopped, which felt like an eternity, I asked, "When are you going to start helping me?"

"I have been, I got you to laugh didn't I?"

I looked at him, wondering what he meant, and he smiled again. This time it seemed that it was as if all the mirth in the world was released with that smile and it danced all over me, tickling me to my very center. When the smile vanished from Friend's face the world went back to the way it was before, dark and sad.

"Look Claude, what would you like?"

The world felt less sad at the sound of Friend's voice but I felt uncomfortable hearing my name again. It didn't fit, it didn't feel right.

"Tell me, why do I feel odd hearing my own name?"

"Claude was the name you had in your last life. You are eternal. You've had lots of names. If Claude doesn't suit you, choose another name."

Names started bombarding me until finally one name stood out; Nexus. It felt right.

At first I forgot what it meant ... which is probably why I liked the sound of my new name so much. However, remembering that it meant attachment, almost turned me off.

I ignored my own feelings and boldly said, "Nexus."

Friend laughed. It was the sound of a joyous waterfall, an echoing endless sound. One that you could listen to forever. It was almost a shock when it stopped. It left me a little sad.

"Nexus. Well that certainly suits you. As long as I have known you, you attached yourself to things."

"I did not!"

Laughter again, and with it my desire that it would never end. I felt like acting silly just to keep him laughing.

"Did not, did not, did not!" I said idiotically.

Friend stopped laughing. "I already warned you about wasting your energy."

I sobered immediately.

"Really, don't you know what you are?" he asked.

That was a difficult to answer. A few moments ago I was human, but what was I now? Indeed, it was hard to describe the differences between being alive and being dead. I still felt like me. I experienced instant frustration, and then anger. One thing was for certain; I experienced emotions much more quickly and intensely. Friend looked at me and with that look, appeared to understand everything about me.

I lamely shook my head, no.

His smile brought me right back to an even keel.

"You are a consciousness," he said.

"Okay, I think therefore I am. No sur prise there."

"Stop being sarcastic. You are a consciousness operating at a certain level. When you acted at the human level of consciousness you organized all the lower forms of consciousness to keep you at the human level. Just as the higher levels of consciousness organized the multitudes of human consciousness across the planet."

"Huh?"

"You were human, right?"

"Right."

"What did that mean to you?"

"I lived, I breathed ..."

"Superficial. You were a consciousness that organized the cellular consciousness of your cells. The cells in turn organized their molecular consciousness, which in turn organized their atomic consciousness, which organized the next lower, and the next lower, etc. The end result being that you were human."

"Wait a second. Are you telling me that cells, molecules and atoms each have a consciousness?"

"Yes, they are totally aware of each other and interact according to 'orders' from higher levels of awareness. If you had a body at this moment, I would tell you to listen to your body and feel the awareness coursing through it. But since you're without one right now, I want you to focus on this small insect crawling across the floor."

Friend was pointing to a small tick-like bug that was making its way towards my former body.

"Concentrate on that bug, and feel its awareness, its every movement."

I watched the bug slowly shorten the distance to my body, when suddenly I felt pulled down towards the floor. Everything appeared enormous, and everything lost its complexity ... the universe became extremely simplistic.

Friend sharply yelled, "Stop indulging!"

I blinked and looked around, "What happened?"

"You joined with the bug's consciousness."

"Why did everything seem so basic?"

"That was that bug's species' consciousness. It's not the same as the human collective consciousness. It probably felt a little strange to you because you have just freshly come from the human consciousness, but I'm sure you've experienced it before. It's similar to when you extended your consciousness during your meditative states, while you were in your physical human body. But had you just lost your spiritual human form while you still had your physical body, the experience would have been similar to the one you just had."

"So you're telling me that everything has a higher consciousness?"

"In a way. Everything is consciousness. There are just many layers, and we all operate at one of these layers. We can of course choose to operate at any of these levels, higher or lower, depending on what we want to do."

"How do we choose where we want to be?" I asked.

"We have free will."

"I don't get it."

"Well, let's say that you were to choose to meld with a newly forming human life. You would then automatically join the higher human consciousness and automatically be in command of the cellular consciousness of the new body, which in turn controls the atomic consciousness, which in turn controls the particle consciousness, etc.

"Now, if the body happened to be male you would automatically tune in to the higher male sub-consciousness and be in command of the male cellular interactions which in turn command the quantum particle awareness.

"If the body happened to be female you would automatically join the higher female sub-consciousness and be in command of the female cellular interactions which is in command of the quantum wave awareness."

I looked at Friend in disbelief. "That's the difference between male and female?"

"Right. At the quantum level males are particles and females are waves, and at the higher level there is a male and female sub-consciousness of the total human consciousness. Of course, anyone can tap in to either sub-consciousness regardless of their biological sex and then will display the behavior of that sub-consciousness, but it is usually easier to stay in the sub-conscious that one was born to."

"You're telling me that you have just explained sexual preference."

"Precisely."

"And males are particles and females are waves at the quantum level?" I asked.

"Not quite. Males act like quantum particle events across the quantum female wave background of the total quantum consciousness."

"Huh?"

"Don't worry about it," Friend said with a smile.

"Okay, you seem to talk about higher and lower levels of consciousness ... are there limits to the levels of the higher and lower levels of consciousness?"

"Yes and no. The lower one goes in consciousness, the simpler the consciousness and the more complex the rules of interactions until one arrives at the beginning of awareness, which some people have nicknamed the big bang, and all the rules of the universe. The higher one goes through the levels of consciousness, the more complex the consciousness and the simpler the rules, until one arrives at the sum of all consciousness, or God, and the one rule ... free will."

I looked hard at Friend. The concepts that he had blown by me were staggering. I had a million questions and the opportunity to ask anything that I wanted and have the answers immediately given. I felt awed in Friend's presence.

"Stop that!" Friend yelled. "I told you to save your energy. You shouldn't give it away so readily."

I instantly shrunk. The outburst by Friend was unexpected. The wonder I had just experienced at receiving so much information was washed away. Friend suddenly smiled; warmth poured over me again. It didn't matter in the presence of that smile how I had come to know Friend ... the important thing was that he was my friend.

Being near Friend made me feel good ... so how come I couldn't figure out who he was? This was an obvious difference between my alive and my dead existence. When I was alive, I never forgot a face, but now I couldn't recognize Friend. It was as if some part of my thoughts were missing ...

I stopped thinking about my dilemma and went back to what Friend had just said about God.

"So, is God made up of all consciousness ... including mine?"

Friend slowly spoke, "Yes," but quickly went on to add, "GOD IS EVERYTHING. Everything has consciousness and God is the sum of all consciousness. So you are part of God, but let's just say that you are a part that is aware there is a whole. You are also a sum of smaller parts that are aware of their collective consciousness."

"But wait a minute ... if I'm dead how can I be the sum of smaller consciousness if I no longer have a body to command the lower consciousness?"

"Your consciousness in its present state is the residue of that which you had in life and thus it has the memory of all it was before."

"What?"

"You are a memory with free will."

"That's it?" I asked.

"Not really, but that's the best answer you can understand at the moment.

"Until you figure out what you are doing."

I blinked, my spirit eyes, realizing that it was a conscious decision to do so, because being dead meant I didn't have eyelids, then I asked, "What do dead people do?"

"Lots of things. Generally things they want to do. Rarely the things that would be good for them. Although some of them just ask a lot of questions."

Friend smiled and I laughed. One of those good, hearty, roll-on-the-floor type laughs. Honestly, I couldn't think of anything I wanted to do, whether it was good for me or just plain stupid. I scanned around the hut where my body was placed. I looked where my body was lying and saw that flowers had been laid around the hut. I didn't remember seeing anyone put the flowers there. Suddenly I saw my youngest grandchild, Rose, placing some flowers at my former feet.

I asked Friend, "How come I didn't notice anyone bringing flowers in before?"

"It takes energy for the dead to notice the living, just like it takes energy for the living to notice the dead."

I looked at Rose again, and saw that she had been weeping ... tears were still on her cheeks ... but I heard her speaking and deduced that she must have been talking to herself for a while.

"Grandfather, Grandfather, I know you can hear me. Why don't you answer? Bobby wants us to move to the sacred cave and I know in my heart that it is wrong Please give us a sign as to what we should do."

"I want to help her." I turned to look at Friend and saw him slowly shaking his head, no.

"You're only fooling yourself if you think you can actually help anyone. She will be fine ... everyone has their own path to follow You can not help her, just as I can not help you."

"That's nonsense ... you've been a great help to me already. You've told me things that I could never even have imagined."

Friend looked at Rose then looked at me and said, "That is not actually help. I can tell you everything that goes on in the universe but that would be totally meaningless to you. The only information that is useful to you is the information that you take to your heart and use. I could tell you what to do next, but that too, is useless, because it did not come from you, and you would not know how to proceed. You could tell your grandchildren what to do, but you are better off connecting yourself to the human consciousness and answering their questions according to your awareness of that consciousness."

I looked around and saw that Rose had left the hut. I didn't see her leave, which annoyed me to no end. How could I be so unaware?

"Awareness is something that needs constant work. You must apply your energy to it full time before you notice any benefits."

Again Friend knew exactly what I was thinking.

"How do you know what I'm thinking?"

"Awareness."

"What?"

"I see the energy of consciousness and I've had enough experience of tuning into the greater consciousness to interpret what someone is thinking. Anyone can do it, even the living."

"How does one see these things?"

"Well, you don't use your eyes. You use your inner awareness. Your eyes can get in the way. Right now you are still using the attachment to your body to interpret the world. You are still seeing the world as if you had eyes. Let go ... use your awareness."

I started to sense the world differently. I saw it as energy connected through lines. But it was too weird for me and I knew I preferred to see it as I always had. Or had I seen it that way before? I was confused again.

"Focus on what you are doing," he continued.

I thought of Rose, my son's only child, and how connected to the earth she was. I knew she was right. Bobby, the eldest of my daughter's four children, didn't understand the danger of moving to the sacred cave. I wanted to help, but how do the dead convey messages to the living?

"It's a waste of time," Friend said.

I looked at Friend and was about to ask him something when he continued, "... and no, I'm not going to tell you how to talk to the living. Figure it out for yourself."

Annoyed. That's how one feels when someone is reading their thoughts. The novelty that someone can actually do it wears out quickly and all that's left is one annoyed personality.

Being human meant that no one invaded one's thoughts and ultimately one had to deal with that aloneness. Friend was looking at my thoughts like someone reading an open book.

"Stop that!" I shouted, with my fists firmly planted on my hips.

"Okay, I'll stop. I just wanted to show you that it could be done."

I realized that I hadn't told Friend what it was he was to stop doing, but I knew that he knew what I wanted him to stop doing, and he said he would. I didn't feel any better because Friend was at this very instant reading my thoughts. I looked at him and he smiled. I had to laugh. I put all my effort into that laugh. In fact, it was the most enjoyable experience of my new existence. Friend had started to laugh with me, and the thought of being dead and laughing with someone else who was dead seemed to me the most hilarious thing in the universe. When we finally stopped, I asked, "Can I prevent you from reading my thoughts?"

"Yes."

Friend just sat there and didn't say anything else, because I knew that he wasn't going to answer my next question without me actually asking it, thus keeping his promise to pretend he was not reading my mind.

"Well how?" I finally blurted out.

"Connect your awareness to a higher consciousness."

"That's it?"

"Well it's not as easy as it sounds. You have to join your being to that higher consciousness. Remember how I told you that the higher the consciousness the more complex that consciousness is?"

"Okay."

"Well, your concentrating on that higher consciousness expands your being so much that it is harder for someone to look at it and 'see' what you are thinking, unless of course they are at a yet higher level of consciousness. The trick to it, though, is to concentrate on the higher consciousness while still retaining your identity at the lower consciousness. If you are successful, the net effect is that your thoughts appear fuzzy, and the more your thoughts become one with the higher consciousness, the more fuzzy you become."

"Fuzzy?"

"Yes, fuzzy. Harder to see. You forget you are you because you concentrate on being you."

"Wait a second! I don't remember doing that!"

"One of the benefits of being human is being part of the human form or, better yet, the basic spiritual human form. This basic human form allows one to forget that one has to concentrate on this form in order to be human. In fact it pulls one in so completely, that even after one dies, most spirits find it hard to drop the human form and move on to the next step. But to answer your first question again ... connect your awareness to a higher consciousness. You could go for the ultimate and try to become aware of God but I'd recommend first trying to attach to the collective consciousness of the earth or as it is called, the Gaia consciousness."

"How?"

"You do it the same way you managed to find power spots when you were alive. Just stop and feel within yourself until you notice changes within your awareness of your surroundings, all the while having the intent of joining with the Gaia consciousness. You will feel yourself expand and you may become lost as a consciousness and join totally with that higher consciousness. In that case you would no longer want to talk to me. But if you retain the ability to maintain yourself after joining with the higher consciousness, then it gets harder to read what exactly your consciousness is thinking because it is now made up of so many more parts. Just try to imagine what God is thinking ... because God is the ultimate consciousness, it is the most complex. Do you understand what God is thinking?"

It was an easy answer. "No."

"Don't be so quick to say no to that one because you are part of that consciousness. You do have a limited insight. But give it a try. Try to expand your consciousness."

I sat there trying to 'expand' myself, to no avail. I tried to remember what I did during my life when I tried to find power spots. I remembered I had the ability to walk slowly toward places that made me 'feel' good. It was a sort of vague feeling in the pit of my stomach that started to make me feel warm when I was going in the right direction. Like I had just eaten something that wasn't too filling, but left me with the desire to have more. I sat and I sat, but nothing happened. My thoughts started to wander and I remembered discovering the sacred cave and how it was one of the most powerful experiences of my life. I remembered sitting in the cave and the feelings that I experienced and I slowly started to feel like I was expanding. It half felt like I was sitting in the cave at this very instant. I looked around and saw vague shapes of people. I recognized Rose immediately and realized the others were my grandchildren and they were carrying my body. I snapped out of the expanded state I was in and saw an empty space where my body had lain.

I thought back to all that had happened. I must have laughed longer than I had thought. I looked at Friend. He knew what I wanted to ask, but I jumped up and rushed out of the hut. He was right behind me.

He shouted, "STOP!" in such a commanding voice that I came to a screeching halt.

I looked at him rather bewilderedly and meekly said, "What?"

"Let it go."

"What?"

"Your grandchildren."

"I can't."

"If you leave me now, you may not see me again and I have not told you all I could tell you."

"But my grandchildren are in the cave. They don't know what they are doing."

"And why does your ego feel that you can do something to help them, or anyone, in the first place?"

I was taken aback by Friend's words but something inside of me started to boil. These were my

grandchildren, I was responsible for them, I had to do something. Anger filled my
every thought. I spewed out a venomous reply, "I have to go help them because no one else can ... why don't you go hide in a hole somewhere!"

"As you wish." And Friend turned, and as he approached the entrance of the hut he slowly began to disappear, until he vanished completely. I gazed at the space where Friend had been. I had the feeling something was wrong, completely wrong. I shrugged and started to move towards the sacred cave.

2

BRUNO

At first I walked to gather my thoughts and convince myself that I was doing the right thing. As soon as my anger left me, I had a nagging feeling that I should be doing things differently. I felt stupid. Why don't I know what's right? Why do I doubt myself? Why can't it just be straight forward and easy?

Why can't life, or rather death, be like a chess game? Well defined rules with a limited scope of movements which one performs to attain a certain goal. Checkmate.

I stopped and meekly cried out, "Friend."

There was no reply. I shouted, "Friend!"

Several thoughts occurred to me at the same time. One was trivial. I felt like I had just shouted, but I knew for a fact that I had no means of making a sound, or for hearing one for that matter. So what had I just done, and how had I carried on a conversation with Friend? This thought bothered me, but so did another. I had a creeping feeling of being alone. It was somewhat like the feeling I had just before Friend had showed up, only worse.

I was ALONE.

Friend being with me had been more of a comfort than I had known.

When I was alive, there was a connection I had to my body … I realized now, how soothing to the spirit it was.

I knew I should be doing something. I thought of what Friend had said about connecting to a higher awareness and I wondered if this was what I should be doing. But I didn't feel like I could do it. I felt that I was going mad. I had visions of myself being a poltergeist somewhere knocking things over that people had carefully placed on a shelf.

I giggled. I also remembered that Friend had said that the universe did have a well defined set of rules.

This last thought stabilized me. If the universe was understandable, even though the rules were more complex than a chess game, then I had a chance of comprehending them. It was a challenge for me, a game. And I had all the time in the universe in which to figure it out. I was dead, wasn't I?

I started to feel smug and slowly proceeded toward the cave, when I heard a loud voice say, "So dere you are. Knew I felt someone die 'round here."

I turned at the sound to see a strange man. He appeared to be the perfect embodiment of a bully. He was over six feet tall and had muscles bulging everywhere. His face looked like he had been on the worse end of a head-on collision. Talk about intimidation. This guy oozed it. I wondered if this was the way this stranger appeared in life, because he could give anyone weak knees … or maybe was his appearance based on some sort of emotional attachment?

"You coming wid me. Committee won't be half pleased for Bruno to bring back new dead one."

This guy looked like a Bruno. I did have an emotional attachment to that name. I knew a Bruno once, a dangerous guy who befriended me in my youth when no one else would. He had been a great teacher to me.

But my ninety years of experience told me that this guy would not be so amiable, and he was just as dangerous as my previous friend.

He came right up to me and said, "Dat way." He pointed vaguely south.

One problem I have is that I am very stubborn and I do not respond well to situations like this.

The biggest problem though, was my current 'body.' As I scanned it for its preparedness, it looked every bit like it did before I died. I looked half starved, frail and weak. But this was not what I was feeling on the inside. I was no longer hunched over, I was again seeing the world from the perspective of someone six foot six, and I did feel an unusual amount of peppiness that I hadn't felt in quite a long time.

These thoughts happened in an instant. And of course I said, "Just what happens to lie that way ... and who is this precious committee of yours?"

"You find out. Don't be giving Bruno no lip or I give you some of dis."

He had pulled out an ordinary looking gray rod and was waving it in my face.

I wondered what this rod could possibly be, and how could a spirit be holding on to something and brandishing it like a weapon.

He shouted louder "Now move," and he wildly pointed past me "Or I drain energy right now."

"Now look, I'm sure we can come to a ... "

My words were cut short as Bruno whacked me over the head with his rod. The pain was beyond description. If I had been in my physical body, I'm sure the force of the blow would have broken my skull in two. But I'm positive that the force of the blow had nothing to do with the pain I was experiencing. The pain wracked my very spirit and I'm sure I became weaker after the strike to my head. I felt less able to control my will … as if my attention had been scattered.

He grabbed me by the nape of my neck and with one arm lifted me and started to walk in a southerly direction, easily carrying me suspended slightly off the ground.

I was quite disoriented, but something told me my very existence was at stake. An immense fear grew in me and I realized that death of the body was not the worst thing that could happen to someone. There were experiences that made physical death look like child's play. The worst was having your energy drained slowly until you ceased to exist, and I had only a mild taste of this when my head was introduced to Bruno's rod.

My anger grew until it appeared to form a massive sword in my right hand. I wasted no time or energy on thinking any more. I became the embodiment of a untamed animal that had spent forty years in the wild.

I planted my feet solidly on a small lump of earth and twisted my body like a snake, firmly grasping the sword in both hands and brought it down on the arm that was carrying me.

The arm severed immediately and I dropped to the ground. I rolled to one side and Bruno screamed in pain.

I leapt to my feet. Bruno, looking somewhat surprised, said, "Tougher dan you look, but no one gets away from Bruno."

I pointed my sword squarely at him. Several things caught my attention. I saw him grow his arm back, he appeared to be slightly smaller, and his severed arm was still holding on to my neck.

Bruno squeezed with this third arm, leapt forward and swung a mighty blow. I fell on one knee and pointed my sword upwards and he impaled himself on it, his blow landing on his own severed arm.

As he started to fall over me, issuing a tremendous scream, I forced my way forward and passed him holding on to my sword with all my might, cutting him almost in two. I turned as quickly as any wildcat and finished the process of dividing Bruno in two parts with a wicked swing of my sword.

The bottom part of him fell forward and the top half of him fell backward on top of the bottom half.

The rod fell from his grasp beside me.

Bruno's screams were even louder but quickly ceased, and slowly he stood up, once again whole, and once again appearing smaller.

He looked at his rod and without thinking I raised my sword and smote the rod as it lay between two rocks.

The world exploded.

I was flung back at least thirty feet by the force that was released from the rod. It was as if the wails of hundreds had been unleashed. The sound itself was enough to throw me. I realized something unusual had occurred but it was so beyond my experience that I didn't comprehend it at the moment.

Bruno had been tossed back, at most, five feet.

He once again stood.

I staggered to my feet.

Bruno worriedly looked at me, swayed back and forth, eyed my sword, then made his decision to run.

I assessed the damage to my sword, the top part was missing. I then watched the quickly disappearing figure of Bruno. I wanted to pursue him, but I had a feeling that I shouldn't. I felt open and exposed. I started to run in the opposite direction, then quickly corrected my course to the sacred cave. I would be safe there, and I would find my grandchildren.

3

SPIDER AND BILL

As I ran, I remembered how secure I felt when Friend was around. I felt what had happened with Bruno would not have occurred if Friend had been around.

Just what Bruno was and what he was alluding to, I could not guess. But he made me feel like a pawn in a chess game in which I had fallen off the board. I didn't understand the rules of engagement, but I was certain they were deadly to my soul.

The terrain became familiar. In the distance I saw the Two Peaked Mountain, a name my grandchildren and I used to identify the entrance to a hidden valley. In fact, they were two separate mountains, very close together, but with spurs down from the peaks, giving the illusion of being one large mountain. The spurs were quite formidable and very hard to climb. I had, however, found a way over the first spur, which had been quite hidden by a growth of cedars.

Once I passed the first spur there was a zig zag path between the two mountains that led to a valley that was nearly inaccessible. It had a small lake in it.

My children and I had first hidden there when the bad times hit and we had made that valley our base of operations. We were a nomadic group during the summer, because as our population grew, the valley was not large enough to support our group. We spent winters in there and enjoyed the milder climate and its safety factor.

It was during one of the winters there that I had found the sacred cave. It was behind a particularly dense stand of cedars. I had been retrieving an arrow and was attracted to the cedars. I pushed my way through the tough trees and almost fell into the cave.

I felt that this was a place of power when the hair on the back of my neck stood up. Immediately I knew this was the perfect hiding spot, especially after the trouble we had when a plane had landed in our valley. It was the only time that we had a conflict within the valley.

The cave then became a place of ceremony for me and my children, and eventually my grandchildren. Rose could feel the power in the cave but Bobby could not. He always wanted to live there in what he thought would have been perfect safety.

Bobby never could feel any spiritual events, he could only experience what his body told him. His favorite experience was a full stomach. He could think only of food and had no time for what he called spiritual mumbo jumbo. But he did listen to me and respected what I felt when it came to unseen dangers, although he put it down to instinct. Just what did he think instinct was?

But he was the best hunter and the most head strong of my grandchildren; the rest would follow his lead even as far as to live in the sacred cave. He did not know that it would drive them all crazy, and maybe even drive them to each others throats.

I had just passed the first group of cedars leading into the valley when I noticed the terrain was not exactly as I had remembered it. The colors were wrong and there was a hazy glow emanating from the rocks.

This glow grew the deeper I went into the valley. It appeared to come from the far side where the sacred cave was.

If I had had this perceptional ability when I entered the valley for the first time, It never would have remained hidden from me for so long. Waves of living color danced on the rocks. Their source was within the depths of the earth and it issued out through the sacred cave.

I felt fear for my grandchildren and I ran faster. I surprised myself, for it seemed as if I ran with the wind and I came to the entrance to the cave faster than any one alive could have. I had to remind myself again that my body was dead and I should not be surprised by anything that happened or was appearing to happen.

I looked inside. It was not dark. Light was everywhere.

Full of anticipation, I stepped inside.

"Nexus!" a voice shouted.

I immediately thought of Friend, because who else knew me by that name?

"Come in, come in, you're always welcome here."

It wasn't Friend, but a very strange apparition. He was very small, bald and his beard touched the ground. He swayed back and forth as he approached me and was quite naked. There were no other features beside the beard to make me think he was male. He was devoid of genitals, or nipples for that matter, but he had the feeling of maleness at a deeper level.

"Thank you," I said.

"No need for gratuities, you've been here many times before. Perhaps you would like your usual seat."

He pointed to the place where I always made my ceremonial fire.

There was a phantom fire burning. Without much thought I sat in front of the fire.

I looked at my strange host and asked, "Who are you and how do you know my name?"

"Ah, that's two questions. One thing you should learn right now, especially when dealing with spirits, is to only ask one question at a time unless the fire within you is absolutely clear, in which case you can ask all your questions at the same time. You never could get that one right."

"What do you mean by that?"

"Oh now he's asking vague questions again. You always were muddled. I could mean anything. You must clear your mind and focus on being whole so you can ask what you want with your entire self so the answer you get is what you need. Or else you will get a muddled answer like you just got. Ah, there you are Bill. Come sit and join us."

Another spirit had suddenly come into view and quickly sat beside us. He was tall with dark hair and dark eyes. He was immaculately dressed in a dark blue business suit.

"This is my apprentice, Bill."

I found the concept of an apprentice ghost extremely hilarious, and I started to laugh out loud.

My host quickly became angry and forcefully said, "Stop that idiotic laughing. Bill has only just stabilized."

I looked at Bill and he seemed to be on the verge of crying. My mood sobered quickly.

But now I had so many questions floating through my mind. Who was my host and his apprentice? How did he know my new name? How did he know me, and mostly, what was he talking about? I sat there another moment and tried to collect my thoughts. I took a deep breath, cleared my mind and asked, "Who are you?"

"That's better. You got it now .... My name is ... Spider."

"Spider?"

"Yes. That's what I said. What's the matter, have you gone deaf?"

"I'm dead, how can I go deaf?"

"There are many types of deafness."

I paused for a moment before going on. "Okay, why are you called Spider?"

"You know ... weaver of webs ... planner of schemes ..."

I thought about what he said for a minute then went on. "How do you know me?"

He gave me a wild grin and said, "I've always known you, and besides, who did you think was answering all your questions when you came here?"

"That was you?"

"None other."

"But you do not look anything like I pictured you."

He suddenly jumped up and over the fire, land ing right beside me. He clasped my head between his hands and turned my head towards his, and closely examined my face.

"That's strange ... you look just like you imagined yourself to be."

I was taken aback by his actions and his words. In fact I noticed that Bill had begun to giggle. I felt like I was the butt of some inside joke.

Spider jumped away, just like some huge jumping spider and sat opposite me on the other side other side of the fire.

"What do you mean by that?"

"Hold on ... I thought you had some other questions first ... or are you getting muddled again?"

Oh no, not the mind reading thing again. But all I could think about was the Spider's appearance. When I came here during my life, I always saw a tremendous and quite frightening apparition that almost scared me to death every time I saw it. I thought that the only thing that prevented it from tearing me to shreds was the protective devices against spirits that I carried with me.

Collecting my thoughts once again I asked, "But how did you know my new name?"

"I told you already that I have always known you so why shouldn't I know what you are calling yourself now?"

That answer did not do a thing for me.

"No really, who are you?"

"Wow! Is that a loaded question. I am who I am." He cackled insanely for a moment. "Or just who do you expect me to be?"

He made me slightly nervous.

"But I thought you were a hideous being who lived in the depths of the earth, and only came out when you were summoned here to this cave, during ceremony?"

"I was," he replied.

"But how come you don't look like that now?"

"I could if you want me to."

He pulled out a rod identical to the one Bruno had carried and he looked at me menacingly. I felt instant fear. I looked around for my sword for it was no longer in my hand.

"Looking for this?"

Spider held up my sword in his other hand. He began to creep towards me. I scrambled back until I came to the wall. Spider leapt up high with both hands raised, screaming a wild battle cry. He landed right in front of me, handed me my sword and said, "But only if you want me to."

I stared at him blankly. Bill broke the silence that followed with wild laughter. He slowly clapped his hands, fell on to his back holding his stomach and continued laughing, clearly unable to stop.

Spider capered back to his spot around the fire.

I returned to my position close to Bill, who had now composed himself, and I carefully placed my sword beside me. I noticed that Spider's rod was nowhere to be seen.

Spider started talking again as if nothing had happened. "I am only what you expect me to be."

I felt confused.

"I appear to you only as your expectations are ready to perceive me."

"So are you Spider or are you just Friend looking like Spider?"

"I am Spider. Friend is someone else even though we are the same person."

"How can you be the same person and someone else?"

"Easy. It all depends on your perspective. Operating at the level that you are currently perceiving, I am Spider and Friend is Friend. But at a higher perceptional level we are the same, just as you and I are the same, and you and Friend are the same. Yet we choose to operate at this lower level so we can discover things, do things, and actually have some fun."

"Why would I want to perceive you as frightening?"

"So you wouldn't get too close to me."

"Huh?"

"So we would remain separate beings."

"So we won't merge?"

"We've done that before, in fact everything once merged, but we decided to split. That's what the big bang was all about, don't you remember? And now we have to learn everything all over again. Fun isn't it?"

I paused, looked at Spider and just reveled in how much fun I wasn't having.

I wondered, "Do you know Friend?"

"I told you. At a higher level I know everyone and do have access to that knowledge, but at our level, no, I've never met the person."

"Friend told me that one can join with a higher consciousness and become part of that consciousness. Is that what you're talking about?"

Spider clapped his hands very rapidly then pointed to me and said, "Yes, that's it. You got it!"

"So where is your consciousness?"

"That's obvious, right here with you."

"OK … now just why are you here with me?"

"That's easy too. To be here with you."

"What?"

"I'll make it easier for you. It's fun here."

"I do have the feeling I'm being made fun of."

"Everyone who has been human has that feeling."

"So there are other spirits that have never been human?"

"Oh yeah, lots."

"How many are lots?"

"Oh … an infinite amount."

"Okay," I said sarcastically. "Do they like to have fun too?"

"Maybe … I don't know … I don't care. Humans are my favorite subject. They lead such tragic and comedic lives. Take Bill, for instance. He was eaten by his children and he can hardly get over it."

I looked at Bill. He nodded his head in agreement, stopped, looked sad, started to cry, then laughed out loud.

"That is right," he said, "nibbled me down to the bones they did. Those ungrateful bastards." He scowled.

Spider smiled and said, "Yes, Bill had a hard life."

Bill stood up and started pacing. He soon started talking as if cued to do so.

"I was an accountant before the bad times."

I snickered, half expecting Bill to begin a Monty Python sketch.

He turned to me and said, "No really, I did good work. I was honest and believed in what I did."

"What? Working with other peoples' money?"

"Yes, I saved a lot of people money. Taxing people is nothing but organized theft.
I ..."

Spider jumped up and forcefully said, "This is irrelevant, isn't it Bill?" He then looked at me and said, "Don't get him riled up, I just recently got him stabilized."

They both sat down, Bill cleared his throat and continued. "Anyway, I was living quite contentedly with my wife and three kids when the world suddenly went crazy. I remember it was in the second year of the global crop failures; just after the second prison population got wiped out by disease, and before the nation-wide prison riots and mass escapes that caused the imposition of marshall law, that was when the real trouble started for my family.

"I remember waking up one night in our home ... hearing gun shots ... then screams coming from outside. I ran to the front window of my house and saw a sight right out of a horror movie. There were looters of every description, size, and age coming up the street with torches. They looked half starved ... wild with drug crazed energy. Some had already reached old Mrs. MacPherson's house across the street ... she was running out of her home. She was completely immersed in flame, as was her house."

Bill paused here. I could see he was reliving that night.

He continued, "I saw dark figures throwing bags onto pickups. Some were already running across the street towards my house, when a military vehicle appeared at the other end of the street firing into the oncoming crowd. Many fell, but the crowd seemed to have no fear, they fired back. Someone had dynamite, which they threw and disabled the vehicle. It kept rolling forward and came to a stop in front of my house. The remaining soldiers were torn apart. In the last moments of the soldiers' lives, a bullet came through my front window. The sound of my glass breaking and the fact that the bullet grazed my head, acted as a wake up call to me. I had been standing there as if I had been watching a movie, but now I came to life. My wife came out asking what was going on. I shouted to her to get the kids dressed and get out the back door within five minutes. I grabbed my gun and a gym bag full of food and we fled."

Bill looked at me straight in the eyes and said, "The whole city was on fire ... chaos was everywhere." He buried his face in his hands and wept.

I thought about what Bill was re-experiencing, and remembered a few things of my own. I had heard many stories like this of the bad times, as we came to call them, but I had not experienced them myself. I had gone into the woods with my kids a year before the first world food crop failure and before the Russian civil war looked like it was going to go nuclear.

When Bill recomposed himself he continued, "My wife wanted to find her parents before we did anything else. It was impossible to use the car with a burning military vehicle in front of the driveway, so we hopped the back fence and made our way through the suburbs to the wild scrub land behind our neighborhood. Others were fleeing the rioters and looters, too. Some of them were very trigger happy in the dark. Matthew, my oldest son, who was sixteen at the time, was real good at spotting them and we did not have any major encounters."

Bill stopped for a moment, looked at something at the other end of the cave and then turned his head slowly as if he was watching something go by. I couldn't see what he was looking at, which annoyed me slightly. I turned to see what Spider was doing. He was just looking at me with a very wide grin … this annoyed me even more.

Bill started again. "We finally made it to my in-laws. They had been in one of the many quarantined zones during the initial stages of the imposition of marshall law. Their house was on fire and they were dead, lying face down on their meticulously manicured lawn. My wife became hysterical. She had maintained her composure up until then, but the sight of her parents brought the unreal events of the night home to her.

"We had keys to their still intact car, and used it to get out of town via a back road which led up to the mountains. I had a cabin hidden away in Oregon where we stayed for a while. The neighbors were great. We formed a small community that pooled resources and protected each other. There were the small groups that tried to steal everything but we had a network of radios that kept us in touch with each other and kept the community together. It was not until after two years of living off the land that the big, well-armed gangs showed up and started picking us off one by one. I knew then that we had to live away from any roads, so I decided to take my family deeper into the mountains.

"I could not believe the throng of people that already were living there. Food was scarce and competition fierce. Most of the people that we met did not try to kill us right away, but they sure were not friendly and did not like to see anyone else living where they were. They tried to drive us back to the former civilized areas, but we ended up deeper into the wilderness. Years passed. Winter was coming on fast and we decided to stick it out in a cave until spring when my life fell apart. Life had been very hard for the past ten years, the last four being the hardest. We had survived and stayed fairly well fed. But our food was running out.

"My sons and I were out hunting, when three men entered our camp, stole most of what we had and took my wife and daughter. I was enraged. We followed them for two days and then caught up with them. We were outgunned and I used up the last of our ammunition in that fight. I think I got one of them but I was wounded in the leg and my sons had to drag me back to the cave. My wound began to fester. My sons were getting edgy. They blamed me for not being able to get their mother back. My oldest son Matthew wanted to go after the abductors. I told him he had to check the traps, bring back food and nurse me back to health, so we could all go after them. We argued almost daily about what should be done. At the end I got so angry I struck my son across the mouth. He snapped. He attacked me so violently I had no chance. He pushed me so fiercely out of the cave, I tripped and fell backwards. I landed on my neck ten feet below the opening of the cave. I never woke up. "

Bill started sobbing here. Spider reached over and patted him on the back and said, "Remember what I said.

Talking about your death is good therapy for you, Bill. It helps you to let go. You did the best you could and that's all anyone could do. Be proud of how long you lasted. Not as many made it as far as you did. "

Spider had a odd smirk on his face as he sat back and watched again.

Bill straightened up with a new look on his face. Harder and proud. He continued, "I found myself back in the cave yelling at my son. He was crying and ignoring me. I found that I could no longer touch him. I saw them bring my body back into the cave and realized I was dead. I could not get over how stupid Matthew had been. I ranted and raved for days. My body froze in the heart of winter. My sons had found nothing new to eat. Matthew sta talking about eating me. James, my youngest would have nothing of it. But they became more and more hungry, and then James got sick. Matthew started to cut my body up, cooked it and force fed it to James, lying that it was something that he had caught. Matthew used every piece of flesh, and with the birds they caught, managed to keep themselves alive until spring.

"I followed them wherever they went. I had nothing better to do. I found that I could irritate Matthew by trying to touch his face, apparently the last contact I had with him left a permanent mark which I could manipulate. But I got bored even of that. Those months of being in the cave with them, unable to communicate, nearly drove me nuts. Only the anger that I felt over Matthew killing me and eating me kept me there. I wanted to know what would happen to them. So when they decided to go and search for my wife and daughter I got interested. I wanted them to do it. My sons would be heroes and I would be proud of them. My wife would guide them again and I would have some peace. I followed them back to where we had had the fight with the abductors, but just before we got there, a rock slide came down and crushed James to death. Matthew had managed to jump behind a rock and avoid being hurt. Matthew could see nothing but the hand of his brother beneath the rubble. After he realized he was dead, he covered what was left of him up and started running.

"Meanwhile, James stood sheepishly beside me unable to look me in the eye. I had no time to comfort him. I just grabbed his hand and dragged him along after me. Matthew did not have to run far because the abductors had a winter camp not far from the place of the fight. He ran at them screaming and waving his knife. I caught up to him and tried touching his face. This only seemed to make him madder … and he ran faster. The men in the camp at first seemed worried … then amused. One of them fired at Matthew, then another. They hit him. He went down … got up, and staggered at them. When he got close they fired again. He stayed down. They came up to him. He screamed at the top of his lungs, frothing at the mouth. They shot him again then threw him into the river. I saw him standing beside the river. I yelled at him, 'that was a stupid thing to do' and I thought he was a disgrace. He looked at me crying then ran away. I stood there numb. James stood beside me crying, not knowing what to do. I went to the abductor's cabin. I saw my wife, lying on the floor dying from illness and my daughter, obviously pregnant, was wiping her forehead. She was crying too. She had seen Matthew die."

I couldn't take it anymore. I had to say something. "Spider, why are we listening to Bill's story?"

All Spider would say was "For good reasons. Keep listening."

Bill continued on, after a nod from Spider. "I looked

at my wife and daughter and just cried. I heard the men talking about leaving this place but complaining how they could not leave the woman because she was too sick. One of them got mad at this statement and walked over to my wife and shot her, splattering blood on my daughter. He coldly said, 'We do not have to worry about her any more.' They left, half pulling my daughter away. She no longer cared what happened to her. My wife took a while to die, but when she did, I saw her jump up enthusiastically as if she had been just freed of a large burden. She saw me and gave me a hug. I slowly came out of my stupor and hugged her back. She seemed so full of life, even though her body was dead. She was practically dancing when she pulled me outside the cabin. She let go of me and said 'I never imagined it to be so beautiful.' She had opened her arms wide and appeared to be drinking in the scenery. She looked up and said, 'Oh, Bill do you see it?' I looked, but saw nothing. She was mesmerized, never taking her eyes off of the sky. She said 'Look there's …' and her voice became garbled. Her spirit started to fade. She looked at me one last time, the look of ecstasy on her face turning to puzzlement, then she disappeared completely."

Bill paused for a moment, looking again like he was watching something happening in front of him then he continued. "I sat there stunned. I watched the river. Even James had deserted me, around the time the man shot my wife. I did not know what had happened to me, why everything had gone wrong. I must have sat there for years. One day two spirits approached me. One of them talked to himself a lot and called himself Bruno."

I stopped him and asked, "A big guy that looked like he'd been hit by a truck?"

Bill replied, "That is an adequate description of him." Spider cackled a laugh of extreme amusement. I peeked at him from the corner of my eye trying to figure him out when Bill continued, "He started talking about a committee of spirits who had found a way to ascend and they needed my help."

I looked confused.

Spider said, "They used to persuade spirits to join in the beginning."

I didn't feel any better after his explanation.

Bill got a bit more emotional when he continued. "I told them I was not interested in any committee. This made Bruno mad and they tried to grab me. I started running. They kept after me like blood hounds. They chased after me for hundreds of miles until we bumped into a gathering of spirits near a waterfall. They immediately went into their sales pitch and this gave me a chance to get away. Even though I was curious about those two and the gathering at the waterfall, some instinct told me to get away from them. I wandered north for a while, until I came to a gorgeous mountain that glistened in the sun. To my surprise there was a small gathering of spirits sitting near the top, softly chanting. They were friendly and invited me to sit with them. I asked what they were doing and they told me they were trying to ascend, by gathering the energy of the sun, stars and earth. I asked them why they were doing this, none of them had a good answer, I found myself sitting among them trying to ascend as well. I also found out that most of these spirits had had an experience with the gatherers of the committee, as they came to call them. One of them, Bob was his name, told me that he thought that the gatherers were devil worshippers when they were alive and had made alliances with evil spirits. I did not know what to make of it at first, but Bob really believed what he was telling me. He said he tried to get close to where the committee was located and he saw a huge one horned spirit prowling around. That was enough for him and he went straight to the mountains."

I interrupted here and asked Spider, "Just what is this committee?'

"Patience, patience," he replied. "Just let Bill finish his story then I'll get to your questions."

Bill looked at Spider, who had nodded again, and Bill started, "One day, though, we saw a group of gatherers running towards the mountain. Bob grabbed me and told me to run. Most of the others ran also. Some stayed. I saw those who were behind us get overtaken by some gatherers and beaten by them with small rods. Their screams motivated us to run faster. There were two still following us, when in front of us, we noticed Bruno. He was smiling and twirling his rod like a baton. Bob ran straight for Bruno, and before Bruno could swing at him, Bob threw himself at his legs, knocking him over. Bruno grabbed him, but Bob struggled valiantly. Bob looked at me for an instant and yelled at me to run. The other two caught up to where Bruno and Bob were struggling and quickly had Bob pinned. Bruno commanded the other two to get me as he said 'no one gets away from Bruno.' The other two let go of Bob and started to come after me. I had been standing there deciding what to do, when Bob lurched free of Bruno and grabbed the other two. They were still moving toward me but at a much slower pace, dragging Bob behind them.

"Bruno, having recovered, began to wickedly hit Bob with his rod. Bob screamed horribly but never let go. In between his screams he yelled, 'Run, you fool.' I ran.

"Bob must have let go, because the other two eventually followed me, but Bob had given me enough of a lead. I ducked into a small crevasse and they ran by.

"I stayed there for a few years before I came out again. I had wormed my way deep into the earth. Spider told me that is why they missed me because they have not learned how to look into the earth. I eventually came out and started to head north, but I had not seen the last of Bruno. He had waited for me to come out, and the chase was on again. This time though he seemed much faster. He had almost caught me when, as we passed a large cave, the spirit of a bear jumped out and lunged at Bruno. The bear started taking chunks out of Bruno and devouring them. Bruno seemed unfazed and just hit him with his rod. The battle was quite ferocious but I stopped watching when a spirit of a wolf came up to me and bit me on the ankle. He trotted away and turned to see if I would follow. I did, and he led me straight to Spider's cave. It was strange but these were two of the animals I had dreamed of when I had stayed in that crevasse. "

Bill looked up from the fire, looked at me, and said, "Spider comforted me over the years and taught me many things, even about you. I always wondered what had happened to Bruno but I understand you have met him as well, which means he survived the attack of the bear. Which I think of as bad news, because what does not destroy you makes you stronger, *and all what we need is a stronger Bruno*."

Spider laughed at Bill's sarcasm. He laughed so heartily that he even made me smile, which only made him laugh harder. Spider went on for quite some time when he stopped quite suddenly and said, "You have finished for now Bill, go to your dance. "

Bill stood up and was starting towards the back of the cave when he stopped and slowly turned, as if he had been watching something go by slowly and it had now stopped at his feet. He was looking intently at this something close to his feet.

I got annoyed and said, "What are you gawking at? "

I crossed my arms to emphasize my annoyance.

Bill looked at me and said, "Your grandchildren, can you not see them?"

4

SPIDER

"What?" I exclaimed, "How come you can see them and I can't?"

Spider jumped over the fire, and landed so that we were face to face, with him squatting over my crossed legs. The more I leaned back, the more he leaned forward, keeping our noses only two inches apart. He wryly said, "It's because while you are in this cave, all you want to perceive is me. And the only reason you saw Bill was because I introduced him to you. So without further ado, may I introduce to you your grandchildren."

He bounced into the air from his squat and did a little dance beside the fire. He pointed down with palms up, to the figure curled up close to what I saw now was a real fire.

"Here is Rose."

Suddenly I recognized her. She looked extremely tired but peaceful in her sleep. Spider now stepped delicately over her, moving about four feet on the tip of his toes. He again pointed down.

"Here is Robert."

Spider used his true name, but I always called my eldest grandchild Bobby. He was sitting next to the fire with his head on his knees, gently tending the flames with a heavy expression on his face.

Spider then did a back flip and landed behind Bobby.

"Here is Daniel."

Daniel was curled up in some large furs, snoring contentedly. He was the second oldest, and Bobby's brother.

Spider then jumped onto the wall, clinging like his namesake, and nodded with his head down to the sleeping figure of someone sitting against the wall with furs at her feet.

"Here is Melissa with her daughter Lolita."

Melissa was the oldest daughter from my daughter's four children. A baby was at her feet, amongst the furs. Melissa and Paul must have named their child Lolita. I stared at the baby. As I watched the sleeping Lolita, all the hopes I had when I was alive came back to me ... the dream that somehow my grandchildren could survive and rebuild the world.

I couldn't watch her long though, as Spider continued his antics.

Spider did his longest jump across the room, doing what seemed like a dozen twirls in the air before landing almost on top of another figure.

"Here is Mary."

Mary was the youngest sibling of the four, but still older than her cousin Rose. She was stretched out to her full six feet, lying just like the log she appeared to be imitating.

Spider then casually walked over to the entrance of the cave and said, "And here are your other pupils, Peter, Paul and Michael."

These were some of the others that had joined our

group at one time or another. There had been many over the years, some died, some left, but these three were among the longest that had stuck with us. Paul was the oldest of the three. They all had spears in their hands, with more close by. They were half asleep, half listening for outside noises.

Spider looked at me closely, having crept up to me without my noticing. I had been scanning all the living people in the cave. He jerked his head while looking at Bill, as if telling him to get lost. Bill continued his way to the back of the cave. As I watched Bill go, he broke out into a jerky dance, and I noticed that the cave seemed slightly darker as he left. I also noticed that the some of the light appeared to follow Bill, but the light following him was a lot less than the light that was around Spider. I noticed that the rocks had glowed as Spider had moved toward me. The closer he was to them, the brighter they glowed.

After a while Spider apparently got tired of looking at my ear and finally asked me, "So how did you like Bill's story?"

"It's hard to believe that so many tragic events could happen to one person."

"They didn't. They happened to his whole family."

"Okay. Granted, but still, I thought my life had been hard, but compared to Bill's ... it was easy."

"That's what makes it so fun being h uman, you never know what's going to happen next."

"Fun? FUN? Are you a sadist or something?"

"No," Spider said simply.

"Well, what possibly was fun about Bill's tale?"

"You are not looking at the bigger picture, you are only looking at the details and getting caught up in them. Of course it must not have been too pleasant actually experiencing the moments that Bill related in his story, but if you look at the whole of Bill's life it was good, and it had a lot of lessons in it. So what did YOU learn from his tale?"

I stood up and paced about a bit, but I couldn't get past the 'details' as Spider called them.

"I still can't stop thinking that here is a man with a tragic life."

"Nexus, you disappoint me. Can you not see that Bill had something miraculous happen to him, but he chose not to see it, and instead chose to carry on with the feud he had with his son."

"What do you mean?"

"His wife ..."

I stared at him stupidly.

"Her death ..."

I still didn't know what he was getting at.

"She ascended."

"Ascended? What does that mean?"

"It's like winning the lottery of the death game. She did it. Whenever you witness an ascension there's a chance you can go with that spirit, even if you are still alive. But no, Bill chose to mourn the loss of his wife and thus he could not see what she saw and felt. He chose instead to hold onto his existence as he knew it, and clung to petty grievances. So what if his son ate him! He should just forgive and go on from there, but he held on to that event and never let it go, and so he missed out on what was happening right in front of him. Then he gets another opportunity to ascend, and instead he gets caught up in the comedy that is now encompassing the planet, that new fad, the 'committee.' That's why I say it is a lot of fun. Humans! Something about being human makes the spirit go funny ... that's just the way it is. I've seen plenty of humans ascend, some even before their bodies died, but a lot of you just don't get it."

"Is this something I should be doing?" I asked meekly.

"Should? There are no shoulds. Do you want to or not? Do it or don't do it, but don't 'should' it."

"Okay. Do I want to do this? Is it something that is good for me? And why haven't you done it?"

"Which question do you want me to answer first, the first one or the last one. Focus! You're almost as bad as you were when you were alive."

"Ahh, the last one."

"Don't assume anything, I may have or I may not have."

I didn't know what to make of this answer. So I thought a bit about what Spider had just been saying and asked, "How come you made it sound like you were not human, when you said 'a lot of you don't get it.'"

"I'm not."

I looked at him again with suspicion. "Well, just what are you?"

"I already told you, I am exactly what you expect me to be."

I wanted to scream. His answers were so evasive. There was a lesson in here somewhere, but damned if I knew what it was. I started to withdraw and go blank. Spider looked at me and shrugged, then looked blankly back at me. No thoughts came to my head. I stared at Spider for I don't know how long. His eyes began to look like dark pools of cool water and I felt I could stare at them for eternity. It took me a while to realize it, but I was staring at a reflection of myself.

A mirror. Spider was a mirror. I wanted him to reflect my thoughts. I got it.

"You are a mirror!" I shouted.

"Okay. Crude but effective description. I am an image of your thoughts that you see, to understand what you have to understand."

"Huh?"

"If you didn't understand that, then call me one of your teachers."

I felt stupid. It was crystal clear when I thought of him as a mirror but when he tried to explain it to me I got lost. Was it that Spider was a manifestation of my own thoughts that was trying to tell me what to search for?

"It's not that hard. You are only making it harder because you feel that is the only way that you can learn anything. I'm a helper, okay? Just leave it at that. Be present. Do you see your grandchildren now?"

I searched the cave but could see no one, but I did see where a shallow grave had been dug and filled up again. It had a rock with a few words etched in it. 'HERE LIES OUR BELOVED GRANDFATHER'.

"I don't see them, where did they go."

"They stopped sleeping in here months ago. Bill has been having some fun with them so they moved out."

"Months?"

"Yes, you turned into a vegetable for a few months before you woke up and called me a mirror."

"You can't be serious when you say it was months ago, it felt like only a few moments."

"I'm very serious."

To counter this point Spider jumped up, danced a little jig, then sat down again.

"I only take you as seriously as you take me."

"I take you very seriously."

"No you don't. You only give a part of your consciousness. You are totally absorbed in yourself. You don't even notice what's going on around you. Months go by before you even acknowledge I'm here."

"Months? I still have problems with that."

"Your perception has altered slightly since you died. As a spirit, you have to pay more attention to time than when you were alive, or it can sneak right by you. You don't have a body to remind you to eat, drink, have sex, etc. and prevent you from blanking out like you did. Believe me, a lot of people that are alive do it most of their waking moments. They're different when they sleep, that's usually when they have fun."

"Okay, I promise to pay more attention and be more aware."

"Don't give me empty promises, just do it or don't do it."

"I don't make empty promises," I said.

"Are you sure you don't? Look at your grave and tell me what you see."

Flowers. Somehow flowers had been laid on top of the grave.

"How did those flowers get there?"

"Rose came in and placed them there. She walked right behind you."

I looked at him and frowned.

"Okay, how do I become more aware?"

"Well, if you were alive it would be easier to teach you, because you would get feedback. You could just stop and listen to the sound. The sound that is in everything. And you could unfocus your eyes and see everything. And you could feel everything with your heart. The pulse that runs through you, runs through everything. If you had learned this when you were alive you would have found it easier to let go after you died."

"I did learn some of that during my life. And I can let go," I said emphatically. "If you could let go, you wouldn't be talking to me right at this moment. And if you did learn to do some of the things I have mentioned, you did not take them to your heart and live that way, you only did it on special occasions, like when you used to visit me in this cave."

I felt cheated. What exactly was going on? How could months pass by while I was trying to figure something out. I had to satisfy my curiosity. I got up and went to the entrance of the cave. Outside I saw snow clinging on the cedars. Winter. I also noticed a thin column of smoke in the distance. This disturbed me, because I had taught my grandchildren better than to allow their camp fires to be seen, and if it wasn't them, then someone else was in the valley. I went back inside.

"Okay, you seem to be so smart about this death stuff, tell me a few things."

Spider smiled a smile that went from ear to ear, which gave him an unnatural appearance.

"What would you like to know? Keeping in mind that you have been very scattered so far in all your actions towards me, and your questioning of me, I will offer you a little help. Go back in your thoughts to a few months ago, to the first time when you saw me as a mirror."

His words irritated me a little. A few months ago indeed. I had just had the revelation of the mirror a few moments ago. But I tried anyway. I remember looking into his eyes and seeing the depths of ages. There was something very comforting about that. Staring into them made me forget all else. My reflection was ever present, but I had no awareness of myself. It was as if I experienced all of everything but had no motivation to do anything. However, the most important thing was that the normal way of thinking had ceased. Thoughts didn't flow through in the usual way, it was as if thoughts existed somewhere else and if I allowed them to, they could flow through me. I remember now that this is what was happening to me, but at the time I felt as if I was just blank.

"I remember. I wasn't just sitting there, I was everywhere."

"Good. You did experience the mirror effect but it took you a long time to realize what you were doing. If you could have retained just a small amount of self awareness while you were communing, you would have remembered more and had more control of the experience. But here is something that I want you to remember. Anyone can be your mirror, you just have to be aware of it. All you have to do is project the thoughts of what you want to know, and if you listen or use your awareness, the person you are talking to will tell you what you want to know, whether directly or indirectly. In fact, this is happening all the time, but most humans are oblivious to it, even though the information they are searching for is often repeated to them over and over again. That's another reason why I like humans. They are so stupid and yet so brilliant at the same time. A real paradox."

He cackled with glee and then made an eerie face at me.

I tried to ignore his feeble attempt at humor, but Spider had a way of changing his appearance that made a chill go down your spine, even if you didn't have one any more. So I asked, "You make it sound like it is a good way to learn, to mirror."

"Good? GOOD?!! IT'S GREAT! It's one of the best way for humans to learn. Just blank out, forget about yourself, connect up the to higher consciousness and talk. Talk without realizing what you're saying and the most profound things can come out of your mouth. I stopped thinking centuries ago, all I do now is have fun."

Bill walked from the back of the cave that was hidden from view, closer to the fire and said, "Are you finished your talk yet?"

Spider replied, "Are you kidding, we've only just started, why?"

"Well, I'm a little concerned about Nexus' grandchildren."

I perked up and asked, "Why, what's wrong?"

"Most of them are gravely sick and Rose keeps coming in here every day to talk to you. I think you should talk to her and ease her mind, she's so sad."

"I would talk to her if I knew how. That's what brought me here in the first place."

Spider looked at me and laughed. "What's so hard about talking to the living?"

"I don't know. I've never done it before. What do you do? What are the rules?"

"Boy, do you ever like to make things hard. It's just as hard for the dead to talk to the living as it is for the living to talk to the dead."

"Are you sure? Can you help me?"

"Yes, and okay. Watch it, that's two questions." He glared at me then continued, "So, step by step I want you to tell me how you went about talking to spirits like me when you were alive."

"Well, first thing to do is relax. Slow your breathing and listen to your heart. Let your heart be your pulse. If you can't get your heart to be steady and even, then use a drum or a rattle and let that be your beat. Next is the hardest part, you have to stop your mind from having any thoughts. This was always the most difficult part for me."

"Yeah, I know." Spider smiled at me.

"I usually concentrated on the sound of my drum until all I was thinking about was the sound of the drum, then since this was the only thing I was thinking of, it was then easy to stop thinking about that because that was my only thought I was thinking."

"Wow, you do have a convoluted way of thinking. Why don't you just say 'quiet your thoughts' and go on from there."

"Okay, you quiet your thoughts. Next you have to energize yourself in some way" I said.

"You don't have to do it during your drumming, you can do it before you start."

"I know, I know, but you told me to tell you how I did it."

Spider smiled and said, "Okay, I won't interrupt you any more."

"So, as I said, you energize yourself in some way. You can chant, sing, dance, or you can face the sun at dawn or dusk. You use the power of your voice, the power of your body or the energy of the sun. All that's important is to feel the energy move through you. Now you are ready to communicate. From what I remember Spider, you were hard to talk to. You were always vague in your answers to my questions."

"The vagueness didn't come from me, it came from you. The clearness of your intent, when you were asking me a question, was not always there. Your mind was easily distracted."

"Okay maybe. But the next most important thing to do is, as you say, have a clear intent about what you want to talk about or ask," I said.

"And have only one thing on your mind at a time," Spider scolded me, then continued "How was I to know what question you wanted answered, when you had maybe a dozen or so on your mind? I always picked what I thought was the most important one. You have to be careful, because there are lots of spirits out there, and 99% of them are just 'dying' to talk to the living. Some of them tell you the darnedest things."

"Yeah okay, okay. So make sure that you only ask one thing at a time, you've been on me about that since I got here. But what do you mean about other spirits? Since I've been dead I've only seen four others, including yourself," I said.

"There are millions, billions, an infinite amount of them all around you. You're just so unaware that it's painful to watch you. Look at the rocks, see how they glow."

I had noticed the glow of the rocks before, but now I paid closer attention. The glow appeared to waver slightly, and pulse almost imperceptibly. In fact, the more I focused on one spot, that spot tended to fade a bit, as if something was trying to avoid my gaze. I could almost see something scurrying away, as if it was frightened. I tried touching the rocks with my hand. In focusing on being able to touch the rocks, I noticed an electric feeling that diminished when I was successful in touching the rocks and not having my hand simply pass into them.

"There seems to be something there, but it doesn't appear to like me."

"That's because you do not resonate with them. You should be good at it, because you could easily find the spots where the spirits of the earth congregated. You called them power spots."

"How do you resonate?"

"Just feel the pulse."

"Of the rocks?"

"Yes, the whole planet vibrates. Stop and listen for a moment."

Spider cocked his head to one side and put his hand to his ear, as if listening.

"It's not hard. You do it. All vibrations make a sound, just tune in."

Spider was making strange hand movements, in an attempt to encourage me. I quieted my mind and tried to feel the 'pulse.' The world moved. It frightened me a little. Spider was moving his hands quicker and grimacing a little. I tried again. I quieted my mind once more and felt the world moving. It felt like an earthquake. The earth was screaming at me. I realized that that sound had been present all my life and I had ignored it when I was alive. The earth wants you to notice it. The sound it gives off is like a symphony of thousands of musical instruments in perfect harmony. How could anyone miss that noise?

Spider said, "Good, good, you're getting it now."

I opened my eyes and said, "How did you know what I was hearing?"

"Well, the sound is louder to the dead who choose to listen than it is to the living, but look around you, what do you see?"

At first I didn't know what Spider was talking about, then it hit me. The cave seemed brighter. The rocks all around me were glowing. I saw the small moving shapes within the rock that had eluded me before. They all had individual faces. They were smiling at me, as if they were glad to be in my presence.

"What are they?"

"Rock spirits."

"What do they do?"

"You'll have to discover that for yourself when you are on your own. Before you got distracted again, you were trying to figure something out. You were supposed to try to talk to the living."

"Yes."

"But you may find that talking to the living is similar to resonating with the earth. Just resonate with the living, and follow the steps you described, as to how you talked to spirits when you were alive."

"Don't I have to wait until one of my grandchildren comes back before I try to talk to the living?"

Spider laughed a good hardy laugh. Bill put on an enormous smile.

"If you want to limit yourself, that's your own business, but the short answer is no."

"What do you mean, limit myself?"

"Well, beyond the obvious, if you feel you must actually be 'seeing' the person you want to talk to, you can go out and find someone. But watch out for the gatherers."

Spider snickered, then continued, "But as for waiting for something alive to talk to, what are you, blind? Even though it is the depths of winter outside, there are millions, billions of living things in this cave."

"No, I want to talk to a human."

"What! Are you prejudiced or something? Even though I enjoy talking to humans immensely, it doesn't mean I completely ignore every other life form or spirit. Anyway, I don't want to dictate to you how to think, but if you try to talk to anyone you want without moving, you might have some success."

"What? Just start talking?" I asked.

"No, concentrate on that person, and have nothing else in your mind. Then slowly introduce the topic you wish for discussion, or eavesdrop onto what they are thinking and add your thoughts to theirs. They'll think it was their idea and go on from there. Spirits do this to the living all the time. Mostly the living don't have a clue what's going on and usually pat themselves on the back for having a great idea. But sometimes people notice that there are actually other voices that tell them things. If they don't get locked up in an insane asylum, they find that they have a valuable resource. There are countless spirits who want to help the living. They will do anything that you want, if you just notice them."

"Why?"

"For lots of reasons. One because its fun ... another, because when the living concentrate on the dead, they give them some of their energy. And to a spirit, that's an important one, especially if they haven't figured out an alternative source besides the living," he replied.

"You make it sound like spirits are vampires."

"They can be. They attach themselves to the living because they don't know any better. But most give you something in return, in order that you will like to have them around. Sometimes spirits give you what they think you need, which is not necessarily what you want."

Spider and Bill exchanged a glance, and both smiled.

"I know of a woman who was on the whole, just a normal woman. She moved into a quaint old house with her two kids after her husband died. Now, this house had had a spirit in it. This spirit got on perfectly well with the previous owner ... an old woman who lived out her days in the house and acknowledged the existence of the spirit by holding seances and asking the spirit questions. This spirit wasn't particularly bright and he made up the answers to any question he didn't know and gave answers he knew would please the woman."

"Is this a fairy tale?"

"No, this is reality as far as any one can tell."

I looked hard at Spider to measure his sincerity, but that was impossible. I was wasting my time. He smirked then continued.

"Anyway, this spirit got his energy from the living, and when his source died he got hungry. He was soon frustrated when the new inhabitants took no notice of him. After about a year of being ignored, he knocked a book off a shelf. This event was noticed by one of the kids who told her mom. Knocking things off of shelves is not an efficient way of gaining energy for spirits. So after a few more attempts the spirit gave up. The woman noticed something strange was going on, but didn't attribute it to the spirit. Now, enough time had gone by after her husband's death, that the woman started to wish she had someone as a sexual partner again. The spirit noticed that the woman was devoting a lot of time to these thoughts, so he decided to visit the woman when she was in bed."

"You're not going to tell me what I think you're going to tell me."

"Oh yeah, he did. He did it over and over. All the time thinking that this was what she wanted. Of course, the woman didn't understand what was going on. The spirit, however got what he wanted ... to be noticed. This set many things into motion. The woman at first thought that she was just having a bad nightmare. But when the spirit came back every night and took longer and longer at what he thought was satisfying the woman, she snapped! She went to therapists, counselors, and finally religious people. The latter were convinced that evil spirits inhabited the house, and when they heard that her child had seen a book knocked off a shelf, they arranged to have an exorcism."

"You make it sound as if there are no evil spirits."

Spider frowned and said, "There really aren't. Most spirits are just misunderstood, but I have to admit that some have an agenda that is not compatible to humans. And this could be judged as being evil. Evil is a human definition."

I wasn't convinced by what Spider said, but I listened intently.

"So, anyway, the day of the exorcism arrived. The priest did all his rituals, read from his texts, and tried to bring the power of God to banish all evil from the house. The spirit was a little intrigued at what was going on, but was not excited about it, until he noticed that the priest was focusing all his attention on the spirit. Now, the priest was a powerful man and as he put all his effort into the exorcism, a vast pool of energy formed that was available to the spirit. The spirit happily moved into the pool. As he did, the sudden input of energy into the spirit caused his perception to change. He immediately ascended and never bothered the woman again. The priest happily felt the satisfaction of a job well done and the woman was left to ponder the nature of spirit. So there was a happy ending all around regarding that evil spirit."

Bill clapped his hands, gave a small laugh and said, "Spider, Nexus must be rubbing off on you, or possibly attaching to you. You are getting just as distractible as he."

"So I am. So I am. Now, where was I?"

"You were trying to teach him how to talk to Rose. She seems to be asleep now, maybe that's the best start he can have with communicating with her."

"Asleep! What good will that do me?" I said.

Spider answered, "Novices like you find it easier to talk to the living through their dreams. Just answer all her questions and keep it short."

"Okay, I'll try."

5

ROSE

The first thing I tried to do was relax, but not having a body, I found that the difference between being relaxed and not being relaxed had to be totally a state of mind. So I merely thought I was relaxed, and I was. The next part of the process, hearing my heart beat, was impossible to do. I was perplexed. Relaxed, but perplexed.

"How do I hear my heart beat?"

Spider grinned, "Just hear it."

"But I don't have one."

"If you don't have the imagination to hear it, why don't you use your drum?"

"Drum, what drum?"

"The drum you always carried," he said.

"I hate to tell you this, but I seem to have left it in a previous existence."

Spider bounced around the room like a giant ping pong ball, landed right in front of me, grabbed my ears, wiggled my head from side to side and said, "Stop trying to be funny. You're no good at it. Of course you have your drum with you. Everything you had left an

impression on you. Some things which had a lot of energy
have a lot of spirit. Like your drum and your sword. Just think that you have your drum in your hand and see what happens."

I concentrated for a few seconds and, presto, my drum was in my hands.

"Wow! But is it any good?"

"Why are you asking me? Try it."

I tentatively hit it a few times. The sound was better than ever. In fact, the sound resonated so beautifully that each vibration of the drum never seemed to die away completely. It was as if part of the sound went into the earth and joined the symphony that was already there. I started to sing. My voice too, joined the symphony, and I was carried away. I floated to the spot where Rose slept in our winter lodge. She looked so peaceful. I gently called her name. Her body remained motionless but a spirit body sat up.

"Grandfather!" she yelled with joy.

"Rose!" I shouted right back.

She leapt at me and gave me a great big hug. I immediately noticed that I once again looked like I did when I had died. Old and bent over, wrinkles lining my face and hands. Ever since my meeting with Bruno, I felt youthful. Now I was as I was at my death.

"Grandfather, why haven't you tried to talk me earlier? I felt your presence for these past months ..."

Her voice trailed off from the obvious mix of emotions she was feeling.

"I've been close, and watching you."

I almost felt like I was lying, but I'm sure she wanted to hear that.

"I've had a lot of things to learn before I could come to you."

"I'm glad to see you Grandfather, but I have the need of your advice. There are strangers in the valley. They hunt all creatures in the valley, not caring if they destroy the land. Bobby wants to come at the strangers at night when they are asleep and kill them."

"WHAT?"

"He says that the time for hiding is in the past, and it is time to fight for our land."

"Where has he been getting these ideas from?"

"I know not. But he has got Peter, Paul and Michael on his side. And only I oppose him openly. He tells me I am just a woman and a child and do not know about such matters. He belittles me openly before the others."

Hearing all this would have made my blood boil, if I had any. None of this was part of my teachings to him. I could only assume that it was one of my other pupils that put these ideas in his head. I didn't suspect Paul, because he always seemed so level headed. He was never very forward, and I think he was just following Bobby because he is extremely loyal. Peter was loyal also, but it took me a long time to get him to drop his violent ways. Michael was always quiet and shy, but he was the closest in age to Bobby, and usually never too far away from him. He was my prime suspect. He was the one who always caused problems among the women.

"The land belongs to no one. How does he think that he has a claim on it? We must live in harmony with the environment or else we will destroy what's left of it. Doesn't he see the mistakes of our ancestors?"

"He sees, but he doesn't tolerate any opposition or competition."

"And I always told him to respect everyone's voice in all matters, woman or man. Why does he now no longer listen to you?"

"I tried to take your place as spiritual guide, but he

says that my advice is worthless. He claims that my inability to talk to you shows that I am not capable of filling your shoes. I tried … ”

She started to cry. I held her close once again and said, "You have done the best you can do. Do not fault yourself in these matters. What I do want you to do though is give a message to Bobby from me. But I will have to tell you something that only he and I know so that he will believe you. DO NOT use this information for your own gain! "

"I will not" she said softly.

"Do you remember twelve winters ago, when the snow stayed on the ground longer than it had in many years? You were just becoming a woman then. "

"Yes."

"Well do you also remember, food was really scarce that year and we sent out the hunters daily, and most returned with very little or nothing at all? "

"Yes."

"Bobby had always been the best hunter among us, and remember how he didn't bring back much either? "

"But wasn't that the year that he found that elk carcass frozen in the snow, which saved us? "

"Yes, you remember well. But there was a problem with his story. I noticed we were all starving, but Bobby didn't look like he was suffering much from the lack of food. He ate his meager share like the rest of us. But when he went out to hunt or check the traps for a few days with little or nothing, he returned well nourished. I questioned him and he replied that he ate only his hunter's share while out in the wild, to sustain himself. I questioned him no more, but I did follow him the next time he went out on the hunt. He went alone, and he was very careful in making sure he was not followed, which I found strange. He traveled for two days then waited a half a day watching behind him. He then tried to hide his tracks, forgetting my lesson that it only makes them more obvious. He then went to a place he had obviously stayed many times before and proceeded to dig up an elk carcass."

Rose's face showed distress, because she couldn't believe that Bobby would withhold food from the rest of us. This was a sacred event among us, the sharing of food.

"I watched him for a while. He made a fire and ate. He stayed there for two days, eating to his heart's content. There was plenty of meat for all of us but he showed no signs of preparing the carcass for transport back to our camp. So, on the second night, after he went to sleep, I crept up to his fire, without him noticing, and tended it for the night."

Rose now had a wry smile on her face in anticipation of what I would say next. She, too had been on the receiving end of my lessons.

"Bobby slept like a log until dawn when he awoke and saw me there. At first he was slow on the uptake, for he must have thought he was back at camp. But when he realized where he was he immediately jumped to his feet and shouted 'Grandfather! What are you doing here?' To which I nonchalantly replied 'Oh I was just in the neighborhood and thought I would drop in to see what our best hunter was up to.' Bobby then went into some inane story about tracking some deer that were close by. I let him go on for several minutes saying about everything that he could think of. He didn't stop talking for five minutes, hardly pausing long enough to take a breath. I think he felt that if he kept on talking and never gave me enough time to say anything, he would escape unscathed from his serious offence."

Rose now laughed. I bet she just loved imagining the

thought of Bobby getting caught with his hand where it wasn't supposed to be.

"He eventually stopped talking about hunting, and was going on about the weather, when he noticed me scratching at the earth where the carcass was buried. You should have seen him. He turned pale. He tried to say he was about to go on a hunt, and asked me to go hunting with him because he needed my advice. I ignored him and started to dig a bit harder, saying that this bush was a good bush for medicinal purposes, and that I would join him in a few minutes after I had retrieved a few roots. I said these roots were good for aiding in the digestion of meat. He looked like a wild, trapped animal. He ran around to the other side of the bush and yelled 'its easier to dig over here Grandfather!' even though there were rocks there. He bloodied his hands digging trying to out dig me, because I had sped up. When I found the skins that he had wrapped the meat in, I said 'What's this, hairy roots?' He stopped and began to sob. He told me everything. How he had surprised the elk and put his spear straight into its throat, killing him in short order. He told me how weary he was after the brief struggle and how he did not want the wolves that found him to dig up the kill while he went to get help to bring back the meat. So he stayed with the carcass and fed until he felt better. He told himself he would use the meat to make himself strong and better be able to bring back food for the rest. He then cried until the sun had risen far into the sky."

Rose knew the severity of the punishment I would have to deal out would be harsh, because there were few transgressions worse than holding back food.

"I tried to tell him that he was being very foolish, that he might just as well have taken a knife to our throats, and killed us outright, rather than watching us die slowly from lack of food. But all he could say was that he wouldn't do it again, please forgive him and please don't tell the others. I promised that as long as I lived I would not tell another soul. That promise I have kept because I am no longer alive, and you are the first one I have told this story to."

"But what punishment did you give Bobby?"

"Well, I told him that after he carried all the meat to our camp by himself, he would then see what the world would be like if we were no longer with him. So I told him he would have to stay away from all of our group and live in the wild by himself until the fall, when he should return to us, with as much food as he could carry. I told him to meet us in the valley."

"I remember, you told us that Bobby had had a vision, which I had found hard to believe, and that he was to live alone for the spring and summer following his vision. We were all happy with Bobby for bringing us all enough meat to survive the rest of the winter. But we were all sad to see him go. I remember when he returned in the fall, we gave him a hero's feast, for we were all happy to see him and all the food that he brought with him. I see now that he didn't deserve it."

"Oh no, he did deserve it. He learned his lesson, but again I remind you not to use this story for anything else but for the message I now want you to give to Bobby."

"Yes Grandfather."

"Bobby really was better after his time alone in the wild. He was greatly improved in his outlook as to the survival of our group, and he generously shared everything he had. That is why I am so surprised by the story you have told me."

"I swear it is true."

"I believe you, little one."

"Grandfather, you have said yourself that I am no

longer a little one ... ”

“Quite right, but for a moment there, I saw you as you were when I still had the strength to lift you. But to more important matters. Give Bobby these messages. First, he is to remember his place in the world. All are equal in counsel, and everyone’s voice must be heard. Second, the land belongs to no man, so it is not worth fighting over. Third my advice is to hide, not fight. But if he feels that there is no other choice but to contest the valley with these strangers, he must not attack them like a coward in the night. He should go to them during the day and issue a challenge that they should leave the valley and if they refuse, then meet them in battle. ”

“I will do this Grandfather. ”

Rose was tiring and her spirit body beg an to fade.

I cried out, “I love you granddaughter. ”

Her mouth curled up in a small and she faded completely. Her physical body turned in its sleep and issued a large sigh. I stood there for a moment longer, then I heard a voice.

“Nexus. ”

I found myself back in the sacred cave. Spider and Bill were looking at me intently.

“That’s pretty good for a beginner, ” Spider said with a large grin. “But you taxed your granddaughter too hard. You have to be careful with the living. She did well to maintain her contact with you for so long, but don’t count on it in the future. You have to be quicker and more precise in what you want to say, because the living are easily distracted. She must be a focused sleeper to have stayed attached to you for so long, or her desire to see you must have been great. ”

“It felt like we were both alive and talking normally. ”

“To you it did. But to her it was a dream. And she could have experienced other things that the living feel when they are asleep. But even for you, was it truly like you were alive?"

"No, there was one point when I actually saw her as a little girl."

"Yes, her spirit picked up on the fact that you still consider her as a child, and it accommodated that thought by her appearing to you as a young girl."

"So that's what you told me before, that your appearance is what I expect you to be."

Spider capered about the cave singing, "He gets it! He gets it!"

Bill watched Spider for a while and commented, "Nexus, sometimes I don't understand what you are thinking."

"What do you mean?"

"Why do want Spider to appear as he does and why do you want him to act in such a bizarre fashion?"

"I don't want him to. He just is that way. He's crazy."

"I beg to differ. When I was his main focus, he was the model of seriousness and sincerity."

I looked at Bill in disbelief. To imagine Spider acting in anything but the bizarre fashion he did was beyond me.

Spider yelled at us, "Stop it you two, you're splitting me in two."

He wavered for a moment, then the two halves of him walked away from each other. One half laughed like a lunatic, while the other had the manner of a clean cut business man in a suit.

The clean cut version simply said, "Bill we need to talk. We have to find some time to discuss some important matters, but first I must finish with a trivial matter. It won't take much longer."

The lunatic Spider laughed even harder, which I

didn't believe was possible. The clean cut version of Spider merged with the now rolling-on-the-floor version of Spider. When they were whole again, Spider jumped up and said, "Okay time's up, it's time you got moving and finish what you have set in motion. Go play with your grandchildren and when you are satisfied with the results, come back and see me."

"But, but ..."

"No buts, just go."

"What do you mean?"

"I don't mean anything."

Spider lightly picked me up and tossed me out of the cave. I fell to the ground, feeling no pain. If I had a human body, I'm sure it would have hurt. He briefly reappeared at the entrance of the cave, and threw my sword at me, narrowly missing me, and said, "And take your junk with you."

I heard giggling come from the cave, then a serious voice which trailed off, "Now Bill, where were we ..."

I sat in front of the cave debating what to do. The sudden expulsion by Spider had taken me totally by surprise. I scanned my surroundings and saw the cedars that I had seen over many years. They were different. They oozed life and I could see it even in the dormant stage of their winter existence and the damage they had sustained from the radiation fallout of the Russian civil war. The wind made them dance, and it was magic. Each tree, every branch down to the smallest twig had a light that shone from within. They pulled the light from the very earth, and with the light came a sound. A sound so beautiful that tears came unbidden from shear joy. If I had been alive the joy would have killed me because it was so intense, but as a spirit I could enjoy the intensity. Life was so magnificent that I now understood its attraction to spirits. I looked at my body and it was once again young. The energy to sustain me was coming from the earth and beyond. All it took was an awareness to see it. I felt like I could let go and dissolve into that light and sound. But something reminded me of Rose The longer I thought of her, the fainter the sound, until it was gone. The trees looked like trees again, I grabbed my sword and I was up and running to find my grandchildren.

6

SID

I saw smoke rising in the distance. It wa s an obvious choice for a destination ... besides I was curious about the strangers who had managed to find this valley.

They chose for their campsite an open area next to the lake, close to one of the small creeks that come from springs in the mountains.

My grandchildren should be in a shelter that we built in a secluded part of the valley, close, but not too close, to a spring which feeds the lake on the opposite side of the lake. They should be safe from detection for a while.

The strangers were all lying around, obviously enjoying the sun after having bathed in the lake. Fish were being smoked in a crude stick teepee covered in small animal hides. There were five strangers in total, all male, dressed in deerskins. They were skilled woodsman by the evidence of all the objects lying around the camp. There were wooden and stone tools and weapons. There were also inverted stomachs that were used for water containers and turtle shells for food preparation vessels. They had sacks of grains and rope made from plants

All seemed okay, except, I found it strange that I couldn't identify the animal used for holding the water.

These men appeared to have had a good teacher who knew a lot about the wilderness. But when I peered behind some rocks, I saw all sorts of animals in various states. There were far to many for this small group for food. They should be preparing them for preservation, but most were lying there. The weather was warm for a winter day, as was usual in this valley. The meat on these animals would spoil unless they got to work fast. This was wrong and I understood why Bobby was so anxious to rid the valley of these strangers. I was about to go and find my grandchildren and talk to Rose again, when I heard.

"Hey Sid, check it out, we got company."

I turned to see five grotesque human-like apparitions. Their skin was all mottled with bulging cysts. They had hair in the wrong places and none in the right places. Some of the cysts on their heads resembled stubby horns.

They had quickly surrounded me and were poking at me, all spouting incomprehensible little noises resembling animal sounds. They were circling me at an even pace and I was beginning to have trouble focusing. I raised my sword. They stopped instantly and stood back. The largest among them said, "We don't mean no harm. I'm Sid, this is Ralph, Ernie, Barry and Clem."

He pointed to all the rest around me, but they were so indistinguishable from one another that I'm sure I would not be able to tell one from another later on. Sid was distinguishable because his horns looked more like actual horns and he was half a head taller than the others. None of them struck me as being very bright and none of them seemed dangerous, either. I lowered my sword. Sid was their obvious spokesman and leader.

I addressed him, "My name is Nexus. Glad to meet you."

When they heard me say this, they made noises like

happy children who had heard something that delighted them. They clapped their hands, jumped, spun around and giggled.

"We're glad to meet you, too" Sid said with a big grin. "We don't get to meet too many dead ones who talk to us."

"Why is that?"

"Don't know."

I wanted to say its because they were so repulsive, but I was polite.

Sid took a side glance and said, "You don't like the way we look."

I got all apologetic and said, "No, no. It doesn't matter to me at all."

I cursed myself silently for not being able to let go of my hang up on appearance and realized that Sid was capable of reading my thoughts. Why could everyone do this except me?

Sid frowned and said, "We don't choose to look like this but live ones that feed us make us look like this."

"What do you mean?"

Sid looked hard at me, it was sort of like watching an old computer working, before he said, "Live ones see us when they feed us, and they want us to look this way."

I was having trouble with the whole situation because I just stared at Sid blankly. I was having trouble formulating a question or a response to what Sid had said.

It was a while before I said, "What do you mean, the live ones feed you?"

"When they kill things."

"Yes go on," I said, not liking what I was hearing.

"They kill things and we feel full."

"What do you mean?"

Sid looked at me with squinted eyes and said, "Are

you stupid or something. I said full. We get strong and big."

I gazed at Sid with disbelief. I couldn't fathom how a spirit could say nonchalantly that he gets fed by things dying. Then I laughed. Well, when I was alive I fed off of the remains of many organisms. Why would it be different for spirits that are dead. All animal life on the planet relies on the death of other life, plant or animal. Why would another layer of feeding at the spirit level surprise me. Still it had a ghoulish feel to it that I couldn't fully accept.

"What does it feel like, exactly, to eat?'

Sid looked somewhat perplexed and asked, "Why? Don't you eat?"

"Not since I was alive."

Sid asked as shrewdly as he could, "How long you been dead?"

Even though it felt like only one long day, I knew by the passing of the seasons that I had been dead for months. But I didn't know exactly how many months.

"Less than a year."

"Oh I see," Sid said and nodded his head knowingly.

"Why? Is there something I should know?"

"Yeah. You haven't started to fade yet, so you are not hungry yet."

I couldn't imagine eating, nor getting hungry either.

Sid continued, "And there are no new babies and all the animals are dying, so there is no room inside live ones, so we have to eat. Else there would be nothing left of us. We've seen some who didn't eat. They slowly fade away 'til you don't see them a'ymore."

This whole conversation was making me curious. I wondered how many spirits did this feeding. From what Sid had told me it didn't sound as though eating was his first choice. His first choice was the desire to be reborn in another body. But with the massive die off of life on the planet, the competition for babies must be fierce. I could see how Sid and his gang could easily be pushed out by more competitive spirits. But the mystery that remained was, how did spirits feed? And was the fear of non-existence so keen among spirits that they felt the need to feed to avoid fading away? I know the feeling Bruno had given me, that deep set fear that my existence could be snuffed out. Was it real or an illusion? Sid claimed to have seen spirits fade away. So did Bill. But Spider said that that was a happy event. I had seen Friend disappear but I'm pretty sure that he was still around. Could I take what Sid was telling me as the truth? Something about his whole situation was blurry. Something didn't ring true. I just couldn't put my finger on it.

"Well, I'd like to be able to stick around, but I've got to find someone."

"Who you have to find?" Sid asked seriously.

"My grandchildren."

"Why you have to find them?"

Good question. What was I doing? Spider had kicked me out of the cave and I realized I had nowhere to go. The message I gave to Rose should have been sufficient instruction to help my grandchildren. I now know that there was nothing in the sacred cave that could harm them. So why was I going to see my grandchildren? Just because I have nothing better to do?
Because I am a homeless spirit that requires some familiarity to stay sane?

I stared at Sid, and almost crying said, "I don't know anymore."

Sid put his hand on my shoulder, and said, "You could stay with us."

Immediately there was a mixed reaction among the

others. Some were saying yes, and some were saying no. Judging by the argument, Ralph and Ernie were for me staying, Clem was dead against it, and Barry changed sides after anyone presented their side of the issues by saying 'he's right you know.' Sid started shouting that he was the leader and he should be able to make the decisions. But Clem pointed out that they had agreed that Sid was only the leader when it came to non-member issues, and the subject of new members was decided by everyone. Everybody else at that moment said, 'Oh yeah.'

One thing I did notice about this debate was that Clem seemed to have the best memory, and was the cleverest of the bunch. Almost too clever.

I really began to doubt the value of joining this group and said, "No, it's okay I think I should go find my grandchildren anyway." I really didn't have anywhere better to go.

Clem immediately said, "Maybe we can help you find 'em, are they close?"

Barry said, "We can help, we can!"

For someone who seemed so nice at first, Clem was really beginning to bother me. Either he wanted to get rid of me so badly that he would do anything to do so, or he had something else in mind. The others just looked at me saying nothing, waiting on my decision.

"No, I don't need any help, and besides my grandchildren are far away." I felt I had to lie for some reason.

Sid said, "Are you sure? There's plenty food here."

Clem hissed something softly to himself, which I couldn't quite make out. But I looked again at all the wasted meat lying on the ground, and made my decision that this would not be the way I would spend my time as a spirit. There must be better alternatives.

"No I must go now."

I started to wave goodbye, but Sid put his arms around me in an affectionate bear hug.

Then he said, "Goodbye."

The others said their farewells and each of them hugged me. Clem's embrace was not as friendly or as earnest as the others.

7

CAT AND VALKYRIE

I resumed my journey towards the camp where my grandchildren and I stayed in the valley. Looking back, I saw Sid and his group watching where I was going. I deliberately headed in the wrong direction until I was out of their sight. I don't know why, but I felt better having done so.

I took my time walking through the woods. After all I had heard and learned, I was still not much closer to a plan of action than when I had died.

A chess game certainly ... but what kind of a pawn was I?

I had not been paying much attention to my surroundings, but when I approached a clearing that was familiar to me, I was shocked at what I saw. Apple trees cut down. My grandchildren and I had planted these very trees. Now none remained. Why had they been cut down? I looked around. There was no snow on the ground. Spring was almost here, but there would be no apple blossoms this year. A lot of wood work had been done here. Many branches remained. Some had been burned in a fire. What was left of one of the trunks remained. It appeared that someone tried to fashion a spear shaft, and the end split when they tried to put in the spear head. This was sheer waste. I stood and fumed.

Anyone who has spent time in the wilderness should know that the best spears are not made from mature trees that stand alone in the middle of a clearing. The best spears or bows are made from young trees that grow in a clump competing for survival.

The trees that make good spears are special. They strive for life. They grow slowly because they are in competition with their neighbors. Their wood becomes tough. Not like the wood of a tree that has things easy. Out in the open, growing with no competition, their wood is not as strong.

You must ask the tree if you can take its life to help you. Thanks must be given. Offerings left, and respect must be given to the life that gave itself to you, so that you can survive.

I felt like going back to Sid and telling him of the harm his 'live ones' were doing.
They had no respect for life. The trees, the animals, nothing. I began to wonder if Sid could comprehend what these strangers were doing to the valley. He seemed like a child, and I imagined myself talking for months, maybe years, to try and make him understand. By then the damage done to the valley would take a generation to heal. And what good would explaining anything to Sid do, anyway? Would he be able to make the strangers understand what they were doing? It would take years. No, this had to stop. I would find my grandchildren and tell them to get rid of these ignorant men.

I rushed as quickly as I could to our hidden spot in the valley. It was at the base of the two mountains that came to a corner in the northern part of the valley. A massive rock slide had come down and filled the space between the two mountains. The spring that led to the lake was close to the slide but free of any rubble. A short climb over the rock slide revealed a miniature of the valley itself. It had a small pool of water in the center, that dried in the summer. It had a mixed variety of trees and a clearing where we had built our home. It was a comfortable, long house with a high roof. It had taken us a full summer to complete because we had to bring in all the materials from outside this isolated part of the valley. The 'Nook' we had called it.

I entered the Nook. It seemed strangely quite. It was daytime, but no one was about. There was usually some activity going on … food preparation, mending clothes, making rope, making new tools, something, anything … but there was nothing. I went to the lodge. The door was closed. This should not have stopped me from entering. Spirits and ghosts can walk through walls, right? But I found the door to be solid and no amount of pushing or shoving would budge it. The walls of the lodge were just as impermeable as the door.

This was a real puzzle. What procedure should I use to figure it out? I wasn't standing there long when the door opened and out came Bobby. I rushed past him before the door closed and was rebuffed by an invisible barrier just as hard as the solid one before. I stood there half dazed as Bobby closed the door through my body. Nothing about the door was special, but something was keeping me out.

Bobby relieved himself and re-entered the lodge. I took a whack at the barrier with my sword. I heard a moan within and I thought better of taking another swing.

I sat down. I was in an unstable emotional state. I stared at the ground. Nothing was there. I looked at the sky. Nothing was there. I looked at myself. My body was once again old, lifeless and faded.

I cried, a cry of self pity.

Where was I to go? No where. What was I do to? Nothing.

I needed some answers. Why did I leave Friend before he told me? I cried harder. Tears flowing freely down my cheeks. Spirit tears on a spirit body, falling to the ground and disappearing when they landed.

I caught some movement out of the corner of my eye. A wildcat was creeping stealthily through the plants. It was staring right at me. It looked in every way like an ordinary animal. I looked behind me to see if I could see any small creature which could be the focus of its attention. I saw nothing. I looked back at the animal. It met my gaze. It waggled its head in a strange manner then pounced, landing almost on top of me. It quickly sunk its teeth into my leg, then jumped as quick as lightning back into the undergrowth.

I yelped in pain, and got to my feet as fast as I could. It was already watching me struggle to get back to my feet. I raised my sword and readied myself for any other movement by this wildcat. It approached me slowly, moving very cautiously. It was stalking its prey. Me!

I held my sword firm. A growing fear crept over me. The cat stared me in the eyes and pounced. I swung. Somehow I missed. The cat landed on my leg, and sunk his teeth in again. Pain shot through every part of me.

The cat leapt away as quickly as before.

I rubbed my leg, then advanced on this cat. This had to stop before I became a pin cushion. I leapt at the cat and swung my sword down.

The cat easily moved to one side, avoiding my blow. I swung in a wide arc, trying for any part of the cat. He jumped easily over my swing, leapt at me again, and bit me on the same leg.

He leapt away, like lightning. I had begun a swing, while he was on me, and had to stop from hitting myself. The pain hit me again.

The wildcat was sitting about ten feet away, licking one of his paws, totally ignoring me.

I rushed at him. He didn't move. I swung my sword and it passed right through him. He continued licking his paw.

I swung once, twice, three times. Each time my sword passed harmlessly through him.

The cat continued to lick his paw, throughout my attack. When I had finished, he put his paw down, then looked at me. He quickly leapt at me, before I could react.

Again my leg was the focal point of the wildcat's teeth. I stifled a yell. I backed away, and said, "What did you do that for?"

I only half expected a reply, when it said, "It serrrves you rrright forrr wasting so much enerrrgy with yourrr tearrrs of selfishness."

The wildcat talked with a long roll on his r's that sounded like a deep purr.

I looked at him with great suspicion. He was alive and yet was talking to me.

I asked, "How can you see me and talk to me?"

"I have eyes and a voice."

"No. I mean you're alive, right?"

"What do you mean?"

"You're alive and an ordinary animal, right?"

"I am an animal, as you so aptly put it."

"Well, how can you see me? I'm dead," I asked.

"Dead?"

"Yes, not alive. I have no body."

"It looks like you have one to me."

"It's my spirit body," I said.

"Okay."

"Well, it's not like yours."

"Why not?"

"Yours is alive."

"How so?" he asked.

"You have flesh. I have none."

"Then what did I just bite?"

He had me there. It still stung where his teeth marks showed on my leg. I had no explanation for what was going on.

I asked slowly, "Who are you anyway?"

The cat licked one of his front paws then said, "I am who I am.

This was a frustrating conversation.

"What can I call you?"

"Whateverrr you like."

I wanted to call him Annoying, but I thought I would actical, so I called him Cat.

"Okay Cat, tell me what you are doing here."

"Talking to you."

"Arrrrgh!" I screamed. "You're driving me crazy."

"Why?"

"Because you're not answering my questions."

"I am. But not in the way you desirrre. You can't expect a lengthy explanation frrrom a cat."

"Okay. What has brought you here?"

"You have."

"Why?"

"To tell you something."

"What?"

"Something you should know."

"What is it?" I said exasperated.

"Something that you alrrready know."

"Okay. What is it that I already know, and that you have come from who knows where, to tell me?"

"You arrre acting stupid."

"That's it! That's what you have come to tell me?"

"Yes."

"Well, no one can say that cats lack moral duty. I mean if I saw someone acting stupid, I'm sure I would cross the entire universe just to tell them."

The cat just ignored my raving and casually started to lick its back. This has a profound effect on someone who is trying to talk to a cat. I mean, what do you say? 'Excuse me, you're being rude' or 'What does cat fur taste like, anyway?' I didn't want to talk to him any more. But my curiosity got the better of me. Why would a cat bother to tell me I'm being stupid? I sat and thought about what I was doing before the cat came.

I asked, "I was trying to get into this lodge. Can you help me?"

"Not while you arrre being stupid."

"Okay Cat. Let's just pretend I wasn't being stupid. Could I get into this lodge?"

"Of courrrse."

"Okay, then explain to me how to get into the lodge?."

"I can't.

"Why not?" I shouted.

"Because you arrre being stupid."

I placed my face in my hands and rubbed my eyes, hoping this would provide me with some insight as to how to talk to this cat. It didn't help any. I did resolve, however, to recommend to anyone I met in the future, to never try to talk to a cat. It's not worth it.

"Cat, can you tell me, without frustrating me any further, why am I being stupid?"

"Maybe."

"What does that mean?"

"Yes, I can tell you why you arrre being stupid, but

no, I can't help you frrrom getting frrrustrrrated. "

"Fine, just tell me what you know. "

"Do you want the long verrrsion orrr the shorrrt verrrsion?"

"What do you mean?"

"Of everrything I know. The long verrrsion orrr the shorrt verrrsion?"

"No, I don't mean that. I want to know why I am stupid?"

"That could take a long time. "

I wanted to strangle this cat. But I took a moment to contemplate and I understood how to proceed from here in the conversation. Be very precise and ignore the delivery of the answer.

"No, I mean how was I being stupid with regard to my attempts in entering the lodge? "

The cat sat on his hind legs, braced himself on his forelegs, stood absolutely motionless, stared me in the eyes and said, "Tell me something. Have you been in this lodge beforrre?"

"Yes, many times. "

"When was the last time you werrre in therrre? "

I was about to say last winter, when I was still alive, when I realized that I had just met Rose in there and had had my conversation with her.

"I was just in there. "

"Yes. "

"Well, how do I get back in?"

"Just go in. "

"But I can't, I hit some sort of strange barrier when I try. "

"It's not strrrange. You put it therrre. "

"I did? How?"

"You taught yourrr grrrandchildrren how to put up prrrotective warrrds to keep out spirrrits, and you believe that it actually worrrks."

With that the cat got up and walked away.

I jumped up and followed him, while shouting, "Wait!"

I tripped over my sword and I fell flat on my face, inches from the cat.

He said nonchalantly, "You should put that thing away beforre you hurrrt someone with it."

I said quietly, "How do I do that?"

"Just put it back wherrre you got it."

"Where was that?"

"Why inside you, of courrrse."

The cat quietly walked away and disappeared into the undergrowth. Now I cursed him for leaving. He was so frustrating to talk to, but he left me with two nagging questions. What did he mean by the protective wards I believed worked. Of course they worked. They kept me out didn't they? And what did he mean by saying my sword came from inside me and I should put it back there?

I got up and went back to the lodge. I pushed experimentally on the door. It was as hard as ever. I couldn't just walk in. So I retreated a bit and thought. Surely I had enough information to figure this one out.

I looked at my sword. It had first appeared during my conflict with Bruno. I never took the time to closely examine it. It was still notched from the time I had struck Bruno's rod.

As swords go it was large, almost six feet long, yet it was marvelously light. It had a unusual gleam. The more I looked at it, the angrier I became. I remembered every moment of the fight with Bruno. I felt every ounce a warrior. I was youthful, full of energy and dangerous. I started to dance around with this sword, swinging it in wide open strokes. It was as if my dance had steps to it, orchestrated on a scale that was larger than myself. Fighting was an art. When one is alive and in a fight to the death, being in perfect harmony with your weapon is essential. But what does a spirit do with a sword? And why do I have one?

These questions made me stop swinging my sword. I guess this sword was my protection. I would not use it to fight a war. I had no need.

Suddenly I heard a scream, more a battle cry, and a huge scantily clad woman jumped out from behind a tree. She was seven feet tall, and what was worse for me was, she had a sword that gleamed like sunshine, and it was as long as she was tall. She was clad in some sort of plate mail armor which barely covered her immense chest. Her back was bare yet she had shin and forearm guards. Her hips were more exposed in what seemed like chain mail panties. Her hair flowed down her enormous shoulders and her eyes glowed with an inner fire. This was someone you would never want to meet under combat conditions.

She raised her sword and with swift, graceful movements closed the distance between us. She swung a blow straight for my neck. Fortunately, I had my sword raised in front of me, and even in my stunned state I managed to block her blow. The force with which she struck forced my sword close against my body. The edge drove into me, causing me a slight discomfort. The force of her blow had also sent me back several feet, which again was fortunate for me, because this stunning vision of a Valkyrie had spun and swung again, narrowly missing me by inches. She advanced again.

I realized my only hope was to recapture those fleeting moments when I had felt like a warrior, because here was someone who totally outclassed me. I had to be a warrior whether I liked it or not, and join her in battle.

With no time to think, I leaped backwards to prepare myself, and started my dance again. With what was only a momentary delay, she had leapt forward and continued her attack. We had both swung simultaneously, but she had masterfully changed her swing mid-delivery and met mine head on. There was a terrific noise of metal against metal and another of rushing wind, as our two swords met. I was slow with my next blow and before I had half swung she had completed hers and cut me across my chest.

She repeated this maneuver at will. After several cuts across my chest, I finally got into the rhythm of her strokes. All that could be heard was the constant sound of metal and wind.

I dared not break this rhythm with an attack of my own, because I didn't want to risk being cut across the chest again. Though they hurt, my wounds didn't impair my ability to move or to fight.

As we moved throughout the Nook with our sword play she did not change her pattern of attack. She used a simple left-right attack swing, and I was parrying each swing with my sword.

But after what felt like an eternity of this, she altered her swing. I got cut across my chest again, until I caught her rhythm and was again successfully parrying her.

I did not get tired, but the monotony of the situation was affecting me. The only thing that kept me focused was the pain she caused when her sword hit me.

She continued with her new swing for a while, then varied by going back to her old swing. Occasionally she would hit my chest until I had learned all the variations she tried.

But now she introduced a spinning swing into the mix of the previous two swings.

I was hard pressed to match this new maneuver, I

was barely getting the rhythm of this new stroke when she introduced another stroke, then another, and another. Until her full arsenal of moves had been tried on me.

I'm certain that this went on for days. My chest had many lines going across it. I managed somehow to match the blows made by this expert swordswoman with an adept placement of my sword. I got a nagging feeling that I was being toyed with. She had now broken into a repeating pattern of swings that I could easily defend against, because I knew what her next maneuver would be.

But just as I was getting complacent, she threw me another loop. She now offered a pause into the routine of trying to hit my chest. It caught me totally off guard. I almost didn't defend myself when she resumed her series of blows. When the next pause came, I was better prepared, and placed it in as part of the sequence of her moves. Up until now, her reigning down blow after blow upon my sword had felt like a strange sort of dance, but this pause in her swings felt discordant to the flow of movement.

The pauses served as such an annoyance that after a while that I gathered my courage, and aided by my anger, I swung at this Valkyrie with a blow of my own, during the pause in her swings.

She deflected my blow easily, but instantly the rhythm of our combined movements felt like a perfect dance. We continued for a short time like this, with her offering swing after swing and I returning only one swing in this sequence. When suddenly she offered another pause. I didn't swing the first time she did this. Soon, I inserted another of my own swings. Now she offered pauses throughout our routine, and each time I swung the moment she did not. Now the dance became freer and we exchanged blows at will. It was as if my skill was the determining factor in how we fought.

A new pattern emerged. It was as if fighting with this woman was a totally natural thing to do. We understood each other. We were connected. I began to enjoy myself. I was dancing a sword dance with this large woman just as easily as making love to her. Both are extremely dangerous activities, because one mistake here could easily result in the loss of my head, due to the skill and grace with which she performed.

I smiled, then laughed. A laugh of pure joy. The pleasure with which we were performing our dance was immense, and that pleasure bubbled out of me.

But now I noticed our surroundings were becoming shrouded in unusual fog. It masked everything around us. All I could see was my opponent, eventually the fog became so dense that it was difficult to see even her.

The concentration I needed to counter her blows and deliver mine was becoming unbearable. I began to lose my rhythm, and again she began to hit her mark. My chest once again began to hurt.

I tried to regain my form, but the harder I tried the more often she cut me.

I began to get frustrated again. I wanted to recapture those moments of perfect balance. But now my anger caused by my failure to regain the moment, made me swing wildly. I just wanted her to stop hurting me and go back to the dance we had.

Suddenly the blows to my chest stopped. My swings met with no resistance.

I stopped and listened. There was absolute silence. I couldn't see or hear anything.

Then a blood curdling shriek came from behind me, and I felt her sword enter my back. I saw it come out my chest. The pain was enormous. I fell to the ground. I dropped my own sword and curled up in a fetal position, trying to move not at all, because pain would course through me with the slightest movement.

I lay there with tears in my eyes, feeling sorry for myself. Not only had I lost a perfectly beautiful moment in the battle we had just enjoyed, but I had also lost all sense of purpose. Nothing was important any more. I was just going to lie here for eternity, in the fog, with a sword sticking through my body.

I lay there for what seemed like hours when I finally looked at the sword. I could only see about eighteen inches of it sticking out of my chest, but the part of it I could see was beautiful. It shined like starlight in the fog. It came to a most exquisite point, which had a perfect crystal-like appearance.

The beauty of the sword roused me a bit, and I reached behind me to pull it out. Every moment was sheer agony, but I slowly began to move it back out through my body. Until eventually I was free. I jumped up immediately. The fog had completely disappeared. I was now enraged. How dare she do this to me? Not only did she abandon our dance but she left me in ultimate pain. I grabbed both swords, and started to swing both of them. One with each arm. I couldn't find any rhythm with the two swords. I just hacked wildly with them. I vowed to have her head. I cursed her and eventually fell to the ground when she didn't magically appear.

I sat there again not knowing what to do. I had another puzzle to figure out. What was this all about anyway?

I looked at the two swords. My original sword had an angry look. This new sword had a beautiful look. It shone as bright as the sun. It reminded me of that stunning Valkyrie and her dance of battle. My sword looked ugly in comparison. Every time I looked at it, anger welled up in me. It was as if my anger and my sword were connected.

I thought again about what Cat had said, 'put that thing away before you hurt someone with it.' Without thinking any more about it, I placed my sword against my chest and began to thrust it deep into my chest. There was a slight pain, but the sword did not come out the other side of me. It simply got swallowed up inside of me. My anger was back where it belonged, no longer out where it could hurt someone. I realized that anger could be a useful tool. When I directed it at myself it could serve to motivate me, but if my anger was directed at others, it was usually destructive.

I realized that the Valkyrie's sword was a gift, as was her dance. I could fight better than I ever had, but I would never again fight in anger. I now had a weapon that I could truly defend myself with. I no longer needed to fear anything. If I felt the need to fight, I could.

It was as simple as that. If I did chose to fight, I would not hold back. But I knew that fighting would never be my first choice any more. I thanked the Valkyrie and the universe for providing me with this peace.

Next, I started to figure out how to get into the lodge. I resisted the idea of trying this new sword on the invisible barrier. This was not its purpose. There had to be a way. I had been in the hut before. So I would just duplicate what I did with Spider to get to see Rose again.

There was only one problem. I remembered leaving my drum in Spider's cave. I was not holding it when Spider had thrown me out. But maybe I didn't need it any more. Maybe I could go through the steps of trying to get to Rose without needing to hear my drum. Maybe the pattern of my life habits were ingrained in my spirit, and everything I learned to do in life was available to me in spirit. I might just have a built in drum beat. I decided to give it a shot.

I quieted my mind and tried to remember playing my drum. It worked instantly, at first the sound was faint, but then it built to a loud, steady drum beat. It was as if my spirit had a built-in stereo, and I was playing back something from my life. The spirit does contain life experiences!

I listened for a while to the drum. I looked up and saw the sun. I could look at it without any harm to me. I started to sing. I sang to the sun. I felt its warmth as if I were alive ... and that warmth penetrated me. It was an energy boost. I could feel the massive power being generated inside the sun and I understood how it could power all things on the planet. I wished that this feeling would go on forever.

My song began to change. At first it was what I felt inside, but then it matched more what I was experiencing with the sun. A new dance. The sun and I. The fire from the sun and the fire within my spirit were in harmony.

I thought of all the days I had spent out in the sun. I felt the life it had given me. I remembered my family and the times we shared outside.

I thought of Rose, and there she was.

8

GRANDCHILDREN

I was inside the lodge, looking down at Rose. I stopped my singing and my drumming. I scanned the interior. It looked like my grandchildren had made only a few changes inside.

The lodge was a simple log construction, one large room with many sleep compartments stacked over each other against the wall. There was a fire pit in the center and a small hole in the steeple like ceiling to let smoke out. The lodge always smelled of fire.

Everyone except Rose had the scars of some unknown disease. Strange pock marks dotted them all. The disease must have passed a while ago, and they were quite recovered. Rose seemed exhausted.

I noticed that Bobby was missing. And since the last time I saw him he was entering the lodge, I realized that my time with the Valkyrie had taken longer than I thought.

I also noticed the remains of several geese. Spring must have fully arrived for the geese to be back. They usually took longer to make their way into the mountains than elsewhere.

Since I died, my greatest annoyance had been with my perception of the passage of time. I know that my fighting with the Valkyrie had taken some time, but more than a month?

I also noticed that someone had been busy making articles for battle. There were many new spears, and shields made from rawhide.

Rose awoke. She seemed to sniff the air like an animal. She sensed something was different. Her eyes became glazed and she looked at a point at the far end of the lodge. I knew this was her way of listening.

I softly said, "Rose I am here, watching you."

Rose smiled and got up. She began to prepare the morning meal. Others heard her and got up to help her. The bustle of the morning activities made me homesick. I wanted to again experience the feeling of being alive, and being among my grandchildren. Not that being dead doesn't have its rewards. It's exciting and quite a learning experience. But something about being alive was special. I had a full life and accomplished many things, yet there was something missing. Either it didn't feel right to be here or it wasn't right for me to be here in my present state. Was I longing to be alive again? Was this a trap that the dead fall into? Watching my grandchildren doing just ordinary daily chores sparked jealousy. I could no longer enjoy these simple pleasures. It made me realize that the teachings I had received in my youth … to treat every moment like it was your last … was something I should have stuck to much closer.

I could no longer wash the back of my head with cool refreshing water. I could no longer share my morning meal with those I loved. Even tending the fire was something I missed. These were considered ordinary things when I was alive. Now they seemed like the utmost in pleasure. Was it because I was denied them now that I so envied the living? I came to the same question again. Was this a trap?

Friend had told me 'to let life go and get on with it.' But again I asked, 'get on with what?'

I began to regret not having listened to Friend. My whole dead existence probably would have been so much easier.

I stopped all thoughts when I noticed Bobby came back. He was carrying two more geese. Everyone congratulated him except Rose. I noticed her eyes met Bobby's and she left the lodge. Bobby put the geese down, then made some lame excuse about fixing some rope he was using and followed after her.

I was curious and followed them. I noticed that the invisible barrier only worked one way. It only stopped me from entering, not leaving. I made doubly sure by trying to enter again, without success.

My oldest and youngest grandchildren walked to the entrance of the Nook, and sat down on some rocks. They were obviously continuing an ongoing debate.

"We're going to do it tonight."

"No, Grandfather was against it. We should go south!" Rose said forcefully.

"No, we have to do something else."

"Not attacking the strangers like assassins in the night. Grandfather was against it."

"I don't believe you. Grandfather taught us how to survive. More than anything, he wanted us to be able to live safely, where there was plenty of food, so we could have children of our own," Bobby said strongly.

"Grandfather also taught us to live in harmony with our surroundings. Not to needlessly kill anything," Rose countered.

"This is not a needless situation. If we do not do something soon, there will be nothing left in the valley to eat."

"That's all you care about, your stomach. Can't you think of anything else? Grandfather was right. He told me, before he died, that you need a woman. That's another good reason to go south," Rose said.

Bobby turned red. It was an obvious sore spot with him. He knew that was what he should do, but he could be stubborn.

He turned away from Rose, calmed himself a bit then said, "Everyone's better now, we have to make a decision."

"And we'll have to do it together, Grandfather said so."

"I still say we should fight."

"No, leaving the valley is what we should do. You know this to be true. Why do you fight it?"

Bobby looked Rose straight in the eye and said, "This is our valley. It has served us well over the years. It provides the best shelter against winter. It has always had lots of food. And best of all is the fact that very few people know about it."

Rose sighed then said, "Bobby, the food is disappearing. The strangers have killed plant and animal alike. We can find somewhere else. There must be even fewer people in the wild by now, let's go south."

"Paul was the last to join us, and he said that the southern mountains were still crawling with people."

"That was fifteen seasons ago. Surely there must have been changes down south. What about that strange disease that was just through here. Maybe they all died," Rose said earnestly.

"That's just another reason we should stay here. What if there is some killer sickness just waiting for us.

No, we should stay here, and that is another reason to get rid of the strangers. I tell you that sickness we all had came from them."

"We don't know that."

"How else do you explain it?"

Rose gritted her teeth and said, "I can't."

"So are you agreed then, that the strangers must go."

"I still say we should leave."

"No, there is no where else to go. We stay and we attack tonight."

"I won't let you, I'll tell first." Rose said with a hiss.

Obviously, she had already told my story to Bobby.

I saw Bobby's blood boil. He obviously didn't want the rest to know of his past. But I could not help but get angry with Rose. She was using the information I had told her to get her own way. This was just as wrong as what Bobby was proposing.

"Okay! Have it your way. We'll just keep hiding until we all starve, because I'm not going to leave this valley!" Bobby said angrily.

Rose started to cry and shouted, "I'll not starve because of your stupidity. If you want to fight, let's do it the way Grandfather said. We'll issue the strangers a challenge, and if they don't leave then you can have your blood." Rose said quietly to herself, "I only hope it won't be our own."

Bobby then said, "We are agreed then, finally. Let's propose this to the group together, and see what the rest say. The sooner we decide, the sooner the problem of the strangers will go away."

Bobby got up and went back to the lodge. Rose wiped her face, then followed after him.

All I could wonder was, what had I started? And how would it finish? I was more worried for my grandchildren than I had ever been before.

I followed Rose and Bobby back to the lodge. I t ried to talk to Rose. I kept calling her name, and trying to get her attention, but nothing worked. I felt quite useless. Here I was with loads of advice, but unable to communicate it.

Bobby wasted no time when he got back to the lodge. He called a meeting outside. It was very short. Bobby did most of the talking, with Rose sometimes agreeing. Her voice was very sad.

But a consensus was reached very quickly. Only Melissa voted against fighting. The rest had apparently made their minds up earlier, and were just waiting for this meeting to vote for a fight. It seemed the only real debate was about how to fight the strangers. Either Bobby's way or the way I suggested. When Bobby supported Rose as to how the fight should be approached, the debate ended.

There was a great flurry of activity the rest of the day, as my grandchildren prepared for battle. It had been decided that they issue their ultimatum at dawn tomorrow.

I tried to get in the lodge again by just walking in, without success. I had to concentrate again on my drum, and clear my mind. But this time I concentrated on what the lodge looked like from the inside. I had difficulty maintaining an image, even though I had spent many winters in there. I still found myself outside. So I concentrated on the many activities that we had performed inside the lodge. The more I thought of each of my grandchildren, the clearer the image became, until I slowly became aware that I was again inside the lodge.

It had taken me quite a while to get inside. Most were preparing for sleep. I could tell that there was great tension and anticipation in the air. Most were unable to fall asleep easily, except Mary. She could sleep under any condition.

When Rose had finally fallen asleep, I decided to try and talk to her in her sleep again.

Once again I set my internal drum beat in motion and quieted my mind. I thought of nothing else except talking to Rose. This wish went on for quite some time without success. Until well into the night she rose from her sleep, and sat up and looked at me.

I quickly said to Rose, "The fight tomorrow. Are you ready to do what you must do? "

She looked at me and began to cry. Her spirit body quickly vanished, and I was alone again, watching my sleeping grandchildren. I had wanted to say more than that to Rose.

I stopped my drum and sat for a while. I was startled to here a voice behind me.

I turned and Bobby said to me, "I will make you proud of me tomorrow, Grandfather. "

I replied, "I am already proud of you grandson. "

Bobby smiled broadly and his spirit body also winked out. I knew that was what he wanted to hear, but I would have said more if I could.

I heard another voice from the other end of the lodge. I turned to see Paul sitting next to his body.

"I come to join you Grandfather. "

He looked immensely sad, but accepting of his fate. He too winked out.

Paul affectionately called me grandfather, partly because he never knew his own grandfather, and partly out of respect. Paul was the kindest of all the others that had joined us.

I turned back to Rose. I was surprised to see her staring at me.

"Granddaughter, you were wrong to have tried to influence Bobby with the knowledge you gained from me. In spite of that you must find another way to stop this fight tomorrow."

"I didn't," was all she said before she again winked out.

'I didn't'? This was beginning to annoy me. Why weren't my grandchildren sticking around long enough to speak with me? It was like playing peek-a-boo with those that you love. I understood now what Spider meant about the living. Their concentration on the spirit world isn't very focused. I was fortunate with my first conversation with Rose.

I remember when I was alive, and wanted to talk to Spider. I used to take a long time preparing myself. I had to be in a good state of mind before I was really successful in hearing anything. And it ultimately came down to how strong my intent was. I can see now that my grandchildren were not actually trying to talk to me. They were dreaming, and in their dreams, they had a wish to see or talk to me, but then they easily got distracted by some other thought, and they moved on from me in their dream. This thought made so much sense to me that all frustration left me. Knowledge easily eases frustration.

I got up and moved closer to each of my grandchildren. I tried to kiss each one of them on the forehead. It was strange, I felt only partly successful with some and totally unsuccessful with the rest. Those with which I felt partly successful, moved, smiled, or sighed and appeared to be more restful in their sleep. I felt like this was all I could do, and tomorrow, I would only be an observer to the events that would unfold. I resigned myself to my role and sat by the fire and sang songs all night. Some happy, some sad, but mostly songs from my heart. Occasionally one of my grandchildren would suddenly appear beside me and join in, or sometimes they would laugh, then wink out just as quickly. I enjoyed those fleeting moments.

As I sang, and looked at each of my grandchildren, I remembered events from the past.

First was Bobby. He appeared before me and sang with me. The song brought me to a time when he was twelve years old. It was his first hunt. He went ahead through the forest. I saw him moving silently from hiding place to hiding place.

He had watched me do this many times before. From a distance, I could see his nervousness. He was as tense as a bow string.

He carried three short spears in his left hand. He had practiced throwing these since he was small. He crept close enough to throw. Even at twelve, he showed the skill of an expert hunter.

I could see that Bobby had picked his target, a yearling deer. The deer, although slightly nervous, didn't show any sign of getting ready to flee. Bobby transferred one of his spears to his right hand. He readied his throw. The deer tensed, and Bobby threw. The deer ran, but the yearling faltered. A spear was sticking into its rear leg. The mother turned back to see what was wrong with her fawn. Bobby chased the fawn through the woods a short way. It was having difficulty running. Bobby raised another spear and plunged it into the deer. The deer struggled to the ground. Bobby stabbed at the deer without thinking. He plunged his last spear into the deer's neck and held it there. The deer struggled a bit then stopped moving. Bobby had watched in horror as the deer died. I ran up to him. The mother deer, also having witnessed her fawn's death, ran away when I got to Bobby.

Bobby looked up at me. He had tears in his eyes. He had witnessed the deer die. He turned and threw up.

When he had finished, I mildly scolded him. I asked him if it was a proper way to show thanks to the spirit of the deer, by throwing up after killing him.

I also told him that he should try to kill an animal he has hunted as quickly as he can. No animal should suffer during his hunt. And after he killed any animal, he should honor its spirit as best as he could.

I told him that he should be proud that he was able to kill an animal on his first try. His mother and father would be happy that we had fresh venison for our meal that night.

I remember his face when he came back into our camp. No one was ever prouder of an accomplishment than he when carrying in his deer.

The song finished and Bobby disappeared.

During my next song, Daniel appeared. I remembered an event that happened in the same year that Bobby had his first hunt. Daniel had a habit of wandering far away from camp, and although he never got lost, he always made us nervous.

But once he did wander too far. When he didn't come back, his father Kurt, and I started to track him. I got alarmed when his tracks were joined by two others. I got confused following them. They were wandering in a strange way. They would travel a couple of miles in one direction, then turn at ninety degrees and travel another couple of miles.

Something else had caught my attention. Daniel's tracks disappeared. One of the strangers had picked him up and carried him. They went without stopping. They traveled in a huge square around our camp.

Night came. I worried about what the two strangers were doing.

I waited for the dawn and tracked them once again. They were making straight for our camp. Only my daughter was left in camp. The rest of us had gone out to search. We ran back to camp.

It turned out we had nothing to worry about. It was Paul and his mother. They had found Daniel and were bringing him back. Paul was carrying Daniel because he had sprained his ankle running through the forest.

Paul's mother was an expert herbalist and she knew plants well. They had survived utilizing her knowledge. Paul's mother had gained wisdom from living in the wilderness for many years. We enjoyed each other's company and her knowledge helped us to be more comfortable from then on.

Paul was a strong young man. He took to my granddaughter Melissa right away. They became inseparable. Lolita was the result of their meeting.

Paul's mother proved to be a great healer and teacher, but her time with us was short before she died.

The song changed again. Daniel disappeared and Melissa took his place.

I remembered the day when Melissa, with a most grave face, called a group meeting. I thought that something must be very wrong. She announced to the group that our lives would be changed forever. With a worried face, she announced that she was pregnant with Paul's child. Paul had been in on her joke and had kept his composure. But when Melissa broke out in a smile Paul started laughing.

We celebrated well into the night, dancing and singing. We all cried openly. The news of an upcoming birth had an uplifting effect on all of us. Everyone was happy.

I was especially proud. This was what I had lived for. I felt a sense of completion. That was probably why I stopped clinging to life after Melissa's baby was born.

Again the song changed. Melissa was replaced by Mary.

I remembered the time when Mary had gone into the forest by herself. We knew she wished to have time alone, and we didn't get worried until the her third day away. We had not heard any rumor of her through the forest, and we decided to search for her.

It didn't take us long in following her trail to notice that she had started to run. She had known that she was being followed. We saw grizzly tracks following hers. By studying the tracks we saw that she had managed to elude the bear in some clever ways. As we moved down the trail we heard a cry. It was Mary and she was calling out from a high place. We saw her in the distance, up an enormous tree. And down at the bottom was a huge bear. When it saw us, it ran straight towards us. Paul, Bobby and Daniel and I. We split up and the bear chose Paul as his target. Paul quickly climbed the nearest tree, but he had chosen his refuge poorly.

The bear stood at the bottom of the tree and started pushing. The tree swayed and Paul had trouble holding on.

The three of us on the ground fired our bows. The grizzly became enraged. It bit at the arrows then charged at us. Daniel was his next target. Daniel found a large comfortable tree to climb. Bobby and I continued to shoot arrows. The bear was frantic. It noticed Paul was climbing down his fragile tree and ran back there. Paul climbed back up again. The bear pushed the tree so hard that it fell over. It fell slowly, then got caught in a neighboring tree. Paul came crashing down, followed by many branches. He was tangled and was unable to get away.

Bobby and I had shot at least a dozen arrows into this bear, but it started to look for Paul in the fallen branches.

Then to our surprise, Mary showed up, and was yelling at the top of her lungs. The bear turned and charged at her. Mary carried a bow she had made and a short spear.

She stood still and aimed an arrow at the charging bear. She let it go at point blank range. The arrow disappeared into the bear, but he kept on coming. Mary dove to one side at the last second. The bear skidded to a halt and ran back at Mary.

Bobby and I ran into the open and fired two more arrows at the bear. Bobby's arrow hit the bear in the eye. The grizzly ran over Mary and narrowly missed her with his paw. Bobby put another arrow into the bear at the same time Mary stabbed it with her short spear.

The grizzly stopped. It looked about for a few seconds, then fell to the ground.

When we cut the bear open, we found that Mary's arrow had gone straight through its heart. She probably killed it with that arrow, but it took a while for the grizzly to realize that it was dead.

Mary and Paul suffered only minor injuries. But that day Mary proved she was a warrior.

The song changed again. Mary disappeared. She was replaced by Rose.

I remember the small face of Rose, ever so serious, following me around. She was nine years old and she was helping me tend to Daniel, who had a bad cold.

Rose would gladly run off and get items I needed as I tended to Daniel.

It was during this time that I broke my medicine bag. To me, it was only a bag. I would repair or replace it when I had time. To Rose, the damage was devastating. She thought that Daniel was going to die.

I went about my business and thought no more about it.

The next day, Rose came up to me with a gift.

She handed me a new medicine bag that she had made. She had gotten the hide for the bag from Melissa, and the sinew for the stitches from Bobby.

She made me proud of her, and from that day on she devoted herself to learning everything about herbs and healing.

I kept that pouch with me until I died. I used it for special mixtures of herbs that I used during our ceremonies.

I looked at her with great fondness, then Rose too disappeared.

I stopped singing. The pre-dawn came quickly.

I saw Bobby awaken as if he had heard an alarm. He jumped to a listening position, looked at the weapons at his side in the near darkness and proceeded to wake the others.

Very little talking went on. Everyone ate and prepared their weapons for the upcoming uncertainty. What would their day hold? The tenseness and anticipation of the unknown emanated from their bodies. I could actually feel their mood.

Only Melissa stayed behind. She clutched Lolita with great concern. She waved to the others as they left. I saw tears in her eyes when I went past her to follow the war party.

They moved at a great pace until they got to the lake. Bobby had everyone wait while he went forward to scout the camp of the strangers. I followed him along the outskirts of the lake. He traveled silently, like all good woodsman.

He came right up to their camp without being noticed by any of the strangers. But he didn't escape the notice of Sid and his gang. They were extremely curious. They came over quickly to where Bobby was watching the sleeping strangers. They had noticed me, but seemed immensely more interested in Bobby.

Sid came over to me, barely letting his eyes stray off of Bobby and said, "Hi Nexus. Knew I wou' see you again. Who's this?"

"This is my oldest grandchild."

Sid turned his head to me and stared hard. "What he do here?"

Sid was quite concerned. I felt a little apprehension in telling him Bobby's mission, but I answered him, "He's here to tell your live ones to leave the valley."

"Why?"

"Well, he feels it is his valley, and that your live ones do not treat the creatures in the valley with respect."

Sid looked at me as if he didn't understand.

"I mean that your live ones waste food, and they are taking an unfair share of what is in the valley. Soon there will not be enough left in this valley to support anyone."

I thought I had expressed myself quite well, but Sid still looked like he was having trouble comprehending what I had said.

Sid did manage to say, "But the live ones feed us."

"It's immaterial that they feed you. They can go somewhere else and feed you, but they do not have to kill so much to feed you."

Sid looked doubtful and I felt that Sid did not understand the concept of waste. He couldn't comprehend the minimalist ideal. To live in harmony with nature and only take what you need, and in the best way, in a way which causes no damage, and in a way that would improve the earth.

"Live ones must kill to eat," Sid said.

"Yes, but they kill everything they find without thinking of what effect they are having on the balance of life."

Sid simply repeated his premise, "You must kill before you can eat."

I really didn't feel like getting into an argument with Sid. It was a waste of time.

I merely said, "No, Sid. There are other ways of doing things, and I hope you take the time to learn about them."

This time Sid really did give me a strange look. I know now what an alien would see if it introduced itself to an earthling. Sid thought I was from another planet. I wondered how he had lived his life. But I was not as curious now as I would have been when I first died. The only thing I was curious about was the fate of my grandchildren. I was becoming weary of being dead. It was an endless task. I was absolutely positive that there had to be something better than the existence I was now experiencing.

I looked at the others. They were following Bobby back to the other side of the lake, where he went to get the war party. Dawn was near. I stayed where I was. Sid stood beside me. He no longer felt the need to talk, for he was deep in thought. I couldn't tell what he was thinking. I hardly felt responsible for his heavy thinking but what else could it be?

Dawn came. I saw Sid's gang and the war party approach. The spirits were jumping up and down with extreme pleasure. The humans were approaching cautiously. Bobby raised his hand and the war party stopped. He whispered something to them and they all shouted at once, the cry of the wild, at the top of their lungs. They were wild things in human form and they unleashed this energy.

The strangers leapt to their feet in utter astonishment. They were confused as to what was happening. They quickly grabbed their weapons and looked around.

Bobby and his group had been standing between the strangers and the rising sun, so were hidden from their searching eyes for a while. After they spotted them they lined up with their spears held in front of them.

This evoked a strange response from the spirits. They ran behind the strangers and started to make unusual hooting noises. Sid was participating, but not as enthusiastically as the others.

Bobby now walked forward and said, "Who are you? Why are you in our valley?"

One of the strangers replied, "What makes this your valley?"

"I have lived here since I was young. My grandfather brought me here to live and taught me everything about this valley. I know every inch of it. I will fight any who question my authority as to what is right for this valley."

Those were fighting words if I ever heard them. The spirits hooted with even more enthusiasm.

A different stranger shouted out, "We don't listen to anybody. We decide ourselves where we go."

The first stranger had some harsh words for the second speaker, then shouted back to Bobby, "Let's not be hasty, maybe we can come to some consensus here."

"It's very simple. You leave and there will be no trouble."

The stranger shouted again, "It's rather difficult discussing this while we are shouting. Wouldn't it be better if we discussed these matters sitting down?"

The stranger seemed to be a reasonable person, and even Bobby was swayed by his words. Bobby would avoid a fight if he could.

Bobby looked back at the rest then shouted, "Okay."

My grandchildren walked forward. Bobby extended his hand and said, "My name is Bobby."

The spokesman for the strangers said, "I'm Fred."

The spirits stopped their hooting and looked disappointed. Clem had been the most persistent hooter and still uttered the occasional hoot. But otherwise, all were just listening intently.

Bobby went into a tirade of grievances that he had against the strangers. Fred listened and apologized for all their transgressions. Most of the humans were listening to Bobby and Fred … some of the others were passing comments among themselves. The strangers started to act like hosts and everyone visibly relaxed. Grips on weapons loosened, and the earlier tenseness that was present lessened.

Sid and I chose to sit apart to watch this boring turn of events. It seemed so anticlimactic after last night's anticipation.

I looked at Sid and said, "What do you think will happen now?"

Sid said, "When your grandchildren not looking my live ones will attack them."

"What??!!!"

Sid was surprised at my outburst, but said, "They always do that."

I jumped up and went to Rose. I started to shout at her, "ROSE!!!! listen to me !!!"

But she was oblivious to me. I rushed back to Sid and said, "You have to do something to stop them!!"

Sid looked at me blankly and said, "I can no do anything. What want me to do?"

I felt totally useless. I watched in horror as one of the strangers who was serving water grabbed a spear that was lying behind Michael and drove it into his back. Michael's face had a look of total surprise as the spear burst out of his chest. He looked at it and without uttering a sound fell over. Pandemonium struck the humans. The strangers had the upper hand because they were rehearsed at ambush whereas my grandchildren had had little experience with dealing with strangers. This was my fault because we had always avoided others, and if we were forced to have outside dealings, I was the only one to do it. I had seen friendly and treacherous, but my grandchildren had not.

Fred and Bobby were rolling on the ground, each trying to gain the upper hand. Rose and Mary were trying to poke a hole in one stranger while he was trying to do the same to them.

Daniel had been wounded in one arm but was still fighting. Peter and Paul were fighting side by side against two other strangers. They were the only two to retain their shields as well as their spears.

But what kept me off balance was the fact that Sid and his fellow spirits appeared to be dancing with the strangers. It was as if they were attached to the humans like shadows, and were helping their movements. They kept behind the humans, but whenever it looked like one of my grandchildren was going to score a fatal wound, the spirits moved in some exquisite movement and my grandchildren missed or caused only a minor injury.

I saw that the battle would turn against my grandchildren any minute. I acted. I jumped at the nearest spirit with the sword the Valkyrie had given me. It happened to be Clem. He saw me coming and detached himself from his human. Clem was much faster than I. He had no weapon to defend himself, but I couldn't catch him. And if I turned my attention from him, he was back with his human in an instant. The best I could do was keep this spirit from his human.

And then, matters turned even worse for my grandchildren. I saw Daniel receive a spear in the chest. Mary fell with a spear to her belly. Peter was wounded in the arm. Bobby had received a few blows to the head and was unsteady on his feet. Rose's opponent no longer had his spear, it was still in Mary, so she was forcing him to back up. Paul was fighting Clem's human and he had wounded him in the side, causing his reactions to be slower. At least my keeping Clem at bay was allowing Paul to get the upper hand. Paul hit his opponent on the side of his head with the shaft of his spear, and dazed him. Paul then took in the overall situation and yelled, "Run!!"

Rose and Peter started to back off. Bobby refused to give ground, in spite of the fact he now had two opponents. Paul ran towards Bobby's adversaries and threw his body so both would be knocked off their feet. It was a good thing too, it looked like Bobby would have been killed in another second. Paul used the momentum from his run to bounce up to his feet. He pushed Bobby and again gave the order, "Run." Bobby stared at him stupidly for a moment then started to shuffle after Rose and Peter, who had already begun to jog away into the forest. Paul stood his ground, keeping all five strangers at bay for a few seconds, then he turned and fled. The strangers all stopped to get new weapons then they ran after what was left of my grandchildren's war party.

Paul saw that Rose and Peter were heading back to the Nook, but realizing this would be folly, yelled, "The Rock! The Rock!"

He was referring to a large rock that stuck out at an unusual angle from the side of a mountain on the other side of the valley. Rose and Peter changed their direction almost 120 degrees and started to run faster. They had been waiting for the others to catch up, but were now running for what was a perfect defensible position.

I had watched the entire spectacle with some detachment after Daniel and Mary were stabbed. I now looked at the fallen bodies of my two grandchildren.

Daniel was vainly trying to pull the spear from his chest. Mary was lying in a fetal position staring forward blankly, but her eyes kept closing. She kept forcing them open, but each time they remained closed just a little longer. It was as if she was fending off sleep but losing the battle. She opened her eyes one last time and she looked right at me. She tried to say something, but closed her eyes and began to cry. I had seen her cry only a few times in her life and seeing her like this pierced my heart. I looked back to Daniel. His breathing was heavier and I knew he too would lose the battle.

I was surprised to see Michael's spirit body standing over his own lifeless body. He had the same confused look that I must have had when I first discovered I was dead. We both exchanged glances, but said nothing to each other. What was there to say?

I started to run after the strangers, but I was unable to catch up to them. The spirits had resumed their hooting. My will to follow them was draining away. I had run faster than this before, but a wave of oppression was weighing me down.

Paul had caught up to Bobby, and was helping him to run. Bobby was very unsteady and stumbled a couple of times. Paul looked back and saw the strangers closing the gap between them. He let go of Bobby and stopped. Bobby stopped a few paces later and looked back. Paul yelled, "Go on. Run!"

Bobby turned bright red with anger.

Paul yelled again. "It's no good if you're dead too. Look after the others. I'll delay them for a while. We can make a stand at The Rock."

This made sense to Bobby because after a short pause he staggered away as fast as he could.

Paul stood facing the oncoming humans. He raised his shield with one hand, and held his spear in the other, and shouted. It was a heart stopping cry. It was as if he called all the energy of his spirit and released it all at once. The strangers slowed and the spirits stopped hooting. When the hooting stopped I felt I could run faster. I was gaining on them. I was determined that Paul would have whatever help I could offer him.

Paul put his shield in front of him and pointed his spear straight at the strangers. They were almost upon him. I had almost caught up to the strangers when the spirits started hooting again. I tried to ignore the sound and the effect it had on me. I fought against the pressure it caused and swung my sword at the leg of the closest spirit. It was Clem. I hit his hamstring or the spirit equivalent and he went down, yelling in pain.

At the same moment Paul yelled again and charged forward. He deflected a spear from Fred with his shield, then fell to one knee, lunging his spear to the full extension of his arm. Clem's human had also lunged his spear at Paul, but his aim was high. Paul's spear went straight under Clem's human's rib cage. He stopped in his tracks, gurgled some blood, then fell … dead. Paul tried to run, but he was jumped by one stranger, then another, then another. They knocked him senseless.

Rose and Peter had waited for Bobby to catch up to them and then watched what was happening to Paul. Bobby started to yell obscenities at the strangers, but Peter and Rose dragged him away. An injured Peter, a dazed Bobby and Rose were no match for the four remaining uninjured strangers.

I knew Bobby would now do it his way. They would not see him before he killed them. He could walk up to a deer and be just two feet away before it would notice him.

Two of my grandchildren and one whom I considered my own, now lay dead or dying.

All because I insisted that they do things my way.

I followed the strangers back to their camp. They carried a semi-conscious Paul ... all the fight was knocked out of him. The spirits also followed them back. I no longer felt the need for combat. However, Clem didn't come near me. In fact, he limped along behind the others who no longer wanted him in their group. If he got close to the group, they shoved him until he hung back. When we all arrived back at the camp, the spirits kicked and swung at Clem until he went back into the woods.

I asked Sid, "Why did you kick Clem out?"

Sid looked at me like I was stupid and said, "His live one died."

As if this explained it. I asked again, "But why does he have to leave?"

"There isn't enough food with one less live one."

Apparently their feeding went one on one, and they didn't share. Why then had Sid wanted me to stay and offered food as an incentive at our earlier encounter?

The humans tied Paul up and examined the dead bodies of the war party members that had fallen in the camp. They had brought Clem's human's body from the forest.

I saw no spirit bodies. Those of Mary, Daniel, Michael and Clem's human were gone, they must not have stuck around.

When Fred saw that my grandchildren were dead, he cursed under his breath and told the others to get rid of the bodies.

Fred then began to put together a crude table. Many logs were lashed together to form a long, narrow tabletop. Four sturdy legs were attached to the flat top. When the table was together, Fred scratched symbols in the ground around the table. He then placed black stones in a circular pattern on the outside of the symbols.

Fred's activities began to make me nervous. I hesitated to ask Sid what was going on, but Sid came up to me on his own and started talking.

"We think you leave now," Sid said.

"Why?"

"You no have live one."

"So, I don't want any of your precious energy."

Sid looked at me doubtfully, but said, "Okay, but you stand over there."

He pointed to the other end of the camp. To emphasize their case all the spirits stood very close together and leaned over me where I was sitting. To avoid any trouble I got up and walked to the other end of camp.

The other humans had returned and made fires all around the outside of the black stones.

Smoke swirled around the table. The sun set. The fires died down and the table was bathed in an eerie red glow.

Each spirit stood on one of the strange symbols.

The humans then brought Paul to the table. He was naked. He struggled fiercely, but he was bound and gagged. He had four humans containing him. He was at their mercy.

I came back to the circle. I shouted to Sid, "What are they going to do to him?"

Sid ignored me. The spirits started to made clicking and hissing sounds. It got quite loud, and drowned out any attempt to yell any more questions.

The humans tied Paul to the table. He could not do much more than shake the table a bit. The humans started a horrible, low, guttural chant. The only word that I could make out was 'death,' because the volume of that word increased each time they chanted it, until they ended with a loud shout, "DEATH!"

Fred then spoke, "O evil one hear our words and receive your sacrifice."

Paul eyes lit up as they removed his gag. Paul spit at Fred. Fred ignored this gesture and merely took off all his own clothes. The others did the same. Each one had a knife and proceeded to cut Paul in sensitive, but non vital areas, until Paul was covered in the red of his own blood. Each human then began to wipe off this blood and spread it over their own bodies.

I went frantic. I had been trying to find so me way inside the circle of black stones, but just like my attempts to enter the lodge, I found an invisible barrier. I held up my sword and brought it down in savage stroke. The noise was tremendous. The sound was as if we were in the middle of a fireworks display. The spirits looked at me with wide eyes. They changed their sound to that hooting noise again. The pressure that accompanied that sound tried to keep me back.

The humans, too, seemed to notice a change in the energy of their environment. They paused and looked around, unsure of what was happening. They started a different chant. It had the names of devils and demons in it.

An immense wave of pressure flowed from the circle. It was a great effort to lift my sword, but somehow I managed. The noise was even louder when I hit the barrier this time. The force of it made me stagger backwards.

The humans swayed back and forth. The blood on their bodies and the red glow from the fires made them look like devils. Fred stepped forward to lean over Paul. He held a knife with both hands and raised it over Paul's body. He murmured something under his breath and then said, "O evil one, receive this sacrifice and give favor unto your servants."

While this was going on, I realized that simply striking the barrier with my sword was the non-thinking solution. Something Cat had said about the barrier around the lodge was the key. I did get in, but it had taken me a long time. I could try to will myself into the circle but it would take time. Cat had said that 'I only believed that the barrier actually works.' So, logically, if I believed that it works and then it does, then if I believed that it didn't work then it won't work. But how could I make myself believe something this quickly.

My mind raced. If I could somehow connect to a higher consciousness then I would believe. I calmed myself. I let my sword fall to my side and imagined myself bigger. Friend had suggested I try to join my consciousness with the Gaia consciousness, and I had been successful when Spider had told me to resonate with the rocks. This had to be the answer.

I looked at the rocks. I noticed a slight glow that earlier I had missed. Then I heard the same sound I had heard when Spider threw me out of his cave. The glow on the rocks was really made up of individual glowing objects that moved in a dance to make the whole of the glow. When I let the sound pass through me with no resistance, the glow gathered around my feet. I now tried to look for the source of the glow. It originated deep within the earth. I followed it with my consciousness. I saw intricate patterns of light and sound moving beneath the surface of the earth. With a mere thought I could see myself traveling through the earth.

This was the solution to my problem. I merely thought that I had traveled through the earth to where Fred was standing … and there I was.

But I was too late. The moment I entered the circle, the spirits gave off a high wail. Sid shouted at me, "I thought that you no want food!! "

I ignored him because at that moment Fred brought down his hands and plunged his knife into Paul's chest. The noise from Paul was like that of the wind being knocked out of him. He refused to scream and stifled any other sounds. He held his breath until he passed out.

Fred swore. He was obviously disappointed with the whole ceremony.

I, on the other hand, was devastated. Paul was dying. His breathing slowed until it stopped.

Sid and the other spirits moved behind the humans and grabbed onto something on their backs. The humans threw their heads back and let out a wild scream. The spirits tensed. Paul died at that moment and the spirits shook wildly. The vibration passed down to the humans. They shook as well. The vibration passed back and forth between humans and spirits. Then the humans slumped to the ground, exhausted. They lay there groaning. The spirits, on though, looked like they just had a cold shower. They looked alert and almost alive.

Paul got up from the table and stood beside me. He smiled and then gave me a big hug.

"Grandfather."

Tears rolled down from my eyes. I didn't deserve his affection. I screwed everything up. If I hadn't interfered with Bobby's plan, Paul probably wouldn't be standing here next to me. I patted him on the back and he released me.

Paul looked all around him and said, "I never imagined it would be so beautiful."

I stared at Paul like he was mad. What was he referring to? I couldn't understand. Instead I had to talk to Sid.

I yelled, "Sid, what you are doing is wrong!"

Sid's vibrations faded and he frowned at me.

"Why you say that?"

"It's wrong to kill people like that."

"We no do it, live ones do."

"You must have some part in it. They probably wouldn't feed you unless you gave them something back."

Sid kicked the ground with his foot.

"Well?"

"We do tell them things."

"Anything else?"

"And help them fight."

"So if you stopped doing these things for them, don't you think they would stop killing people like this?"

Small tears started to flow down Sid's cheeks, but he stopped looking at me and gazed past me to where Paul was standing.

Paul was looking up. His mouth was open.

He spoke softly, "*It's so beautiful!*"

I looked up and saw nothing. I looked at Sid. He, too, had looked up. But now his face had a look of pure joy, and the sad tears which had fallen down his cheeks had now been replaced with tears of sheer joy. His appearance changed from a pseudo-devil to that of an ordinary man. He looked child-like but was quite handsome.

Paul turned to face me and said, "Grandfather let's go home, we can ..."

His voice trailed off and his spirit faded. I could barely see him and could not hear him. He was confused. His eyebrows lowered for a moment then he smiled and laughed. Sid grabbed his hand and the both of them faded completely from view.

The other spirits held their heads and ran around, lost. They screamed at the top of their lungs. I saw Clem come out from the woods with a broad grin on his face, and walk toward the other spirits. They ran to him and huddled around him, grabbing him as if they were lost children. Clem's eyes met mine. He gave me a broad grin. I knew he would continue his work with the humans. I turned away. I wanted to kick the humans as they lay there, spit on them even, but since I could do nothing to them, I left.

I walked into the woods not caring about anything any more. I was more depressed than I ever had been when I was alive.

9

HISTORY

I wandered out of the valley. The trials of my remaining grandchildren no longer concerned me. They were better off without me, anyway. I headed north. I came to a small river and followed it until I came to a small waterfall. I don't know why, but my thoughts seemed lighter here. I stopped and gazed at the waterfall. Eventually I sat down, never taking my eyes off of the waterfall. It was a simple shelf of rock that had worn down with the force of the water flowing over it. It fell no more than six feet and made a happy noise as it hit the rocks in the pool of water that lay at its base.

When I tired of staring at the water, I lay down and watched the sky and its many changes. I took no notice of the passage of time. Sun stars, clouds all passed by again and again. Time passed unceasingly.

I was beyond bored. I was accepting of a fate to just fade away. Then I heard a familiar voice.

"Grandfather!!!"

I looked up to see Rose.

She helped me up then hugged me. We held each other for an eternity.

I asked, "Are you alive and just visiting me?"

She shook her head.

My heart sunk. I asked, "How?"

"I got careless. I fell out of a tree while looking in an empty bird's nest. Fell and broke my neck. Then I looked for you until I found you."

"Bobby and Melissa?"

"Oh, they're still alive. They left the valley and moved south. That's the last I saw of them. Actually I really don't care what happens to them anymore. I just wanted to find you. I felt you needed my help."

She paused for a moment then continued.

"It's funny, I met Mary and Daniel while I was trying to find you."

"You did? Why aren't they with you no w?"

"They said they had joined something called the 'committee.' They tried to convince me to join."

"The committee? Is that all they said?"

"No, when I refused to go with them, they argued between themselves and finally said I could go and they wouldn't try to bring me along because I was family. I said thanks sarcastically, and thought that I'd like to see them try to stop me from finding you."

I wondered at my bad luck. Why were only bad things happening to me? Why would Mary and Daniel get involved with the committee? These questions roused me from my stupor. I had to find out. Rose coming to me gave me purpose again. Even though the thought of her being dead hurt deeply. But it does happen to everybody eventually, and I realized I was going to meet more and more dead people that I knew. Which brought me back to one of the first questions I had had. Who was Friend? I felt if I could answer that question, a lot of other questions would be answered.

I digressed. I tried to imagine Mary and Daniel being friends with Bruno. That was enough to raise me out of my depression and resolve that action had to be taken. If I couldn't save Mary and Daniel from their deaths, surely I could stop them from making a mistake with their spirits.

I looked at Rose and smiled. She smiled back.

"We have something we must do."

"We do?" Rose asked sheepishly. "I was hoping that we could just sit here and I could listen to one of your stories again, like I used to."

I smiled, remembering little Rose on my lap, as we sat around the fire, listening intently until she fell asleep. She used to soak up all the stories I told.

"What story would you like to hear?"

"Well, I always wondered why Grandmother never came with you into the wilderness."

Now I frowned. I never told this story to any of my grandchildren. I felt reluctant to say anything. I sat down. Rose sat across from me, with her back to the waterfall.

When I was quite comfortable I said, "She didn't want to come."

"There has to be more to the story than that."

"She thought it was a waste of time to hide in the wilderness. She said it was useless to avoid doing what has to be done in life. Running away only makes things harder. I told her that if you are killed, you won't have any chance to do things in your life. Her only reply was that you should live every moment as if it was your last, and in that way you accomplish your goals in life."

"You used to tell me how fiery Grandmother was. It sounds like you had quite the argument."

"Argument was the word for it. She said if I wanted to go, I should go. She didn't care if I did something stupid, just to keep her out of it. She was totally against your father and his sister coming with me. In the end I took them, against your Grandmother's wishes. I would have dragged her along too, but she was a powerful woman. That would have been impossible for me to do. "

I started to cry. "That was the most painful decision I had to make in my life. I loved your Grandmother more than life itself. It was so hard to leave her. But I couldn't understand why she chose certain death by staying behind. I had to survive. I wanted a future for my children and grandchildren."

Rose held me close and said, "You loved her very much, didn't you?"

I nodded my head. I felt the pain of her absence as sharply as when I had left her. I wished more than ever that I could see her again ... but the fear of meeting her again extinguished any wish that I had.

"That's why you didn't take another wife! I remember Paul's mother dying when I was young. She died sad. I asked Melissa why she was always so sad, and Melissa said it was because she loved you, but you never returned her love. I understand now."

I looked at her and asked, "How can you understand? You're so young."

"I may have died young, but now I feel old, and I understand so much more."

I felt pain. The memories that Rose made me relive, were too much for my being. Rose must have sensed this because she suddenly changed topics.

She smiled at me then said, "My father and you, did not part on good terms, did you?"

Rose was acting older. She was trying to help me resolve issues from my past.

"No, we didn't. Your father, my son, never got over the fact that I left your mother behind. When he became a man, he went to search for her. He stayed only long enough to get your mother pregnant. I told him it would mean his death to go. He laughed at me, then left."

More tears streamed down my cheeks with this memory.

"It was a very bitter parting. I knew I would never see him again, but I had to say goodbye. He refused to say farewell, saying that he would see me again, and he would bring his mother."

"I never knew my father when I was alive, but now I feel like I've known him all my existence. I know just what he was like, and what he would say and when he would laugh. I know!"

I looked at my granddaughter. She seemed so different. How could she know these things? Death seems to have been kinder to her than to me.

"Your father was a character, like his mother. They were made from the same mold."

"It's strange that the more you speak, the more I understand and see how it actually was. It's almost as if you only have to think it and I know what happened in the past."

Oh no, not again, I thought. Rose could read my mind. How come everyone could do this except me?

"I don't know," Rose said. "But I maybe that's why I feel you need me now. There's something not right about you Grandfather. I can't quite understand what is happening to you. All I know is, I am here, and whatever you need I will to help you find it."

"How come you can read my thoughts?"

"I don't know. Melissa and Daniel asked me the same question when I talked to them. I do know that I feel this strange tug. It's like something is trying to pull me away. Whenever I let the tug pull me, everything is much clearer, but I don't let it pull me completely, or else I feel I couldn't talk to you at all."

"That sounds remarkably like what Friend and Spider told me."

"Spider and Friend. Hmmm."

Rose looked at the ground for a moment then burst out laughing.

"What's so funny?"

"Spider!"

"What do you mean?"

"I'm not sure, but when I imagine what he is like, I get this overwhelming urge to laugh. And when I imagine Spider and you together, I keep getting this picture of this frog like guy bouncing on your head. You look quite annoyed with him, but you don't want to tell him to stop."

I was perturbed at the accuracy of Rose's description of how it felt to be around Spider. "You know Spider is the spirit that lives in the sacred cave."

Rose laughed even harder.

When she regained her composure she said, "That makes total sense for some reason. He tried to scare you out of your wits, so you would pay attention to him. It fits his sense of humor."

I wanted to change the subject, so I asked, "What do you see about Friend?"

"Hmmm. That's tougher. Something about you doesn't want to see Friend as he is. I don't know why."

"Is that all you see about him? Because I feel if I could figure out some of the things Friend said to me, then I would have all the answers to my questions."

Rose frowned and said, "I'm sorry Grandfather. All I can feel about Friend is his infinite capacity for space that he makes for you."

"Nothing else?"

"No, there's nothing clear that I can see. It's like a dark cloud is hanging between you and Friend."

We both stopped to think over what had been said, and sat quietly staring at the waterfall.

Rose was the first to break the silence, "Tell me about my mother."

I thought for a moment, then said, "I really only knew her for two years. She had joined our group by chance. Your mother, Lisa, and her husband, John, were wandering through the wilderness, when Bobby, who was quite young at the time, stumbled upon them. They befriended him and he led them back to camp. They had not done well in the woods and were very hungry when they arrived. They were quite content to join a well organized group. We taught them the ways of the wild, and they adapted. However, on his very first hunt, John was killed by a bear. Your mother was devastated. This was when your father took it upon himself to comfort your mother. They became very close, in spite of the fact that she was at least ten years older than him. Your mother was a kind soul, and I think she grew to love your father in the short time they were together. But your father grew restless and he left to find his mother, not knowing that he was going to be a father.

"Your mother had trouble all through her pregnancy. She died shortly after giving birth to you. It was a long hard labor, too much for your mother. You barely lived. It was a miracle that you survived.

"I think your mother had too many heartbreaks too close together. She missed the civilized world. She hated winter and was always cold. But she had a warm heart, and that was what everyone missed about her after she died."

"Yes, I see her now. Even though I have no memory of my mother, I see her. I know everything about her. Her hopes and dreams. It's strange seeing someone else's life. I knew nothing of the civilized world, except what you and others had told me, but I see it now. It was full of filth, disease and hunger, how could anyone stand it? "

"People are adaptable. The ability to change is one of the strongest survival traits that we have. But it was the resistance to change that probably brought down civilization. But to answer your question directly, most people hated it, but felt there was no alternative, so they simply tolerated it."

"Why did you leave?"

"I saw the writing on the wall. I knew that things would deteriorate. Others saw it as well, and I'm sure they survived longer than most, but died trying to defend territories. I chose to be non-confrontational. We hid from most of the people we encountered. I taught everyone how to disappear when they needed to. Very few of us died in battle."

The day of the fight came back to me and I felt the need to explain myself to Rose.

"I'm sorry for giving you such bad advice."

But she put her fingers to her lips and said, "Shhh. There's no need to talk, I understand. If given the chance I would not do things differently, I would do everything again, just the same."

I felt relief and gave my granddaughter a hug.

"But you must tell me something now. What happened after the fight?"

"Well, we made our way to the Rock, and prepared some defenses. Mostly large rocks we could throw down or roll down on anyone trying to get up at us. I tended to Peter. Then Bobby went to get Melissa. They brought as much as they could carry. Before it got dark we moved to the sacred cave. Peter was too weak to do anything. Melissa was crying to herself and I could do nothing to prevent Bobby from going out to see what happened to Paul.

"So we knew nothing about what happened until Bobby got back. He was very reluctant to say anything, but I prodded it out of him. He said he went back to the lake as quietly as he could. As he got closer, he heard strange chants. When he came to the edge of the woods and could see the strangers, they were all naked and the leader was raising a knife over Paul's body. He cursed himself for not having brought his bow from the Nook. He had intended to get it before he came back to the sacred cave the second time. He wasn't thinking straight from the knocks he had received on his head. The leader killed Paul with a viscious stab to his chest. He saw the strangers do some strange movements then fall to the ground. They writhed on the ground for a while before the leader walked away from the dying fires.

"He saw that the others had fallen asleep. Bobby crept up to the sleeping strangers and killed them silently with his knife. He said killing the first stranger was easy. He slit his throat from ear to ear. He made little noise. Bobby kept him pinned for only a few seconds before he stopped moving. It was difficult killing the other two because they were locked in an embrace. He slit the throat of one, but his movements awakened the other. Bobby had to stab him repeatedly before he died. He was alarmed by the noise the dying stranger had made and he ran back to the woods.

"The leader came back to the fires and saw his dead companions. He immediately grabbed some things and ran. Bobby was torn between following him right then or going back for his bow and then tracking him down. He decided to spend the night at the Nook and rise up before dawn and track down the leader. As he had suspected, the leader had left the valley during the night. It was easy following him because he had stumbled around in the dark. The stranger turned south, to follow the mountain range. He ran all day and caught up to him before dark. The stranger didn't notice him in spite of the fact that he kept looking over his shoulder. The leader of the strangers was now slowed by fatigue and a sprained ankle. Bobby waited until he decided to rest and shot him in the leg with an arrow.

"The stranger panicked and ran away as best as he could. He fell many times in his attempted escape. Bobby ran in front of him and shot an arrow into his other leg. The stranger tried to crawl away. When he was totally exhausted he propped himself up against a tree. Bobby walked toward him. The stranger threw his now broken spear at Bobby in a last attempt to stave off death. Bobby raised his bow, looked at the now cowering form of the stranger and fired his arrow an inch above his head into the tree. Bobby then went over to the stranger, and held him by his hair. He pulled out his knife, stared him in the eye, and plunged the knife into his chest ... just as the stranger had done to Paul. He watched the stranger die, never taking his eyes off of him. They watched each other but neither said a word. The stranger's eyes rolled back and he was dead.

"It was two days before we saw Bobby again. We were worried that he, too, had died. We were all sad when we heard of Paul's death, no one more so than Melissa. But life went on. It was harder in some ways, but easier in others with only the five of us left.

"It was two years before we started to move south."

"Two years?"

"Why does that seem strange to you, we needed to prepare before we moved."

"No, that's not it. I just don't remember two years going by, that's all."

"Well, we moved south. It was pretty much deserted. Very few signs of people. We did find two youngsters, a boy and a girl. Their elders had all been killed by a disease that killed by filling the lungs with blood. They were living like coyotes. We took them in. Melissa then had another girl. She named her Mary, after her sister. "

I bowed my head in thought for a moment and said, "Peter?"

"Yes. He never regained the full use of his arm, but his others parts were in good working order. "

"You sound as if you know. "

"Well, we had decided that we needed to increase the population a bit."

"And you?"

"A boy. I named him Claude, after you. "

"Congratulations," I said. Rose had made me proud.

We both laughed, then I cried. I now had three great-grandchildren. But it was as if I had slept for a few years. What could I possibly feel for the living. They were getting more remote, and time passed so strangely. And here now was my granddaughter. She died when her child was too young to remember her, just like her mother before.

"Do not cry Grandfather. I left my legacy. And you are still well represented among the living. "

"Yes, but how many are there left among the living, and how will they survive?"

"Bobby will find a way."

"Do you really believe that?"

Rose turned away. She didn't answer. A single tear ran down her cheek.

"What can we do?" she asked.

"I don't think there is anything we can do. I can barely help myself, let alone others. Have you tried talking to the living. It's harder than it looks. "

She laughed.

"Well, the living have their hands full. So what about the dead?"

"What about the dead?"

"What can we do to help the dead?"

"I don't think there is much we can do. But one thing I'm going to try and do is find Daniel and Mary, and try to talk them into quitting the committee."

"What's the committee?"

"I'm not sure, but I don't have a good feeling about it. Well, not about one member I ran across, anyway. Bill told me some more about it."

"Who's Bill?"

"He's Spider's apprentice. Spider told me he had had some fun with you, when you lived in the sacred cave."

"Oh was that him?"

"Why, what happened?"

"We all had strange dreams in the cave, all except Mary."

"What sort?"

"Well mine were about you."

"Go on."

"I saw you in a strange lodge. The walls were straight and smooth, as was the floor and ceiling. You were sitting on an unusual chair. It was much too small for you, and it had a table attached at the front. The only way to sit in the chair was to squeeze in from the side. There was a strange looking man with a long white beard standing in front of a large black wall. He scratched on it with a white stone. He was always scratching his fingernails across the black wall, it made a horrible noise, and he always yelled at you to pay attention. You seemed to be under a lot of pressure."

I laughed heartily at what I thought Rose was describing.

"It sounds like you were describing a school room, with a tough teacher in it."

"Scool rooom?"

"School room. When I was young, I sat for nineteen years in a place such as you described."

"Nineteen years?!!"

"Yes, a terrific waste of time. I could have learned everything in only about five, maybe six years. I was extremely bored."

"Why did you stay?"

"Oh, we had to. The wisdom of our elders said that this was the best way to learn. What it actually did though, was take away parent's responsibility to teach their own children. In fact, if parents taught their own children, they were treated with suspicion, and were watched closely. If they were judged as having done anything wrong, their children were taken away and the parents locked up."

"That sounds horrible."

"Of course, if one was rich, one could avoid the laws that the elders put down."

"What does rich mean?"

"Well, people used pieces of paper to get things from others."

"Pieces of what?"

"Paper was made from trees. You could make the tree into very thin strips and write things on it."

"And what did you write on them?'

"All sorts of things. But with money, we wrote how much it was worth."

"Huh?"

"How much value people associated with it. This was agreed by mutual consent."

"So then what?"

"We then exchanged the money for things we needed, food, shelter, sex, you name it ... people exchanged money for it."

"You tell strange stories Grandfather. That's why I always liked listening to you."

"Yes but you see, people became obsessed with the desire to have the most amount of money, because of the perceived freedom that everybody thought this would bring. Most soon discovered that their lives were just as empty after they accumulated money as they were before. Only those that had found happiness and peace first, were happy after they accumulated money."

"Life sounded difficult."

"Oh, it really wasn't that difficult. All that one had to do was try to be the best one could be. It was when one allowed oneself to be distracted or travel down dead ends that one found things difficult."

"That's what you always told us."

"It applies to everyone, regardless of their situation. But it was funny how people came up with ways of thinking about how money should be used. These people killed you if you didn't believe in the system they believed in. I have to admit I was guilty of falling for these ideas when I was young. I was an anarchist, a communist and a capitalist."

"A what, a who, and a what?"

"Don't worry about it, the concepts are not important. Once I started seeing things as an energy exchange, I was better off."

"So there were few people who saw things this way?"

"Sad but true. Very few understood that thoughts are energy. Positive and negative. Very few understood that you could control your own destiny by controlling your thoughts.

Some people realized this and organized methods with which to control other peoples' thoughts. There were political, religious ... all sorts of methods to control peoples' thoughts. The people who were in charge of what people thought wielded great power. They never entertained deviation from their dogma, because that threatened their power."

"Free thinking was not allowed?"

"Precisely. No one was ever taught to question the wisdom of the one in charge. True wisdom comes when one finds out for oneself by trying out knowledge, and not relying on others to give them wisdom."

"How could you even stand living in that world?"

"A lot couldn't. There were millions of distractions and escapes available to most everyone. I fell into many of them. But before I met my wife I tried to escape big time. I went into the wilderness with the intent of never going back to the civilized world. I resolved to either learn how to survive out here or die. I was never going to go back. I was out for two moons."

"So what happened?"

"I lost my tent poles."

"What are tent poles."

"The sticks that kept up my portable lodge."

"Why didn't you just make new ones?"

"Let's just say I just wasn't ready to stay in the wilderness. I went back out to get new tent poles, but on the way my truck broke down. I had to go further out to get it fixed, I needed my parents' help, but they helped to pull me back. But the time I spent out here made me see things differently. I fell back into some distractions, but it was the call of the wild which kept me on my path, that and your Grandmother."

"Grandmother?"

"Yes, as I have told you she was a powerful woman. She saw clearly through all situations. She caused a lot of turmoil in peoples lives, including my own. But I loved it. She kept me from becoming complacent. But there came a time when she became tired of me falling into the same traps over and over. I was stuck. We became separate for a while. I stopped being so scattered and took charge of my own life. I had to change to get close to her again.

"It's funny, some things in life seem so simple when you look back, but were so hard when you were in them. For example, I had injured my foot, before my children were born. This injury caused me great pain for many years. It prevented me from enjoying life fully. I went to many healers, doctors and physicians in order to make my foot better. I bought expensive shoes and expensive inserts for those shoes. The only result was that the pain lessened, but it never went away. I got so tired of the pain that one day I tried to walk differently. The pain was decreased somewhat. I stopped using all that fancy hardware for my foot and just changed the way I walked. In a short time, my foot stopped hurting. I had wasted years living with the pain. And all it took was for me to change my walk."

"It sounds too simple."

"Yes I know, but if you don't like something, just change it. Your Grandmother ... my wife ... always said that those who never changed, didn't really want to. No matter how hard they said that they wanted to. There are no baby steps to change. Either do or don't. And if you don't, then stop complaining. And one day I just took it to heart. It was hard. But after that, life was certainly interesting."

"That was one thing I always wondered about you. Why you changed the way you did things all the time?"

"Well, let me tell you. There was a time when I was in a rut, and I resisted change. I waited until the last possible moment to initiate change in my life ... I may have stayed that way."

"Not you. I can't imagine you that way. No, I see, you're right. Ugh, how could anyone have tolerated you?"

"I tried many peoples' patience, but I was lucky, I had a lot of people who loved me despite myself."

"Just like I love you, too." A strange voice said behind me.

I turned to see three spirits.

"Bruno!! I cried.

10

DANIEL AND MARY

"Glad you remember Bruno."

"How can I forget a mug like that."

I stood up and held my sword in front of me.

"Oho sword is shinier, but committee gave me one too."

Bruno pulled out his rod, but this time it grew longer and developed a point. He laughed a deep harsh laugh. The other two with him laughed a forced laugh.

Bruno stopped laughing then said, "Now no more time for laughing. You come with me this time and bring girlie too."

Rose started to reply but I cut her off.

"If you tell me more about the committee, I may be more inclined to come with you."

I remember Spider said that the committee used to try and convince spirits to go with them by talking and not by hitting them over the head. Perhaps I could find out something useful before I had to do something about these three.

"Okay, we play it your way. Committee real good. Right?"

He shouted this at the spirit beside him as he hit him on the side of the head with the back of his hand.

The spirit nodded with great enthusiasm and said, "Oh yeah, oh yeah," repeatedly.

"So, enough talk-talk now. Let's go."

"Well, I was hoping for a little more information than that."

"What? You no believe Max here. Max no lie."

"No, I would never dream of questioning the integrity of your esteemed colleague. I merely wanted to know what the goals of the committee were."

"Goals to help new dead ones. Right."

Bruno dug his elbows into both his companions' stomachs, as he said this.

They readily agreed, "Oh yeah, oh yeah."

Bruno broke out into a short laugh. The other two followed suit. It was obvious Bruno was hiding something and found this quite amusing. I could only imagine the goals of the committee, and none of them were good.

"What sort of help?"

"Only the best kind."

They laughed again at Bruno's prompting.

This was going nowhere. I gripped my sword harder and was about to leap at the three of them when I had another thought.

"I heard that two of my grandchildren joined the committee. Rose here ran into them recruiting spirits just like you. Is there a plan for relatives who want to join?"

Bruno had a more serious look on him when he said, "You have gran-chillren in committee? What their names?"

"Mary and Daniel"

"Oh dey yours?"

"Yes."

"Then wait here."

Bruno moved away ten feet. He looked like he was sucking in air, then he let out the highest pitched sound I ever experienced. I'm sure it was well beyond the range of normal human hearing.

"What was that?" Rose asked.

"I call gran-chillren."

"How did you do that?" Rose asked.

"Committee teach me."

"Is it some sort of long distance communication ability?" I asked.

"Oh yes. Committee know many secrets. Maybe dey teach you when ... if you join."

I realized that now would be a very good time to control my thoughts. I was just thinking how Bruno would never be able to convince me to join, when he changed his 'when' to an 'if'. I tried to think that maybe my grandchildren could enlighten me a bit about the committee, and possibly they could sway me to be more favorable to the committee. I tried to hold that thought so Bruno would not be as suspicious of me.

Rose inched closer to me and said in a hushed tone, "Why don't we just leave?"

Max said, "Boss I dink dey's getting ready to leave."

"I have no intention of going anywhere until I have spoken to my grandchildren."

This seemed to satisfy Bruno, but Max gave me a nasty look. He was a weasely character.

Rose and I stood quietly together and watched Bruno and his two stooges. This went on for a while, until Bruno started to grumble. "If dey no get here soon, Bruno personally will serve them up to committee."

Suddenly we heard the same high pitch whine, only this sounded like it was coming from a great distance as it was not as ear shattering as the first one we heard.

Bruno smiled and said, "Dey come. Now we see what dey say. You listen good. Bruno be patient with you. Like old times. But not be so patient if don't finish talk-talk quickly."

I could see in the distance five figures running quickly along the river bank. The two in the middle I recognized as Daniel and Mary. The other three were much like Max. The increase in the number of Bruno's companions made me slightly uncomfortable, but instinctively I knew that the only one who posed any difficulty for me was Bruno.

I worried more now for my grandchildren. What would happen to them if a fight broke out? Worse yet, what if Daniel and Melissa sided with Bruno?

It wasn't much longer before the five spirits joined us.

"Ah, Morris, you found them. But you take too long. Bruno tell committee when he get back."

Morris' eyes widened with obvious horror.

"No, please don't. They will make mincemeat out of me," Morris said pathetically.

Bruno delighted in his groveling. Bruno then turned to my grandchildren and asked, "He your gran-father?"

Mary and Daniel both shouted "Grandfather!!" simultaneously, then rushed to hug me.

In the scramble to hug me, I almost dropped my sword. Bruno looked tempted to attack me, but I quickly recovered my grip and gently pushed Daniel and Mary away.

"Grandfather, it is so good to see you after all these years," Mary said happily.

Daniel shook his head in agreement.

It had seemed to me a much shorter time since I had last seen them and that not enough time had passed for me to miss them. "I need you to do something for me."

They looked at me with trepidation.

"I want you to tell me everything you know about the committee."

Daniel took one look at Bruno then said, "The committee is committed to helping newly dead spirits adjust to their dead existence. I've seen for myself how helpful they are to others. I've even heard that after you have totally adjusted to your dead existence that they help you find out your next task."

Hearing Daniel talk like this frightened me. He sounded like someone out of a fifties sitcom, where everything is just peachy keen and nothing serious ever goes wrong. I wondered if it were possible to brainwash spirits?

Mary continued, "We've been going around recruiting spirits that have just died and telling them all about the wonderful work that the committee does. We've already helped three spirits find a new home with the committee."

Rose couldn't take it any more and said, "What kind of crap is that?"

Mary looked offended.

I quickly blurted out, "It's okay, Rose. Let them finish, we need to hear all they have to say before we make any decisions."

"I don't need to listen to this. I've already made up my mind ..."

I interrupted her quickly, "Good, good, then why don't you sit by the waterfall, and be ready to leave. We may have to leave in a hurry, if you know what I mean."

I winked at her, making sure no one else noticed, then continued, "I mean Bruno here is a busy spirit and has a lot to do."

"That's right. Girlie sit down. Let gran-father listen.

"Bruno busy. Must pick up twelve more dead ones before go home."

I hoped that Rose understood my meaning. I wanted to get her and my other two grandchildren away from here. But we were still outnumbered six to four, and I knew Bruno wouldn't let us just get up and say goodbye without putting up some sort of resistance.

"Okay, where were we? Oh yes, you were telling me about helping spirits find new homes. What does that entail?"

Mary continued happily, "Well, newly dead spirits are brought together in groups and these groups form the basis for new family units. Everyone in the committee is like a brother or sister. And if you have any unresolved issues from your life there are hundreds of spirits in the service of the committee that can offer you help."

"Do you believe what you are saying?" I asked.

I looked hard at Mary. She had a glazed look in her eyes, but as we continued to look at each other, she became uncomfortable, until she had to lower her eyes to the ground. I turned to Daniel, who had a stupid smile on his face, and said, "And you?"

Daniel gave more praises to the committee. I tuned out quickly, but giving them the impression that I was paying attention. I noticed Bruno was getting edgy. Mary was looking confused. Rose was alert but waiting. This was getting me nowhere. I decided on the direct approach.

"Daniel."

He kept babbling about the committee, not hearing me call him.

"DANIEL!!!" I shouted.

He stopped. Everyone looked at me.

"I want you to stop and think about what you have been just telling me. Does it feel true to you?"

"What do you mean Grandfather?"

"Well, I'm pretty sure even a small child could figure out that there is more going on here with this committee than meets the eye. One could tell that by your obvious lack of free will and by the reactions of your distinguished colleagues."

"Dat don't sound like you interested in joining committee," Bruno said menacingly.

I spoke urgently, "Daniel, Mary look at me. I want you to choose between the committee and me. I want you to forget about how you died or anything else that traumatized you. It is time to wake up and take some responsibility for yourselves and your own actions. Choose now!!"

"Bruno no like what you saying. Bruno put you in your place. Me going to cut you into little pieces and give each one to chairman himself."

Bruno advanced. His henchman followed behind. Daniel and Rose stood confused. Rose was standing and had her fists ready.

It was now or never. I leapt to one side and swung at the outmost gatherer. The sword passed effortlessly through him, neatly cutting him in two. He screamed a sickening scream, as his upper half grasped at his lower half. He looked like he was trying to put his two halves back together.

The gatherers moved back. All except Bruno.

He shouted to his lackeys in case they were thinking of running away from him, "Get deez two outta here, and take girlie too."

Bruno pounced towards me and brought his heavy sword down.

I met his blow with my new sword. The force of his stroke knocked me to my knees. He raised his sword for another stroke but before he could deliver it. I rolled to one side, clipping Bruno's leg with the tip of my sword. He winced but moved quickly to keep on top of me. He swung stroke after stroke at me, missing only by inches each time. He never allowed me an opportunity to get to my feet, and it was almost impossible to get an effective swing with my sword from the ground. In-between a swing from Bruno I braced myself and kicked with both feet. It was enough to knock him off balance and interrupt his attack.

I did a backwards somersault and landed on my feet. Bruno was already coming towards me with a swing. I knew that my only hope would be to attack. I started a wide swing at the oncoming Bruno. He diverted his swing and deflected mine. We crashed together from Bruno's momentum. The force of his forward motion made me stagger backwards. We both swung wildly at each other as we moved closer. Our bodies came together with our swords in-between us. We each pushed our swords as hard as we could towards the other.

Bruno couldn't resist saying something, "Bruno gonna cut you … and he gonna cut your gran-chillren too."

I said nothing but leapt backwards. We each executed perfect swings and our swords met with a loud clash of metal. I leapt backwards once more. This time when Bruno moved towards me, I dropped to the ground then leapt forward, keeping close to the ground. Bruno's swing narrowly missed my head, but my sword made a deep gash in Bruno's leg. Bruno cried in pain, yet his cry was weak compared to the screams that now caught my ears.

I turned to see Daniel and Mary being dragged away by two of Bruno's henchmen. Rose was struggling with one, while another was hitting her with his rod. The sight and sound of Rose being hit with a rod, coupled with my own memory of what it was like, was almost fatal for me.

Bruno, although wounded, didn't waste any time in trying to remove my head. A wicked swing from Bruno's sword narrowly missed me. Some hidden sense caused me to duck at the last second, but I wasn't quick enough. His sword grazed my scalp and instantly the pain I had experienced the first time Bruno struck me returned. Only this time it was multiplied ten fold.

I didn't have time to indulge in my pain because Bruno started a flurry of swings at my now wounded head. It was all I could do to avoid being hit.

I began to panic. I knew I had to dispatch Bruno quickly in order to help my grandchildren, but I had been on the defensive most of the fight. I heard no more screams coming from my grandchildren, but I couldn't afford to take my mind off this fight in order to find out what had happened to them.

I had to defend against a wicked onslaught of blows from Bruno. He was swinging in an almost predictable pattern. It felt briefly like my fight with the Valkyrie. But Bruno had a few tricks up his sleeve. On one of his swings that I successfully parried, he suddenly moved forward and he brought his sword down along my blade. This allowed me to direct my blade across Bruno's side. I caused a slight wound, but the main purpose of this maneuver was to injure my hands. His blade slid past my hand guard and neatly sliced off my little finger.

I had to let go of my blade with my right hand. The pain in that hand was enormous. I jumped backward to gain time. Bruno was just as quick. He swung at me many times. Each time I evaded his swing rather than parry, for I feared losing my sword. The force of his swings required me to have both hands on my sword.

I had little chance now. So with nothing to lose, in-between Bruno's swings I jumped forward, instead of backwards as I had been doing. I struck Bruno with the hilt of my sword and pushed as hard as I could, trying to knock him off balance. I continued to run past him as he stumbled backwards. I had run a short distance before Bruno realized that I was no longer trying to fight him.

He began to run after me shouting lustily, "Coward. You afraid of Bruno. Bruno gonna hurt you. "

I tried to run in the direction that my grandchildren had been taken. I saw no one else. I didn't think that we had been fighting for long. I'm sure there hadn't been enough time for the others to have traveled far, yet there was no one in sight.

But I had no other alternative except to run. I couldn't fight Bruno with the wounds that I sustained. I had to think of a new course of action, but what?

Bruno was hot on my heels. I was running as fast as I could. Bruno was not gaining on me, but neither was he falling behind.

I had to lose him somehow. I remembered that Bill had lost Bruno twice before. I somehow doubted that he would give up chasing me if we ran into other spirits. But I also remembered that Bill had lost Bruno underground and Spider had said that the committee hadn't learned to see down there. But where should I go? I thought of the sacred cave, but I didn't want to lead him there, or to the hidden valley for that matter. I tried to remember some other cave that was close, because I knew Bruno wouldn't give me a chance to search for one. The terrain was unfamiliar to me. In my depression I had traveled farther north and west than I had previously traveled. The landscape didn't vary much in the far north. Lots of water. I followed the river back towards the mountains. In the distance I noticed a sudden gleam of light reflecting off a point on the nearest mountain.

I decided to make for that point. The mountains soon loomed up in front of us. I started to run up the mountain that had reflected such a gleam. I was amazed that I could maintain the same speed running up the mountain as I could over a flat surface. It took me no time at all to get up to the point I was making for. To my delight a large cave suddenly loomed up. Without thinking I ducked inside. I glanced behind and noticed Bruno came to a halt before the entrance. I went deep into the cave, just barely able to see the entrance and the reluctant Bruno. He swayed back and forth, unable to decide what to do. I wondered where his fear stemmed from. Suddenly the memory of something Bill had said came to me ... about a spirit bear leaping out from a cave and fighting him. Bruno had overcome his fear and was slowly making his way forward.

I decided on a wild plan. I roared like a bear. I thought it a poor imitation, but Bruno stopped in his tracks. I tried to imagine that I was a bear and roared again. This time the effect was more convincing. Bruno turned and ran out of the cave.

He turned and shouted, "You no stay in dere forever. Bruno get you when you come out. No one gets away from Bruno."

I laughed to myself. I wanted to ask him about Bill. I roared again. I enjoyed watching Bruno scamper away from the entrance.

But Bruno was right about one thing. I couldn't stay in this cave forever, and I knew Bruno would wait for me to come out. So what could I do? A thought came to me. I got into my grandchildren's lodge by traveling through the earth. Why couldn't I do that again? I wasn't sure exactly how I did it before but I was going to try again. I was sure I could end up in the lodge again, but how could I land somewhere else? I had concentrated on the inside of the lodge and I had traveled there. How could I get to, say the other side of this mountain? Difficult when I have never seen it. I'm sure Spider would know the answer.

So why don't I go to see Spider? I have a lot more questions to ask him and I was sure he could tell me how best to save my grandchildren.

I quieted my mind, heard my drum and imagined the sacred cave. I pictured in my mind a grinning Spider beckoning me to come. I felt myself travel through the earth at the speed of thought.

"There you are. Have you finished running around yet, or do you still have more to do? "

11

EVIL?

"Spider!!"

"Who else were you expecting?"

"Ahhhhh, you," I said rather sheepishly, but I quickly added, "And Bill! Where is he?"

Spider smiled at me then said, "He's taking his exam."

"Exam!!??"

"Oh yes. Bill likes to takes exams. That way he feels as if he's learned his lessons. We all have our own idiosyncrasies."

"How does a spirit take an exam?"

"Anyway he wants."

"That's not the answer I'm looking for. How does he physically do it?"

"Well, he has no 'physical,' but I think I know what you mean. He's taking a written exam now, followed by an oral exam later on."

"Written? What does he write on?"

"I see you haven't yet learned that you are limited only by your own thoughts."

"What do you mean?"

"I can't be any clearer when I say, YOU ARE ONLY LIMITED BY YOUR OWN THOUGHTS! It applies to the living as well as the dead. Bill created his own test, using his own paper and his own pen. And now he's writing the exam."

"Isn't it a little biased, if he got to write his own test."

Spider looked at me comically, "Whatever do you mean?" Spider spun on one foot, holding his other foot in his hand, while shouting the occasional 'Hey.'

He stopped his strange dance then said, "The entire universe is biased."

He looked at me as if to say, how come you can't see the obvious?

"Look at yourself," he said.

I looked.

"Where's your finger?"

I shrugged.

"Where's the missing part of your head?"

I touched the place where Bruno had skinned my head with his sword. I shrugged again.

"It's a good thing you don't believe that you can bleed to death, or else there wouldn't be anything left of you at the moment."

"Huh?"

"Stop acting so stupid. Do you want to walk around like that for the rest of eternity?"

"No."

"Well, fix yourself up a bit then."

"How do I do that?"

Spider laughed. It started out as a small chuckle, grew to a more robust guffaw, then finished with a hold your stomach, roll around on the floor belly laugh. When Spider was finally able to control himself he stood and said, "I've told you already."

I blinked emphatically then said, “When?”

“Just now.”

“I didn’t hear you.”

“Of course you did.”

“Well, let’s just assume that I’m deaf. Could you repeat it please?”

“I think we don’t have to assume that.”

I scowled, then Spider continued, “You believe that you can get hurt so you did.”

“What’s that supposed to mean? When Bruno hit me, it hurt. It still hurts. I’m missing a finger in fact.”

I held up my hand for effect.

“Oh da poor little hand has a boo boo,” Spider said in a child like voice.

I didn’t appreciate his humor. I never liked anyone who made fun of others’ pain.

Spider sensed my mood. He said in a very serious voice, “I’m not making fun of your injuries, I’m making fun of the fact that you want to stay injured.”

“I’m not choosing to be injured.”

“You’re right of course. Now what did you want to see me about?”

Spider’s sudden change of topic made me suspicious. It was unlike him to give up before he came the point he was trying to make.

“How am I choosing to be injured?”

“I don’t want to talk about it any more”

“Why not?”

“Just don’t.”

“But I want to know.”

“So. What are you going to do. Make me talk. Just try it.”

Spider then proceeded to hop around me, taking the occasional comical jab with his fists.

"Seriously, why don't you want to talk about my injuries?"

Spider stopped bouncing around and said, "Because I'm tired of how easily you indulge yourself."

"Well, I am missing a finger."

"So."

Spider then grabbed his left arm with his right, and yanked. His arm pulled out of his socket and he started waving his detached arm about.

"I've seen a lot worse than a missing finger. And I know something can be done about it, but you won't listen to me."

He opened his mouth wide, really wide, and shoved his arm down his throat. And a second later a new arm popped out of his shoulder.

I stood with my mouth open. Spider reached up to me and closed it for me, then said, "So are you going to put your finger back or what?"

"I can't. I left it on the ground back at the waterfall."

Spider shook his head and said, "I'm bored of this. Just imagine yourself whole again, and let's get on to more interesting topics."

I didn't argue with him any more. Instead I attempted to do what he said. I imagined myself whole. I strained. I grunted. I moaned. Nothing happened.

"Well, at least you make it interesting to watch you. Why not try to remember what it felt like being whole. Remember that feeling, your entire energy make-up and how that felt."

I didn't quite understand him.

"Okay, how about if you try to remember comfor ting someone else when they were injured. What did you do then."

"I tried to soothe them with my words and presence."

"Forget the words, go with the presence part."

"Well, it's like I got all warm inside and I could feel that warmth extend through my hands into the other person."

"That's it. Try to do that again."

I remembered when Rose was young and had fallen and hurt herself. I comforted her by holding her and felt myself become bigger than myself. I never thought of it that way before.

"That's it, you got it."

I looked at Spider. He was pointing at my hand. My finger was back. I touched my head. There was no injury there either.

"So now what else did you want to know?"

"But how?"

"Let it go, we've spent too much time on it already."

I guess I'd have to let it go for now and figure it out later. I remembered why I had come to Spider in the first place.

"My grandchildren!"

"What about them?"

"The committee has them."

"Oh boy that should be fun."

"For whom? You or them?"

"Both."

"Look Spider, all I want is to get Rose, Daniel, and Mary away from Bruno. He can't be up to any good."

"Oh yes, Bruno is a nasty one all right. But why don't you tell me what happened right from the beginning."

"But the committee has got my grandchildren, I have to do something now!"

"Oh, so you can waste time talking about your wounds, but not have time to tell an old spirit a story. I'm sure it will be quite amusing."

"Amusing? There was nothing amusing about it."

"Well, tell it to me and let me be the judge."

I told Spider about my adventures since the time he kicked me out of the cave. About meeting Sid and his gang, going to the lodge, meeting Cat, my fight with the Valkyrie, the happenings of my grandchildren, and Bruno. Throughout my story, I had to pause many times. I had to let Spider compose himself after each of his laughing fits. The story of Cat seemed to be extremely funny to him, sometimes I just said two words when he would break out laughing and it took forever before he could listen again.

When I was done telling my story Spider said, "Well, one thing for sure, your dead existence hasn't been boring so far. Believe me when I say that I have met some pathetic spirits."

"Yes, but maybe just a tad too much has happened to me?"

"Nonsense."

"Well, I didn't appreciate you laughing when I was telling you about the death of Paul."

"It wasn't the funniest thing that happened to you, but I assure you there was humor there."

"You'll have to explain that one to me."

"Oh, certainly. That was one of the most significant events that has happened to you yet. There's tons of material there. Almost enough to write a book, if you were alive that is."

Spider laughed again, which made me smile. Being around Spider made it difficult to take yourself seriously for any length of time.

But I tried when I asked, "Spider, you have to tell me about evil spirits."

"I told you before that most spirits are not evil."

"But there are some then?"

"Spirits have their own agendas. Take Sid for example, would you call him evil?"

"No."

"But he was participating in what you would call an evil act."

"Yes."

"Does that make him evil?"

"I guess so."

"Not really. The humans he was interacting with were undoubtedly, from the human point of view, evil, with a capital E. This is not totally unusual. Even though most humans are neither truly good nor truly evil, there are some that are one or the other. Fred and his gang believed they were in contact with some powerful evil spirits that gave them magical powers in return for their sacrifices. When in fact they only had Sid and his gang … a group of spirits that didn't know about any other options of gaining energy to stave off the loss of their consciousness. Sid would have done anything within his abilities to maintain the status quo, that is until you showed him a better way."

"I did? What did I do?"

"You let him ascend, instead of you."

"What do you mean, instead of me?"

"Paul would have taken you along but you declined."

"I did no such thing."

"Sure you did, you stopped paying attention to him, and let Sid receive the energy instead of you."

I had to think about that for a minute.

"What is ascension anyway?"

"Oh no, I'm not going to get into THAT topic, go find somebody else to answer that question."

"But …"

"No buts, or I'll toss you out again."

Spider looked serious, so I dropped the subject.

"Okay, then tell me something. Fred died, right? "

"Right."

"Well, isn't he now an evil spirit, running around doing more evil from the spirit side? "

"No."

"Why not?"

"Because he ascended."

"What?"

"Just because you haven't done it yet, doesn't mean others can't do it."

"But isn't ascending just for non-evil people? "

"I told you that evil is a human concept."

"What does that mean?"

"Well, before humans, spirits existed but evil did not. And when humans showed up ... boom ... there was evil. That's why I can say that most spirits are not evil. There are an infinite amount of spirits that have not been human."

"So tell me, who are the evil spirits?"

"Dead humans."

"But you told me Fred ascended."

"Yes, but not all evil humans that die, ascend. All human spirits have the same options. Some stick around. And the majority who stick around are harmless."

"So isn't there some head evil spirit or something? "

"Oh yes."

"Is he a human?"

"No."

"Well how can he be evil then."

"Humans call him that. He started out by learning that humans are easy to manipulate. They can give their energy to spirits easily under the right circumstances. Easy food for an enterprising spirit. The problem with humans is to keep them in the right state for energy transfer. Well it turns out, that when humans tend to do things that they consider wrong, they stay more focused and in the proper state for energy transfer."

"So you're telling me this evil spirit business started because it's easier for the spirit to feed when he makes people do bad things?"

"No, he doesn't make them, that's their own choice, but he does let them know it would please him. He could get energy from people who do good, but it is harder to keep people focused in that state of pure goodness than it is keeping people focused in the state of pure evil."

"So this one evil spirit is responsible for all the evil in the world?"

"No, no, no. Once the first spirit figured it out, then millions of other spirits figured it out. Practically every evil group of people on the planet has an evil spirit that they think is the head honcho. Sid was called some secret evil name that his humans gave him, because they thought he was so special. When in fact Sid was just an ordinary spirit who attached himself to Fred in order to get fed. A lot of spirits love to have that relationship with a human. Most humans can't take more than one spiritual attachment, but there are some humans that are so energetic that they can take on hundreds, but they're rare.

"But before a spirit can attach to a human, they have to get noticed. Some spirits will do anything to get noticed. Remember the exorcism story I told you?

"Of course there are many other ways that spirits and humans can interact, but what I have told you is one of the more common ways."

"Yeah, where do you fit in?"

"I told you."

"When?"

"When we first met."

"Okay, remind me."

"I'm here to have fun."

"That's not what I mean. I want to know how you get your energy."

"I just told you."

"What? By having fun?"

"Precisely."

"There has to be more than that."

"Not really."

"Come on. I don't believe you."

Spider began to do one of his dances. When he finished he said, "I don't care whether you believe me or not."

"You mean if I just start having fun I could sustain myself forever?"

"Maybe."

"What does that mean?'

"It means that you might find the connections I did or you may not."

"So there is more to it than you're letting on."

"No, it's quite simple. I suddenly found myself as a consciousness one day and I immediately started having fun. With that realization I connected to the universe and that sustained me."

"That sounds hokey. How can I believe you?"

"You crave certainty, there is none. So I can't help you."

"So why do I keep coming to you?"

"I can only guess that you crave my advice."

Is that so?" "

"Yes. But of course you realize that advice is useless. I really don't care what I say to you, but you care what you hear."

"What?"

"It's true."

Then Spider did something totally bizarre. It reminded me of something I had seen years ago on television when I was a kid. He bounced around the room on his head, while laughing like a maniac. This totally unnerved me.

"Why do you do that?"

"It's what you expect of me, and besides it's fun. You should try it sometime. It would be good for you."

I was about to protest that I didn't want him to do these strange performances on my account, and I couldn't possibly see the benefit of acting so bizarrely, when Bill came into the main part of the cave. He had a broad smile on his face.

"I have finished," said Bill.

Spider went into his very serious voice and said, "That's excellent Bill. How did you do?"

"I passed with flying colors."

"Great. So you're ready for the next part of your exam."

"Yes, any time you are."

"We can start immediately. But first I must finish with some other trivial matter."

Spider looked at me. I knew what he was thinking. He bounded over to me, picked me up lightly and headed for the entrance.

"Wait," I shouted.

"What is it now?"

"You haven't told me how I can help my grandchildren."

"I thought you would have figured it out by now. But I can't bother with that right now. I have an exam to give. But I'll tell you what. Just hang around outside for a while and I'm sure something will pop up."

He giggled then tossed me forcefully out of the cave.

I landed better this time, and I even held on to my sword. I felt like going back in and asking for my drum, when suddenly I was struck on the head by it. I looked back to see a laughing Spider waving goodbye. He went back into the cave and I was once again alone.

I sat and remembered all that had happened to me so far. I really was beginning to wonder why most of the spirits I met were so frustrating in their interactions with me. I wondered if there was something wrong with me. But of course in order to keep my sanity I had to let go of that thought. If there was something wrong with me, then I would just go crazy denying it.

I had just found a nice place to sit when I heard a strange pop sound. I turned and was amazed at what I saw.

Beside me sat a person. He had long blonde hair and a rather large nose. He was meditating. It took me a second, but I recognized him.

12

CHRISTOPHER

"Christopher!!" I shouted.

He opened his eyes slowly and said, "Claude."

We both stood up and hugged each other. I was so happy to see him that I laughed with pure joy. I was surprised to see one of my spiritual teachers in front of this cave. To see a familiar face from the past was very emotional. Christopher Tims helped guide me in my youth.

"What brings you here?" I asked.

"You do."

"So, you're dead too then?"

"No."

"You're still alive?"

"I'm not sure why you're saying still, but yes I'm alive."

"It's been years and years since I last saw you."

"That's strange, because I remember seeing you just last month. You were talking about going on vacation up north somewhere. Is this where you went? It's beautiful here."

I looked at him in disbelief. How could he be sitting next to me if our time references didn't match?

"It is beautiful here. I've spent about thirty years of my life here. So how come you seem to think that it's almost forty years in the past?"

"I am where I am, and you are where you are. Time doesn't mean that much if I want to come visit you. I tried a few times, I saw you, but I guess you didn't see me. It looks like you had to wait to be dead before you could hear me. Your wife is looking for you."

I was surprised to hear him say that.

"She's pretty mad at you and is wondering when you're coming home," Christopher continued.

I laughed. That was a cruel joke. Tears came to my eyes. It was too late to go back now. I wished that I could. Maybe I would have been better off if I had done things differently. But it was no good second guessing. What happened, happened.

"I guess she'll be waiting a long time."

"Pity. She was looking forward to seeing you again."

Tears now started flowing freely. It was as if an old wound had been torn wide open. I started to wail. Words were useless now to describe how I felt. The pain, the loneliness I experienced without her presence near me. All my emotions and feelings I had for my wife came out of me in one huge long scream.

Christopher tried to comfort me, but nothing could stop this hurt from coming out, except maybe my wife herself. But I didn't know if I could face her, after what I had done. Taking children away from their mother is a pretty despicable thing to do.

After much self pity, I noticed Christopher had climbed higher up. He was looking out at the setting sun. At this time of the year the sun would set between two mountain peeks at the far end of the valley, as seen from a point right above the cave. I climbed up to talk to him again. I felt much smaller, but all the events of my dead existence came back to me, and I had a nagging question. I was pretty sure Christopher would have an answer for me, or at least he would try to answer it.

"Do you know what ascension is?" I boldly asked.

"Do you want the short answer or the long answer?"

"Both."

"Well, the short answer is, ascension is moving to a higher vibratory state."

"What's the long answer then?"

"Well, how about I give it to you in a metaphor. Your existence is in a playpen. Some humans stay in this playpen and keep all their stuff with them. Ascension is then losing all your stuff and climbing out of the playpen."

"I think your long answer is worse than your short answer."

"Wait, I'm just getting warmed up. Okay, where was I, oh yeah, in the playpen. Humans, dead or alive, develop ruts, and thus the playpen becomes a self-created prison, but at the same time humans revere and idolize their playpens, because in spite of it being a prison, it is safe and known. Anything outside the prison is unknown and humans think that it must be dangerous."

"Okay, I'll bite; how does one get out of one's playpen?"

"By developing curiosity. Just ask yourself, what is it like outside of my playpen? When you ask this question, eventually your curiosity develops into courage, and this courage will allow you to ascend."

"Where to?"

"Usually to a bigger playpen."

"What good is that?'

"Well, it's not necessarily a bad thing. Once curiosity is sparked, the process continues. Let me give you another metaphor ..."

I groaned quietly to myself. Christopher loves metaphors. I'm sure I could spend my entire dead existence listening to Christopher and he would never run out of metaphors.

Christopher paused and looked at me for a moment. I tried to look innocent.

He then continued, " ... suppose your journey led you to sit in a tree. Your journey would be quite boring if all you did was sit in that tree. Don't you agree? "

"Depends."

"On what?"

"On the view."

"Well, even after a certain period of time the view would become boring, too. Right? "

"Right."

"Okay, now suppose you decide to add a little excitement to your existence, and you wonder what it would be like to jump out of the tree. You say to yourself, I don't know, it looks pretty high, and you give yourself hundreds of reasons not to do it. But you're so bored that you jump. You land okay, you're safe, it was exciting, and you do it again. But eventually you get bored of jumping. It now has become a known, as opposed to an unknown. So you look higher in the tree and decide to climb to the next highest branch. The view from up there is better. The jump down looks more dangerous. Eventually you find the courage to jump. So the process leads you to higher and higher branches and bigger and bigger jumps. Do you see what I'm getting at?"

"Not really, I'm having a hard time understanding what this has to do with ascension. I mean, besides the obvious climbing of the tree, it sounds like you're telling me that human spirits only ascend when they get bored. "

"No, no, no. You're missing the point. Most humans ascend in small steps, by using relentless intent. It takes effort to climb to the next branch, and it takes effort to overcome their fear to jump. The only way that this can be done is by relentless intent."

"I don't think you said that the first time."

"Well, it's what I wanted to say. You have to be relentless in what you intend to do. If you want to ascend, then just keep at it. But remember, you only take what you bring with you."

"What does that mean? I don't have anything, well, nothing except this sword and drum here."

"As soon as you said except, that means you have stuff. But I mean more than just what you are holding. You have concepts and beliefs that go with you. Drop all expectations when you go, and it will be a more fulfilling experience."

"Wait a minute. If you claim to be still alive, how do you know this for a fact?"

"There you go with 'still' again. But a quick answer to your question is … I get around."

"Okay, if you get around so much, and you seem to have a problem with the words 'still' alive; tell me something. What is your view on life?"

"Descending."

"Huh?"

"Descending is bringing spirit into your life. The body is where you visit."

"So where do we live?"

"You're dead and you don't know this?"

"No, I don't know. How am I supposed to know. Is there a newspaper published called The Daily Spirit or how about a library where I could be read all about it?"

"You mean that you haven't been to the library yet?"

"Library, what library?"

"Just look around you."

I looked. High. Low. Behind me.

"And just what am I supposed to see."

"If you don't see it, I can't help you. But I can answer your question about where you live. I'm pretty sure you heard me talk about it before. I call it the essential questions of life."

"Yes, but I'm dead."

"Doesn't matter, it still applies."

Christopher put on one of his big grins and started to speak more slowly.

"These are the questions you should be asking. Where did I come from? Who am I? Why am I here? And where am I going ?"

"Yes, I recall the answers were in a Beatles' song."

"That's right. The one which made reference to a nowhere man. Where did I come from? ... Nowhere. Who am I? ... No one in particular. Why am I here? ... No reason. Where am I going? ... Nowhere. We all fool ourselves with the illusion of separateness from each other. Since we are all one, life or death has no meaning except what we give it."

"I not too sure that that is much help. I mean why don't I just give up now and evaporate into nothing?"

"If that's what you want."

As Christopher said those words he evaporated. Poof. Gone. I laughed. I'm sure he had waited a long time to do that to someone. I just happened to be that poor fool.

So was that all there was to ascension and existence? Spider hinted that all there was, was having fun. Or was this all his existence was about?

What was my existence about? I tried only to survive when I was alive. I tried to leave a legacy. Now some of my grandchildren were alive. I had three great-grandchildren, but how long would they be alive? And when they die will they end up like Daniel, Mary and Rose. With some unknown group like the committee? And what will happen to me?

I had to know the answer to these questions. Surely Spider knew. I felt very reluctant about going back into the cave. I didn't want to interrupt Bill's exam. That's another thing. What could Bill's exam be about? Or maybe that's just what Bill expects. Is that his meaning to his dead existence, taking tests? He exists to have his knowledge tested? I guess any bizarre combination of circumstances could exist.

So then my dead existence just mirrors my expectation?

This was too heavy for me. I wish Bill would hurry up.

"It really is lovely here, isn't it?"

I half expected it to be Christopher again, but I was surprised to see Bill.

"Yes," I said hesitantly. "How was the oral exam?"

"I think I did pretty good. I have to wait for the results though. That is why I'm out here. Spider is evaluating my answers."

"I hope you don't mind me asking, but just what were you being tested on?'

Bill was really serious. He looked at me, then turned to face west, and watched the darkening sky.

"Are you ready for the answer? You may not like it."

"Why? What could be so bad about the answer to my question?"

"Well, that is the problem. Once you hear the answer, there is no going back and unhearing it. So I will risk it. Having studied the matter, I feel perhaps it is time for you to hear the answer."

I couldn't take this. What could Bill be studying that could cause me discomfort? This was ridiculous.

I blurted out, “Well, tell me already.”

“Okay. I but I am pretty sure you will not like it.”

I couldn’t take it. I started to walk back to the cave.

Bill said loudly, “My test was on ... YOU.”

I turned and looked at Bill as if he were mad.

“Me?”

“I told you, you would not like hearing it.”

“It’s not that I don’t like it, I’m just confused. Why would you take a test on me?”

“It is something I had to do.”

“That’s not an answer. It’s not like I’m special or something.”

“You are wrong there. Everyone is special. Spider has taught me that much. But you do have a story to tell. And I have been learning it.”

“You’re making me paranoid. What is it?”

“Well, I hate to say it, but you are stuck.”

“That’s it? That’s what you had to take a test on, to know that I’m stuck?”

“No, but you are really stuck.”

“Okay, I can take being stuck, but isn’t this a bit ridiculous? Why are spirits going out of their way to tell me these things? I’m not going to listen any more. Where’s Spider?”

“Here.”

Spider hobbled out of the cave, like a really old man.

“I’m glad to say that Bill has passed his exam.”

Bill clapped in glee and a huge smile filled his face.

“And as a reward for passing, I now free you from your apprenticeship. You are now free to follow Nexus. Having studied him so hard, you now get to experience him, first hand.”

“Wait a minute,” I protested. “What if I don’t want someone who thinks I’m stuck to follow me? And who’s been putting those thoughts into his head? You? Do you think I'm stuck too?"

"Of course."

Spider grinned like only he could, then added, "Well, you two should be off. You have grandchildren to save, so off with you. I've been neglecting the moss lately and it's been getting a bit lonely."

Bill tugged on my arm and Spider added, "Shoo, shoo."

"Wait. Wait. Why am I being stupid?"

Spider cackled then said, "You should ask yourself that one. Now goodbye."

Spider quickly disappeared into the cave.

Bill said, "Let us go."

"Where to?"

"South."

"What's there?"

"The committee."

13

BILL AND CAT

I said, "Lead on then, if you know the way."

I had to admit I felt curious as to what the committee was all about. I knew little about them except what Spider and Bill had told me, and what my first hand experience with Bruno had revealed.

Bill had heard from a spirit named Bob that the committee were some sort of devil worshippers. Spider said the gatherers of the committee talked spirits into joining, but my experience with Bruno suggests that they just whack spirits over the head with their unusual rods. With just these few tidbits of knowledge, I couldn't guess what the committee does.

"Bill, do you know anything else about the committee?"

Bill walked quite a distance before he said anything.

"Yes."

"Well?"

"Well, Spider told me. They are nothing but a joke, and a poor one at that."

"So it should be easy to walk right up to them and just demand that they release my grandchildren, right?"

"For you? I do not think that you are sufficiently prepared for such a scenario."

"Then can you do it?"

"I think so."

"Good, then you can do it and I'll wait for you."

"No. I do not think so."

"Why not?"

"I believe that you are the one that has the desire to save your grandchildren, not me."

"Okay then, teach me how to do it."

"No. I believe that I am not one of your teachers, I am merely an observer of your drama."

"You're my audience then? Well, how do you feel about audience participation."

"I do not think that would be a good idea."

"Is there anything else you can tell me about the committee besides them being a bad joke?"

"Well, as far as I can tell, they are an organized group of experienced spirits who started to band together shortly after the beginning of the bad times. They prey on naive spirits who are unable to defend themselves, and alter them in some way. One other thing I heard was that more spirits go into the committee chambers than come out."

At that moment, the experience of being hit by Bruno's rod came back to me. I remembered my thoughts of feeling totally drained almost to the point where I no longer existed. With this in mind, I wondered how Spider could think they were a joke.

"They arrre."

I stopped. I knew that voice. I looked around. I couldn't see anything, then the figure of a wildcat moved gracefully from behind a rock. All I could think of was that I certainly didn't need to see Cat at this moment. I already had a follower who thought me stupid. Now the size of that audience had just doubled.

"Cat, what are you doing here? Don't tell me, you wanted to call me stupid again?"

He started to lick his paws.

Bill had not realized that I had stopped, so turned and came back.

"A friend of yours?"

I rubbed my leg where Cat had bitten me and said, "We've met before."

Cat looked up and started to purr. It almost sounded like laughing.

"Bill, this is Cat. Cat, this is Bill."

Bill said, "I am pleased to meet you."

Cat replied, "The pleasurrre is all mine."

I was impatient with this exchange. I wanted to know what brought Cat here this time. The last time he disappeared, I was left with more questions than answers. Then a seven foot woman attacked me. What else could happen this time? A group of flying elephants, with a bad case of the runs, flying by, came to mind. I thought better of my curiosity. I really didn't want to know why Cat was here.

Cat just stood watching me, waving his tail back and forth.

Bill didn't say anything, but looked at me and Cat.

This silence was just as frustrating as Cat's evasive answers. So I said to Bill, "Well, look at the time, shouldn't we be going?"

I gave Bill a push forward. He started to move. But Cat followed behind, keeping perfect pace so the distance between us never varied.

"Are you following us?"

"The answerrr to that is obvious."

"Can I ask why?"

"Cerrrtainly you may."

I forgot to be more direct in my questioning.

"Okay, why are you following us?"

"I have an interrrest in what you arrre doing."

"And what may that be?"

Cat just kept walking and totally ignored my question.

"Aren't you going to tell me?"

"No."

"Why not?"

"Cat's perrrogative."

"What does that mean?"

"It means that a cat has the rrright to ignorre anything or anyone that it wants, when it doesn't want to do something."

"Who made these rules up."

"Cats."

It seemed to make sense. When I was alive I certainly met quite a few cats that acted that way.

"So it looks like I'm stuck with you until you're ready to tell me why you're following me, right?"

"You arrrre most perrrrrceptive."

We walked along for quite some time without saying anything. Cat had an effect on me. I didn't want to talk too much around him. Bill seemed to sense my mood and didn't initiate any conversation. The silence was broken by Cat.

"Nexus."

I turned and answered, "Yes?"

"Would you mind if I asked you some questions about humans?"

"No, I guess not."

Cat purred then continued, "Why did humans devote so much time to grrrass?"

I burst out laughing. Here I expected Cat to be asking me some profound question, and all he wanted to know was why humans like lawns.

"Why ever do you want to know about that? "

"Let's just call it a cat's currriosity. "

"Well, people wanted their dwellings to look better.

I wasn't into lawns very much, so I really don't understand the effort that much either. "

Bill interrupted, "I used to spend one day a week looking after my lawn. "

"Looking back, didn't you find it a waste of time?" Cat asked.

"No, it was extremely relaxing. The smell of freshly cut grass was heavenly. It looked beautiful in the morning with the dew shining on it. In the evening it had a indescribable green color that shone into the soul. The kids used to play on it. We had barbecues there. It had many uses. And we had the best lawn on the block. I watered it daily and bought only the best fertilizers. "

"So beyond having it forrr yourrr own pleasurrre and brrringing out envy in yourrr neighborrrs, it had no otherrr purrrpose? "

"I wish you would not put it like that, " Bill muttered. "But I guess, no. "

"When humans dominated the planet, therrre werrre millions who did this also? "

"Yes, " I answered.

"Werrren't therrre always waterrr shorrrtages? "

"Yes. "

"And didn't it rrrequirre a lot of enerrrgy to prrroduce these ferrrtilizerrrs? "

"Yes. I see what you're getting at. I remember hearing somewhere that North Americans used about one-third of their total water use towards watering their lawns, and about one-half of all fertilizers towards feeding their lawns."

"Why?" Cat asked.

"If you're going to ask me why humans did the things that they did, then I'm going to have to leave you, because I don't want to be held accountable."

"Rrrunning away?"

"No. But I wasn't involved with the lawn thing. As a kid I thought it was stupid."

"Doesn't matterrr. If you saw the stupidity arrround you, why didn't you speak out?"

"I was only one person and my thinking went against the majority. I couldn't change anything."

"If you want to initiate change, you must follow some simple rrrules. Firrrst believe you can change whateverrr you want to change. Second, starrrt small. Change small things in yourrrself beforrre biggerrr things. Thirrrd, once you have changed yourrr thinking and behaviorrr, then you can show otherrrs theirrrr folly by yourrr example. Explain why you have changed and you will be surrrprrrised who might listen to you. But neverrr prrreach."

I was amazed. Cat must have been truly interested in the grass issue, because they were the most words I had ever heard him put together all at once.

"So you really don't seem to like how much time humans devoted to lawns."

Cat stopped to swat at a butterfly then said, "Let's just say, I get annoyed at stupidity."

"I still think lawns are beautiful," Bill said in obvious disapproval of what Cat and I had been talking about.

Cat purred again.

"And I still disavow any responsibility for the human race."

Cat purred louder, then said to me, "If you will not take rrresponsibility forrr what you arrre, then who will?" He then turned to Bill and said, "And if you do not look at all yourrr actions and see how they affect otherrrs, who will?"

Bill and I protested simultaneously.

I said, "I was only an individual, not the whole race."

While Bill said, "Lawns never hurt anyone."

Cat stared at me then at Bill.

"If you trrruly believe that Bill, then I am sorrry forrr you. And you Nexus, have you not hearrrd the teachings that have been thrrrown at you? You arrre the whole rrrace. Any individual of the rrrace is the whole rrrace. All you have to do is join to the collective human consciousness to see what I am saying is trrrue."

Bill and I walked in silence for a long while. I thought long and hard about what Cat had said. I wasn't sure what was going through Bill's thoughts.

What Cat had said was no different than what Friend or what Spider had said. Joining up to a higher consciousness seemed like a worthwhile goal. But the question was how to achieve it.

I noticed Cat looking at me. He had crept up to me silently and had started to pace me at my side.

"It is not as difficult as you think. Just let go of yourrr perrrcieved contrrrol. Yourrr thoughts, while at the moment unique, arrre in fact just a mirrrrorrr of a larrrgerrr patterrrn of thought. Let go and you will be much happierrr."

An unexplained fear came over me. What would happen if I let go? I imagined that if I still had a body, that my body would pull me back. But now it was more scary. If I let go of my consciousness, would I still exist?

"I can't do that. Unless, perhaps, you tell me why I should?"

"Fearrr is the only thing stopping you. I can not tell you anything that will get rrrid of that. You must overrrcome it then experrrience it forrr yourrrself."

"So stop talking about it and just do it, is what you are saying to me, right?'

"Yes."

"Easier said than done."

"No. Just easily done."

We walked again in silence.

Bill was in the lead and Cat followed me. This went on for days, when Cat once again came up beside me and asked another question.

"Nexus. Why werrre humans so unhappy?"

"Oh boy, that is a hard one. There are so many reasons why people were unhappy. I think the main reason was that there were just too many of us. Humans were much better off in small groups. Cities were just too crowded.

"It's best summed up in an adage I once heard. If there was just one person, there was no problem, Add another, and although there were now arguments, agreements could still be reached. But add another person, and all of a sudden you get politics."

"So politics was the rrroot of all unhappiness?"

"No. But to listen to some people, you would think it was. People devised entire political systems whose only purpose when broken down was ultimately to control other people. There was Communism and Socialism, which were the politics of envy. There was Democracy, which was the politics of sloth. There was Fascism and Dictatorships, which were the politics of pride. There were other political systems around but these were the most prevalent. You could also have other forces driving the political system, such as capitalism, which brought the politics of gluttony, and religious zeal, which brought the politics of anger, and then, the best of all, the special interest group which brought the politics of covetousness and even sometimes lust."

"Yourrr statements sound highly political themselves."

I laughed out loud.

"You could be right. But I really believe that the political trap that the modern world had created, really brought on spiritual death to those that got caught up in it. It would have been a better world if people strove to attain virtues such as prudence, justice, temperance, fortitude, faith, hope and charity. I think a lot of arguments could have been avoided."

"You forgot to mention love." A new voice said.

We all turned to see Spider.

14

BILL, CAT AND SPIDER

"Spider," I shouted.

"Yes. It is me," He said very dramatically.

"And who is this?" asked Cat, wryly.

"This is Spider, he's a friend of mine. He lives in a cave, back where we started this journey."

"And who is this lively cat?" inquired Spider with a chuckle.

"This is Cat. He usually doesn't say that much, but lately he's been on a roll."

"Charmed," Spider said as he performed an intricate bow.

"Howdy," Cat replied.

I thought the greetings that Cat and Spider gave each other were reversed.

"As I was saying, Nexus. You forgot about love," Spider said most seriously.

"What kind of love are you talking about?" I asked jokingly.

Spider turned all serious and said, "The deep, dangerous love. The one only the extremely brave or foolish dare to tread. The exciting all-encompassing type.

The Love. The love which puts Only Serious Applicants Need Apply, on the door. And when it comes down to it, the only love that really exists. The others are just pale imitations.

"If you do not put your entire heart and soul into it, then you do not really mean it. You're faking love, and cheating the universe."

Spider put real emphasis on his last two sentences.

"Okay, okay, calm down, I get your point."

"Do you really? How many times can you say that you put your heart and soul into anything you did?"

I do not get angry very often, but Spider irked me with that comment.

"Many times!!"

"Oh really? Name one."

Many came to my mind, but each I felt was too personal to just blurt out to Spider, with Cat and Bill listening.

"I don't have to answer to you about my personal feelings!!" I shouted.

"Well, if you can't tell me, then they probably weren't much of anything anyway, and you're just embarrassed to expose your fakeness!!" Spider shouted back.

I saw red. I raised my sword without thinking.

"Oh, a tough guy. Do you really think you can turn me into pin cushion with that thing of yours?"

Spider started a comical dance, bouncing around while waving his fists in the air, looking like a ridiculous shadow boxer. I had a hard time imagining me actually taking a swing at Spider. In fact, the more I watched Spider, the harder I found it not to laugh.

I laughed, I cried, and I laughed again. I laughed because Spider was so funny. I cried because of all the lost opportunities in my life to have shown more 'passion.' And I laughed again because the universe is so funny in how it teaches you lessons.

Spider smiled and said, "I worry about you my lad, well not really, but I will tell you something anyway, because it may prove fun for me. You will have to show more passion if you keep on your course. The committee, although a joke, does have some passionate members. And unless you are totally committed, heart and soul, to retrieving your grandchildren, don't bother."

"I am committed to saving my grandchildren."

"Well, there are two problems with your last statement. First your grandchildren don't need saving, and second I really doubt your commitment to anything. I mean look at your entire dead existence. You've just been coasting. What have you really done? Nothing. I mean it is not like you haven't had an opportunity to actually do something. But each time, you avoided it, ran away, or just thought about it."

I wanted to object most vehemently, but I stopped myself, and really thought about what had happened to me up until now, and how I reacted to it. Maybe Spider was right.

"Okay then, no more Mr. Noncommittal. I'm going to be decisive from now on, and finish to the bitter end whatever I start."

"So, you're going through with this crazy idea of saving your grandchildren?"

"Yes."

"No more running away?"

"No."

"This should prove fun, right Bill?"

Bill grinned wider than I ever seen him grin and agreed, "Right."

"And can we expect your accompaniment as well, Cat?"

"Most definitely, I wouldn't miss this upcoming display of stupidity."

"Right then, Nexus. It looks like you have three very brave companions to aid you in fulfilling your quest."

With that statement, Spider and Bill proceeded to laugh almost uncontrollably, while Cat gave out a very long purr.

I failed to see the humor in that comment, and I started to walk away. I figured they would catch up to me anyway. Besides it's very uncomfortable being the butt of a joke you don't get.

I walked along for a while before I realized that I had no idea where I was going. I looked back and no one was following me. I turned forward again at the sound of a strange noise. Cat was up ahead, sharpening his claws on a tree. I walked towards him. I then noticed Bill was right behind me, but I had not noticed him approach. Spider was on the other side of me, as well. He, too, had somehow snuck up on me.

Bill had some sort of laser sword in his hand.

He noticed my glance at his sword and said, "I always liked space-cowboy-type movies."

Spider was balancing a large quantity of rocks precariously in his arms, he used his beard to help corral them, but they fell out, one or two at a time, and he stooped down to pick them up.

Spider noticed my observation of what he was holding and said, "We figured you would choose the fighting option, so we just wanted to be ready."

Spider gave a big grin and dropped two more rocks.

I asked, "Can I see one of those rocks?"

Something had caught my eye when one dropped.

He picked one up and handed it to me, "Sure but be careful, they're dangerous."

"Dangerous? How ..." I began to say.

I had felt a strange buzzing from the rock and I dropped it suddenly. The rock quickly disappeared beneath the ground.

"Resonate."

"Huh."

"Don't act stupid, you've done it before."

"What?"

"Resonate with the rocks. If you don't, they can take a bite out of you on their way through you trying to get back to the earth. Remember I told you that the committee doesn't pay much attention to the earth, so these suckers will hurt like heck."

"I didn't feel pain, it was more like a pin prick."

"Well don't forget you have actually resonated before, and have actually traveled through the earth, so they really don't have much of a problem with you. If you did it full time and not just when you found it convenient, then you wouldn't have felt anything at all. Go ahead try it."

Spider handed me another rock. I took it tentatively. I started to hear a small sound coming from the rock, then a beautiful glow which extended up my arm. I was resonating with the rock. I saw two small eyes briefly look up at me. It looked like it was trying to find a way down from my hand. It kept looking at the ground slightly swaying back and forth in my hand, when it suddenly looked harder at me and noticed me staring at it. Our eyes met and suddenly, in a burst of sound and light, the rock disappeared. I felt an explosive rush flow from my hand through my body and down my leg. I felt the rock jump off my foot into the ground. It looked back briefly and vanished beneath the earth. It left me with a tingling sensation all along the path it had taken through my body.

I turned to Spider and said, "What was that all about?"

"Well, when you resonated with the rock, you gave the rock an opportunity to use your spirit body as a conduit for it to return to its natural environment. In effect, you grounded the rock."

"How come the rocks you're holding don't do that?"

"I understand them, as well as resonate with them, thus I can convince them to stay with me. Besides they like me."

Spider began to stroke the rocks as best as he could and made cooing noises to them.

I did notice the glow grow larger.

"How did you get them in the first place?"

Spider dug his hand beneath the earth and pulled out a new rock spirit. In the process though, his sudden movement made him drop most of his existing ones. He scrambled to collect all of them before he said, "You just have to be quick."

Bill laughed and imitated Spider, but he failed to bring up anything when he pulled his hand from the earth.

Spider laughed as well and said, "Bill, I told you they smell you coming, let go, don't try to catch one, just be there when they are."

Bill stopped and just shrugged his shoulders. Bill looked at me and smiled. Spider's explanation meant nothing to me, either.

"Spider, why don't your rocks go back into the ground? You keep dropping them but they just pile up," I asked. It was curious.

"I fool them into thinking I am the ground. If they touch something else that is not the ground, they realize it immediately, and whoosh, back they go. If they were to stay on the ground for any length of time they would eventually go back underground. You fooled the one rock you held for a moment, until it figured out where it was. But if it hit a committee member, stand back. They are totally unprotected from the rocks. I, on the other hand, am totally immune from the committee."

"As am I," purred Cat.

"What do you mean immune?"

"I just pretend to be a rock," Spider said.

"And I just ignorrre any intrrrusions into my space by spirrrits," Cat said.

"Can I do that too?"

"Which one?" Spider asked.

"Either."

"Sure. It's easier to ignore intrusions into your space. Bill! Fire up your sword and try to cut off Nexus' arm."

"What?"

Bill advanced on me, activating his sword.

"Sure," he said.

"Wait a minute. What do I do?"

Bill swung at me. I held up my sword and Bill's bounced back.

"I like my arm. Stop it."

Bill stopped. Spider came over to me and said, "How are you ever going to learn unless you allow yourself to experience things?"

"I'm not yet ready to lose my arm."

"Well, whatever you say, but remember you have to learn how to lose things before you can truly keep them."

"Fearrr, nothing but purrre fearrr," Cat added.

I ignored them both. When we got going again I trotted on ahead a bit. We had been traveling at a slow pace, and had stopped frequently during our conversations. Bill then resumed the lead, and after a few more days he finally said, "We are getting close to the home of the committee."

We traveled close to the mountains most of our journey, but for the past day we followed the coast of the Pacific. We came across some small coastal towns, but now we approached the suburbs of some larger city. Most of the homes were in total ruin. The streets were overgrown, large trees grew in what had once been a busy intersection.

It had been a long time since I had traveled to the former civilized areas. I had heard from people I met that there were still groups of people eking out a living, but this place was obviously desolate, and had a very eerie feeling.

"Spider, are there many humans left alive?"

"Oh yes, millions."

"Millions? Not billions?"

"No, I don't think your race can achieve those numbers ever again. About two million people with the average life span of about thirty-five years is all you can hope for, for the next hundred years or so. Maybe if conditions on the planet improve those numbers might improve, but you never know what is going to happen during a period of mass extinctions."

"Mass extinctions?"

"Surely you must have noticed that there has been a large decrease in biodiversity over the past century. Living in one of the last natural refuges for the past forty years surely hasn't blinded you to this fact, has it?"

"No," I said sadly. "I just didn't want to believe that it could be that bad."

"Just look around you. Do those trees look healthy to you?"

"No, they are just clinging to life, trying to adapt as best as they can."

I noticed too, that there were a lot more dead trees than live trees in this suburb than back where I had lived.

Bill moved even further ahead. He stopped, w for us to catch up to him, then turned to us and said, "Nexus, you'll have to decide how we are going to approach the committee. Do you want to walk up boldly to them? Because I don't think we can go any further without being seen, unless they've spotted us already."

I suddenly felt like there were eyes everywhere looking at me.

Spider said, "Don't worry your little head, Nexus. They haven't found you yet."

I stood in thought for a while, then decided to scout ahead on my own. I had been pretty good at hiding when I was alive, besides I couldn't trust Spider to remain as serious as he had been for the past week.

"I'm going on alone, to see what I can see. I'll be back as quick as I can."

Bill looked disappointed, but Spider quickly said, "We will honor your decisions, but be warned, you can no longer remain hidden like you did when you were alive. Then you could fool the living into missing the living. But spirits are another matter. Your only chance to remain hidden is to resonate with the rocks. I know you can do it. So we will stop here and await your return. Hopefully, you will gain enough knowledge to plan a decent rescue of your grandchildren, otherwise I'm going home. It has to perk around up here a bit. You're too solemn. I need more action and excitement. I will cease to exist if I get bored. I need fun to live."

To illustrate his point, Spider looked sad, and his whole body turned into jelly and sank to the ground as a large mass of ooze. Suddenly a laugh came from the ooze and the mass jumped twenty feet into the air and landed as a whole Spider.

"Good special effects," Cat said.

Bill and Spider broke out laughing.

"Go already," Spider said.

He gave me a hard kick to my behind. It knocked me at least ten feet.

"We'll be waiting here."

15

CHAIRMAN

As I moved away from my companions I looked back, to see them laughing, probably at Spider. I wasn't sure why I decided to go on alone, but it felt right.

I stopped for a moment and thought about what Spider said, resonate or else they will spot you. I tried to remember all the times I had resonated, because I knew that if I let up, I would be spotted for sure. This was one time in my dead existence where I could not afford to be mediocre. I had to concentrate totally on what I was doing.

I started to resonate. The ground beneath me turned brilliant. The light was as bright as the sun. I felt extremely conspicuous. As if I had lit up a beacon saying 'here I am.' Part of the brilliance from the ground crept up over my body and covered me. I was one with the earth.

At first I didn't want to do anything. Because with the glow came love. Love from the earth. It was so all-encompassing that it was hard to concentrate. The warmth of being embraced by the earth is hard to describe. It felt like the first time your mother held you … even if you could not remember that event, it was shadowed in every other time your mother held you …

you go back to that earlier time in spirit and experience it there. All your mother's joys and expectations are felt. So it is with the earth. Even though all the earth's expectations are unconditional except perhaps one, her desire, if it could be called desire, to be noticed.

There was another aspect to the love from the earth that I didn't detect at first, because of my expectations. It was a fatherly love. The earth is of a dual nature for those who wish to see and feel it. It was as though all the strength and wisdom of the father was available for me to experience, given to me through the love of the earth.

It took me a while to remember what I was doing. But having remembered my purpose, I slowly began to move forward. Even though I felt like a brightly burning beacon, I knew that I was protected by the love from the earth.

It was none too soon that I gained this protection, because without it, the sight of what then turned a corner from some old forgotten building, would have put me over the edge. The creature which I now beheld put me on the edge of panic. It was being followed by committee gatherers who resembled those I had encountered earlier with Bruno. What was leading them was what I had expected Spider to look like before I met him as a spirit. It stood nine feet tall with two, two foot long, curved horns protruding from its head. Its skin was grossly mottled and rough. The hands were large enough to crush someone's head with little effort and its fingers had dagger like nails, as did the toes. The mouth was grotesque and was large enough to accommodate a basketball. But nothing would last long with those long, sharp and irregularly spaced teeth. Worst of all were the eyes. They were as large as baseballs and glowed red. Now I understood Bob's story to Bill. This creature matched the classic description of an evil spirit.

If I had been trying to hide from that thing using ordinary methods, I would have given up and run screaming from my hiding place. But I concentrated on resonating and was comforted by the constant presence of the earth. I stayed in place and listened to what these spirits said.

"What are we looking for anyway?" one of the spirits near the back said.

"I heard it was two human spirits, a live cat and a horrible monster," said one.

"And I heard it was two humans, a cat and a huge earth spirit," said another.

It was almost amusing. They got the descriptions of Bill, Cat and I correct, but they thought Spider was something to be feared.

"Be quiet," bellowed the leader, "We'll find them soon enough, they should be here shortly."

The leader was as intelligent as he was deadly. But what worried me more was the fact that these spirits seemed to know all about our movements. I thanked the earth for helping me, but I was still too shaken to move.

If I had a heart it would have stopped beating, when the group suddenly made a turn and headed straight for me. I nearly wished that I could be somewhere else, but I didn't have to worry. Just as they were going to bump into me, the two columns of committee members divided in two and walked the space I occupied as if there had been a statue placed in that spot. When they had past, I was too nervous to turn around.

When one of them yelled it was right in my ear.

"Hey, isn't that a cat over there?"

I heard them run off, then I ventured a peek when I could hear no more. I couldn't be sure if it was an ordinary cat or if Cat had helped me. But in either case I had remained unseen. I could probably walk right into a committee meeting and no one would notice. I just hoped that there weren't many more of those giant spirits about. They totally unnerved me.

I continued my search in the direction that this group had come from. I chose correctly. I soon saw a large line up of spirits. The line was moving slowly down what had to be a main street. On either side of the line stood baton-waving committee members. Their job was to keep the line moving. There was a lot of shoving and pushing, as no one wanted to be on the receiving end of a baton. One committee member would raise its baton in a mock swing, to see the spirits in the line scream and shove and then would chuckle. It was a cruel game.

No one noticed me, so I cautiously proceeded down a side street parallel to the enormous line.

How my grandchildren could have thought that these spirits had good intentions was beyond me. Something rotten was going on here.

Just as I was thinking this, I spied graffiti on a crumbling wall. It read, 'You are now entering hell, repent or forever be damned.'

When originally penned I'm sure this piece of artwork was considered humorous. But the author of this particular masterpiece never imagined that someone would be reading it under these conditions. I was not amused.

As I passed this wall I heard screaming. I ran to where the line rounded a corner to see three committee members standing around a poor spirit, whacking away at her with their rods. The spirit was screaming for mercy, but the attackers showed none. I watched in horror as the groveling spirit shrank in size, deflating like a balloon. Her cries became less robust as she grew smaller. The final hits from the rods sucked up the last parts of the spirit until there was nothing left.

I assumed that all the energy had been drained from that spirit's consciousness and she ceased to exist when her energy was gone. The committee members chuckled and went back to the line. They only had to glance in the direction of the line to cause panic. Those in line scrambled away from the committee member like frightened rabbits.

I could now see the destination where the spirits were being herded. Nothing grew there. This huge complex, with lots of land, must have at one time been beautifully landscaped. Trees had overgrown the lawns, but now all the trees were dead.

In the buildings there were large openings where windows had been. It must have been impressive in its day.

I approached cautiously, going around the building out of the line of sight, to try to find a way in. Because I was dead I assumed I could walk through the wall if I wanted to. But I hadn't really tried that yet, so I was reluctant. I found a window that had not been boarded up and tried to walk through. But just the same as at the lodge I experienced a barrier.

I had not expected a non-physical barrier. This wasn't going to stop me from entering the building. I was already resonating, so I could travel through the earth and emerge just a few feet away, inside the barrier. I looked down and let myself dissolve into the earth. It was impossible to tell how far I went down but it didn't feel far. I stopped my downward motion and started to move forward.

I was surprised to come out on a lower level. I was even more surprised to find live humans here. Approximately twenty of them were huddled in a large room, whose original function was no longer in evidence. There was filth everywhere. These people were slobs and had no standards of hygiene. There was a small fire going in the center of the room and because someone had made one of the huge ventilation shafts into a chimney, the smoke was just tolerable.

Most of the people in this room were asleep, but those awake were consuming a odd looking mushroom. The mushroom was having a strange effect on the humans. They had a stunned look, staring endlessly at nothing, and muttering to themselves.

One of these humans caught my eye. He looked li ke someone I once knew and the more I stared at him, I became convinced I knew him. His name was Hope ... James Hope. He looked much older and much shabbier than the last time I saw him.

He was a young lad when he joined our group, perhaps a dozen years before I died. He stayed with us for only six months and left saying I was a dictator and didn't allow anyone any freedom.

But the way I remember it, he had tried to force himself on Melissa. It was all I could do to prevent the others from tearing him apart, especially Paul. Paul really wanted to do him some harm. I told James that kind of behavior would not be tolerated if he wanted to stay with us.

I had him perform a purification fast lasting three days. He was to stay isolated from everyone until he came to an understanding of what he had done.

He lasted only two days before he stole some food and ran away.

Now here he was in the basement of a building that was being used by the committee for what as yet, were undiscovered activities. Life and death sure are strange.

Stranger still was the fact that he was looking at me with wide eyes. He was a little fearful.

"Grandfather?" he said.

He, as did everyone who joined our group, called me grandfather.

The others ignored his question.

I asked, "Can you see me?"

"As plain as my hands."

"What are you doing here?"

"I am the leader of this group of gatherers."

I didn't like the fact that he called his group gatherers.

"Why are you called gatherers?"

"We scour the city for useful things and bring them back to the Head. He finds uses for everything and rewards us with food. It's getting tougher. There's not much left in the city. Most of the things we find are buried. And because we lost half our group to disease the other groups take advantage of our weakness and take our findings."

"Who is this Head you speak of?"

"He's the one who talks to the great spirit who lives in this place. And he gives us the magic mushrooms that allow us to see him. I don't think the others really see him, but I do. I see spirits all the time. There are thousands here. It is a real place of power. That is why I see you. The magic in these mushrooms has made me strong. Stronger than these weak fools here. Someday I will be a great power here, when I understand what is going on. I watch and I see much."

James was not in full control of his faculties, most likely from eating these mushrooms over a long period.

"What do you see in this place?"

"Secrets. Many secrets. Paths to power. I see it all."

"If you see so much, why are you just a gatherer? Why are you not in charge?"

He looked like he wanted to bite my head off, then he whispered, "There are still too many powerful people here. I have to get rid of them before I can move up to the inner circle."

"You're pathetic. What have you done since you left the woods? Lived a bare minimum existence? With nothing but petty dreams to sustain you? What would you do if you were in charge? Become a dictator? Just like you imagined me to be? Take the best food and have your choice of women? Is that all you can think of? Answer me."

As I was asking my questions of him, his mind snapped. The feeble hold he had on his reality disappeared. He began to cry and then wail. I didn't think my questions had been that harsh, but I must have hit some chord, because a flood of tears came out of James.

I truly felt sorry for him. The other humans in the room barely acknowledged the fact that their leader was crying like a baby. They were more pathetic than James and were so feebleminded that nothing would phase them. Those mushrooms must have an extremely powerful mind altering substance in them.

I figured out that he was made leader because he could hold himself together better after taking the mushrooms. But one thing was for sure, if this group wanted to improve their lot, the mushrooms would have to go.

"James ... James ... JAMES!" I finally shouted.

He regained his composure and answered, "Yes."

"You have to stop eating those mushrooms."

He became defensive and said, "No, they're magic."

"No, they're killing you. You have to stop or else you'll die and you'll end up like one of those poor spirits out there and never be free again."

I really didn't know what happened to spirits here but I figured that if terrible things were going on in here, then James might know about it, and not want anything similar to happen to him.

"And when you are free of them, you'll have to leave this place. Go back to the forest. It is better there."

James now looked like a hunted animal. He crouched, as if he wanted to run.

"Go away, you're dead. I don't have to listen to you any more."

James spat out these words then turned away and ignored me.

I have always had a bad habit of trying to get in the last word, and now was no exception.

"It doesn't matter if I'm dead or alive. Truth is truth. You will die a pathetic death and have a horrible afterlife unless you change now."

I walked away. The door leading to the corridor had long ago fallen off. When I entered the corridor, I had the choice of a long dark passage to the left or a long dark passage to the right. I should have gone back to James and asked the way, but I was angry with him. I should know better at my age. I should be able to ignore his reference to me being dead. Of course I was biased, but if a spirit offered me good advice, I would take it. What was wrong with James? Or was it me? Why was I so angry? I didn't really know. I turned right.

The corridor became progressively darker. No physical light reached this part of the building, yet I could still see. The resonating I was doing gave me a spiritual light with which I could perceive the world. This was not how I was used to seeing the world. The earth itself lit up the immediate environment for me to perceive. The light came from resonating energy lines rising up from the earth, lines so closely knit that individual strands were hard to distinguish.

I had never noticed these lines before. There were little tiny pulses along each line and these lines were everywhere, and they went through everything.

I didn't have much time to marvel at this phenomena because a group of spirits came rushing down the hall. I moved to one side of the corridor, waited and focused on resonating.

"What are we in a hurry for?" one of the spirits said.

"I don't know. The orders I got were to check out all the lower levels for any unusual activity," said a rather large spirit.

Hmmm. Somehow they knew I was here, even though they could not see me. I felt a mild panic, and an urge to flee. But after a moment's consideration, I decided I would stay.

The spirits went by quickly, checking all the rooms leading off the corridor. I waited until they were out of sight before I started to move. I had seen where they came out and made for that door. Behind was a set of stairs leading up.

Up two flights I came to a closed door. I stopped, unsure of what I should do. Should I try to walk through the door? I was just about to try when I heard someone coming up the stairs. It was James. He got to the top, looked at me, smiled, then opened the door, holding it open for me to go through.

He quickly followed me through, looked both ways up and down the corridor and gestured for me to follow him.

"Where are we ..." I started to say, when with a look of panic he shushed me.

He led me down a long corridor that had many office like rooms off one side. On the other side of the corridor was a small auditorium that could hold a few hundred people.

James led me down this corridor, through a door with more stairs that led up, and through a walkway that joined two buildings at the second floor.

James kept low to stay below the level of the windows. I followed his lead, but peeked outside at intervals. I could see the line of spirits filing into the building we were now entering. I saw a pair of the nine foot spirits standing at the entrance of the building. I bent even lower after spotting them.

Once inside the next building, James found another set of stairs, which led us up three more floors. At the top of those stairs, he stopped and carefully peered through a small window in the door. He quietly opened the door and went through. We were now in a short corridor, only ten feet long which ended in a t-junction. He crept to the end on all fours and peered each way. He didn't like what he saw, because he came right back. I went quickly up the end and looked around for myself, in spite of James' protests. I saw another one of the large spirits and a human conversing near the end of the hall. They were too far away for me to hear anything. Besides, my fear was greater than my curiosity.

I looked at James to see what he would do next. He was already at a door in the small corridor that had escaped my attention. He opened it, and I was disappointed to find that it was just a small closet. But James went in and moved the ceiling tile in this small space and pulled himself into the ceiling. When I was up, he reached down and closed the door. It was dark again. But I saw the lines again and so was able to watch James pull himself through a small opening in the wall above the ceiling. When I had climbed through, he reached back and replaced the ceiling tile. He was making his way by feel along the steel girders that held the building together. He skillfully managed to avoid the tangle of wires that criss-crossed this space.

When we came to where a small sliver of light shone through he stopped and peeked through a small hole in the ceiling tiles. When he was satisfied he opened up a tile and jumped down. When I was through he grabbed a nearby chair and replaced the tile. We went through a well furnished office. It was odd that not much had been moved in here. The lower level of this building had been well looted by eager hands.

We left this nice office after James checked out the new corridor as thoroughly as each previous one. This one was well lit by skylights along its entire length. It was deserted. There were only a few expensive looking oak doors to on either side along the way. The corridor ended at a set of lavish mahogany double doors.

James stopped and listened at one of the doors for quite some time before venturing to crack it open. He opened it just enough to look in, then swung it wide and gestured for me to enter. I walked in slowly. The room was well lit by a wide expanse of curved windows that covered two sides of the room. There were also large skylights in the center of the room.

The furnishings bordered on decadent. They were still beautiful and perfectly preserved. James slammed the door behind me. I turned and cursed him. The curse had hardly left my mouth when I heard, "Welcome Nexus, we've been expecting you."

I turned back and saw a rather handsome spirit just coming out from behind a large marble stonework that adorned one wall. There was a alcove there, large enough to hide ten people, but cleverly crafted so that at first it was not apparent.

The spirit that greeted me had well groomed hair, immaculate teeth, perfect skin and was wearing an expensive, gray business suit. He had salesman written all over him.

"Who are you?" I asked.

"Some call me the Head. Some call me the Chairman. It doesn't matter, I'm in charge and that's all that matters."

"No, what's your real name?"

The Chairman broke out laughing. "Their are no real names anymore. Nothing has a real name. Don't you see? We're dead and we've been cheated of our rights. We have to fight and some must make sacrifices so that the rest can remain strong. The others won't let us in, so we'll have to force our way in. We'll have so much energy accumulated that they won't be able to stop us."

"Who's they and where is it they are trying to keep you out of?"

"You must know what I'm talking about. They won't let you in either."

"No, I'm afraid you'll have to explain it to me."

The Chairman looked disappointed.

"We could use you, you know. My reports say that you are a good fighter and have a lot of accumulated energy. So you would last a long time in the up coming battle. We need someone like you. Won't you join us?"

I didn't like the direction of this conversa tion.

"Well, before I can make such an important decision, I'll need to know more about this up coming battle."

The Chairman stopped looking at me and stared at the ceiling.

"The battle at the gate. I see it now. It will be glorious. I will lead my armies through the gate and take my place which has been so cruelly denied me."

"What gate??!!" I said impatiently.

"Why the gate leading to heaven, what gate do you think I've been talking about?"

Well, that certainly made things clearer. I understood now what Spider meant when he said that the committee was a joke. This spirit was mad, totally mad. But now all I could think of was how to get back to Spider. Would I still be invisible to the rest of the committee members now that the Head had seen me? What would he try to do, if I just walked out? There was really no reason to stay here except to find my grandchildren. Maybe the bold approach might work.

"Enough of this, where are my grandchildren? I want to see them now."

The chairman stirred from whatever dreams of glory he was imagining for himself and said, "Of course, I expected that you would be interested in seeing them."

He clapped his hands and my three grandchildren, and two others who I didn't recognize, were brought before me. Each had a large gatherer at either side.

Mary and Daniel looked catatonic, Rose was her feisty self and the other two looked weak and depressed.

Daniel and Mary perked up when they heard Rose say, "It took you long enough to get here Grandfather."

"Sorry, I got held up by my own stupidity," I said while trying not to laugh.

I'm sure Cat would have loved to hear me say that. Rose smiled and the others looked like some hope was coming to them. Rose's spirit was indomitable. She had a look of utter defiance and was quite willing to fight to the last of her energy.

This heartened me and I said, "They're coming with me, release them."

I raised my sword for emphasis.

The Head looked at me with disappointment and said, "I'm afraid that is not possible, they're scheduled for draining, unless of course I'm given a good enough reason to spare them."

Though I have never responded well to threats I knew enough to think calmly and not lose my cool. Because if I failed here, I wouldn't get a second chance.

"So let me see, if I agree to join you, then my grandchildren can go free?"

"No. They would have to stay here, as ransom for your good behavior."

Well, even if he was crazy, he wasn't stupid. Strike down that strategy. My mind raced. I could not think of a good way of leaving this place with my grandchildren in tow. There were too many against us. Perhaps I should join them and try to get us all out later. This really went against my grain. I found myself wishing that Spider or Cat were here to help me decide what to do, because the thought of joining the committee, even though a ruse, was just too much for me.

No!!! No matter what, I would not join the committee. I would have to escape and find another way to rescue them.

I had just taken one step back towards the door when I heard a commotion coming from behind it. Everyone in the room stopped to listen to the strange sounds. At first I thought a train was coming, then I realized that it was someone howling very loudly. Intermixed with this loud howl, were many shouts and screams, and a cat screeching!!! It could only be Spider and Cat.

The door burst open. James Hope came running in with Cat close on his heels. Cat was slightly bigger than usual, like a small cougar. Spider was howling and throwing rocks. When a rock hit one of the now fleeing spirits it exploded into a multitude of colors, then totally dissipated. Bill walked in backwards with his back to Spider. He was guarding the rear from any spirit attack.

The chairman was about to explode with rage.

Spider stopped his howling, nonchalantly entered the room then said, “Howdy, big guy. Hope you don’t mind if we drop in. We have some friends to rescue.”

16

BATTLE

The Chairman didn't like Spider's remark, but he was too upset to say anything yet. All spirits in the hall had fled or were destroyed. James Hope ran out some other door. Cat was licking his paws. Spider was beaming.

Bill was the last one to enter, and when he turned around, his eyes lit up. I heard him shout, "James!!! Matthew!!!"

The other two spirits looked up and they both quietly said, "Father?"

These two were Bill's sons. When Bill first said, 'James,' I was a bit confused, because I wondered how he knew James Hope. But when I heard the name of his other son Matthew, I remembered that he had sons, but I had never really wondered what had happened to them. I realized that they had been gathered, but how had the Chairman known that these were Bill's sons, or even that Bill would show up?

These questions had to wait because the Chairman decided that now was a good time to blow up. He yelled in utter rage, "Get them!!!! Guards, guards ... get them!!"

Five of the ten committee members who had been holding my grandchildren and Bill's sons, charged at the four of us. The others held on to their prisoners. Rose began to flail away with her free hand at the much larger spirit holding her. He ignored her blows as he grabbed for his rod. Rose saw what he was about to do and she grabbed his arm. To my surprise, Rose was holding her own. In fact, she might have been winning the obvious test of strength. If they were alive, there would have been no contest. He towered over her and was twice her weight.

I couldn't watch much of her contest because two guards were taking swipes at my head with their rods. I easily ducked and leapt between my two lumbering opponents. I cut one deeply with my sword as I dove past between the two of them. The wounded guard winced in pain and hesitated. I turned and brought my sword down on my other opponent, cutting him neatly in two, from the head down. On the same stroke, I cut the now recovering spirit's head clean from its shoulders as I raised my sword from the floor in a perfect arc over my head.

Cat, in the meantime, had pounced on another guard and was biting his throat, to the obvious discomfort of the spirit. He tried to hit Cat with his rod and grab him with his free hand, but whatever he tried passed right through Cat. He ended up hitting himself with the rod.

Spider had not moved from his spot. He cackled with glee. A spirit approached him and ended up with a rock between his eyes. This resulted in an amazing pyrotechnical effect. He exploded into millions of pieces as the rock spirit returned to the earth. Spider then freed the non-struggling Daniel, Mary, James and Matthew in quick order with four well placed rocks to their guards.

Bill was well kept busy showing off. As a spirit tried to hit him with his rod, Bill whittled the rod down until there was nothing left but a stump in the spirit's hand. Bill then waved his sword in the face of the weaponless guard, who kept backing up then decided to turn and run.

Cat had let go of his guard and he, too, fled.

That left only the Chairman and Rose's opponent. To my amazement she had slowly maneuvered his rod up to his face and with one mighty effort she shoved it into his open mouth. His scream was a horrible sound. Rose held it there until he was the size of a small child, then released him. He scampered away as best as he could.

I was now feeling pretty good. I turned to look at the Chairman. He had not moved, nor had the look of anger left his face.

I was just about to say something to him when I another voice said, "Oho, Bruno get here just in time to protect Head. Nexus think he harm Head. Bruno put stop to that. Bruno chop Nexus into thousand pieces. Use pieces for bowling pins. Have lots of fun. "

Bruno!!! And he brought friends ... dozens.

"Get out of my way, we're leaving. Either you move aside or we go over your remains. "

I knew it sounded pretty lame. I never was very good at threats ... they never came out right. There's an art to it I never mastered.

As expected, all I got out of Bruno was laughter, which turned out not to be such a bad thing. He was so taken aback by my lame threat that he lost his composure. Before he could recover or say anything back, I leapt at him.

But Spider having heard me, and seeing my actions, burst out laughing. He was on the floor and had a hard time keeping the remainder of his rocks in his arms.

Thank goodness Rose was around. She had already taken a rod that a guard had dropped and now she shouted to her cousins and Bill's sons to each grab one and fight. She charged into the battle behind me. This inspired Bill who charged behind her. Three of us in the doorway caused enough congestion to prevent others from entering, giving our side enough time to prepare.

When I leapt at Bruno I didn't catch him totally off guard, but did manage to get a good chop to his legs. I cut a deep slash down the side of his left leg that almost cut through at a diagonal. Bruno retreated then fell. Unfortunately, others swung their rods from behind the fallen Bruno. And with Rose and Bill on either side of me, I couldn't properly utilize my enormous weapon. If I swung too wide, I would hit Rose or Bill. I had to use my two handed sword as a skewer, which wasn't very effective.

I did manage to stab two other guards before I had to retreat. By this time the others had entered the battle. The entire room was a combat zone. There were opponents for all. Spider had used almost the last of his rocks. He tried to keep the number of opponents down to one each. He threw at committee members who tried to gang up on any of us, and at any new ones who came through the door.

Bruno had skillfully avoided being hit by a rock and came after me. He had healed himself once more. I had just dispatched an opponent when Bruno struck at me with his sword. I just managed to block his blow and we started a dance of blow and counter blow.

I was oblivious to the rest of the battle. It became a blur to me. None of it mattered any more. Defeating Bruno became my only focus.

Repeatedly Bruno swung blows to my torso which I successfully parried. But each time Bruno advanced until we held our swords between us. This became a contest of strength which I always lost. I had to leap back to narrowly avoid the touch of his sword. I was successful three times, then Bruno changed his strategy slightly. With each leap back, I had used the push from Bruno for momentum. But Bruno caught on to this and the next time I was set to leap back, he stopped his push for a moment. I now leapt backwards, but didn't land as far away as before. Bruno then took a swing straight down at me. My sword partially deflected the blow, but it still caught my left elbow, nicking off the end. The pain was enormous. The piece of my elbow that fell off was absorbed by Bruno's sword.

Bruno now had the clear advantage. With the use of only my right arm I was no longer able to defend myself properly.

It would only be a matter of time before Bruno would swing a fatal blow. I was dodging his swings like a trapped alley cat.

Spider noticed my distress and ventured to offer me some advice.

"Nexus, have clear intent ... clear intent ... clear intent."

I didn't have a clue what he meant. Why repeat those words? The only thing on my mind was survival. Survive!! That's it! That's all I had ever done during my entire live and dead existence but that's not what I should be concentrating on at this moment. If my intent was to save my grandchildren, then I would have to change my thought patterns. To save my grandchildren I had to defeat Bruno. No ifs, ands, or buts. I had to devote one hundred percent of my will to defeating Bruno and no longer waste any thoughts on surviving.

Bruno's last series of blows were near misses. I ran to the windows. The sun shone through. I felt its rays on my back. It helped me forget about myself, there were other things in the universe besides myself.

I stared at the charging Bruno. I no longer thought of myself and my survival. I now thought only of my purpose. To think of anything else now meant annihilation. I would save my grandchildren and Bruno would not stop me.

I held my sword in front of me, firmly with my right arm, and loosely with my left. I felt my purpose flow through me. It started in my legs and coursed up through my body. When it reached my arms, my will took control of my left arm and I again had full use of that arm. But the power didn't stop at my arms. It flowed out over my sword. My clear intent covered my sword like a thin film of oil on the blade. It shone with a new light brighter than ever.

Bruno was now upon me. We raised our swords and swung simultaneously. Time flowed very slowly. It took many lifetimes before our swords actually hit each other. I saw lines again coming up from the earth. I saw them flow through me and how they interacted with Bruno's movements.

Our swords hit. I had aimed for the base of Bruno's sword. There was no clash nor sound as before. I saw only that my sword passed straight through his, cutting it as the swords passed each other. My sword then continued on into Bruno. It traveled straight through him, leaving a coat of oil on each half of him.

When my sword had passed through Bruno I noticed a subtle change in the lines coming up from the earth. They wavered slightly when I cut Bruno in two. But I knew that Bruno, whether consciously or unconsciously, could control these lines, and would eventually make himself whole again.

So instead of taking another swing at Bruno, I concentrated on the lines below him, and before his two halves could fall to the ground I swung at the lines and cut them.

The effect on Bruno was that he moved in slow motion, but his face changed from its usual brashness to abject horror, then to absolute peace. He then exploded into billions of small pieces that were instantly swept up by the newly formed lines coming up from the earth. His pieces gave off a gold light from a concentrated cloud of Bruno dust that blew upwards and disappeared in an instant.

I wasted no time wondering at what had just happened. I ran to the remaining committee members in the room and repeated the gold dust treatment on any that stood in my way.

The rest fled. Spider in the meantime, had been watching me, and was jumping up and down on the spot, clapping his hands and laughing every time I created more dust. He again and again cried out, "Good, oh great, look at that one go," to go along with his clapping.

Rose gave me an enormous smile. That smile made my effort worthwhile.

A quick look around the room and I could see only my friends and family ... and the Chairman.

I was about to announce our intention of leaving, when the Chairman, now red, started a high piercing shriek. This summoned his nine foot tall servants. They came through another door at the far side of he room.

My euphoria vanished. Fear now gripped me. I could not face these creatures, they terrified me.

"Run!!!" I shouted.

Spider laughed real loud, but I didn't stay to watch his antics. I was one of the first out the door.

Spider threw his final rocks at the advancing spirits and was the last of our group to leave. He left capering and laughing.

Cat had followed me out of the room quickly, but now took the lead. "Follow me," he said and opened all the doors by leaping at them. The doors swung open as if they'd been hit by a battering ram. He then held them long enough for all of us to get through, then moved like lightning to take the lead again.

Cat found the quickest route out. I could hear the thundering footfalls of the enormous spirits following us. They easily drowned out our own quiet steps, but didn't quite mask Spider's insane cackling noise. We burst out of the building, only to find the line of spirits in our way.

The spirits guarding the line quickly detected our presence and most ran towards us. The few who stayed herded the unfortunate spirits in the line, into groups.

From a distance, more of the demon-like spirits approached with hundreds of gatherers. There were far too many for us to fight all at once.

We moved down along the building looking for a possible escape route. Spider picked up rocks as we went. But it was no use, spirits poured out of all the buildings, cutting off any chance of escape.

We stood in what once had been a rock garden. All the plants were dead. I stood on a large rock, watching the horde approach. It would only be a few more seconds before we would be overwhelmed. Cat was unconcerned. Spider was laughing, as usual. Bill was yawning. I was terrified.

I looked at Spider, but I couldn't say a word. The thought of one of those creatures getting his hands on me was too much for me. Spider looked into my eyes and laughed louder, but he understood my thoughts and he exploded into action. He crushed the rocks he was holding and threw the resultant pebbles at the advancing crowd. There was another pyrotechnical spectacle from that simple toss. He grabbed more rocks and repeated the process. The first two waves of spirits disappeared with bright flashes.

Spider pointed to the ground and said, "Quickly, down that hole."

I looked to where he had pointed. It had been a gopher hole, or perhaps a rabbit hole, and was only ten inches wide.

"How can we get down a hole that size?" I asked.

The words were barely out of my mouth when Bill walked over to the hole and dove head first. His body shrank as it approached the hole, and he disappeared down the hole in an instant.

Spider shouted, "Follow Bill!!" and he continued to bombard the onslaught of spirits with pebbles.

Bill's sons joined their father down the hole. Rose jumped in next, followed by Mary, then Daniel.

Cat said, "Go down, Nexus. I'll guarrrd the entrrrance."

I hesitated. How could I make myself smaller?

Spider yelled, "Just imagine that the hole is bigger. You think too much, Nexus. Just do it without thinking about it."

I squinted my eyes to give myself a different perspective, and dove at the hole as I'd seen the others do. I imagined that the hole was huge. And as my head approached the hole, it did seem to be larger. And to my utter surprise I rapidly shrank just before I actually touched the earth. I rolled a distance down before I came to a stop. Spider was already standing beside me, as were the others.

The natural light that came streaming down the hole winked out. Something covered the hole.

"Cat is sitting on the hole," Bill said.

"He's immune to the spirits, and they can not pass through him," Spider added.

"And it will probably take the spirits some time before they can actually get some humans on the spot to try and chase him away," Bill said.

"I pity anyone that would try that," Spider said with a laugh.

Bill laughed with him as did Rose. She looked deeply at Spider. She obviously liked him.

"Well, now that we are safe ..." Bill started to say.

Spider grinned at me.

Then Bill continued, "... Nexus, you have to tell me something. Why do you seem to have such a hard time with being dead. It is like you went stupid or something."

I frowned, but said nothing.

Bill continued, "You were totally competent in life, well, in your later life anyway. You raised your grandchildren adequately. You had lots of wisdom and were able to convey it. You were adaptable in life. So, why are you so inept in death? I noticed that when you get close to your former life, or life itself, you regain some semblance of your former self, but right now you seem somewhat dense."

I didn't know what to say.

Rose smiled then said, "Bill, I have been watching my grandfather. You're right, he is not himself. It's almost as if part of him is missing."

Spider gave me a serious look, then suddenly struck my head with the front of his hand. It felt like a sledge hammer had hit me.

"Why did you do that?" I shouted.

"Just trying to make you pay attention. But I see I'm just wasting my time," Spider said.

Spider turned to Rose and said, "It doesn't matter anyway. He's about to discover something about himself that should make him better understand what he's doing here."

Spider broke out into one of his wild grimaces. It unnerved me enough that I didn't feel like asking him what I was to discover about myself.

I looked about me for the first time.

I noticed that I could see perfectly well down here. The glow that I noticed before in the Chairman's place was all around us. However, it was strongest at the feet of Spider and Bill.

It was moist and lifeless down here. The earth was full of stones. Whatever animals that lived down here had to contend with a lot of large rocks. It was a maze of twisting passages, with a trail of pebbles leading down one of the tunnels.

Spider capered down the trail. He started humming an old tune that I never did learn the name of. Bill joined in, then Rose, until everyone was humming along.

I thought something was going to happen, and everyone knew what that was except me.

We followed the trail of stones through partially caved in tunnels, under dead tree roots until we came to an opening. It must have been a living room for some small animal. There was decayed plant material, some shiny objects, and one rock in the center of this small space that seemed cavern-like to those of us only six inches tall.

This part of the animal's home was lit better than any other part. The center stone shone the brightest.

Everyone stopped humming and stood staring at the stone. I couldn't see what they were looking at, the light was too bright. Eventually my eyes adjusted and I saw a small figure sitting on top of the stone.

Delightfully, the figure had a warm, friendly smile. The light was strongest behind him, so it was impossible to make out his features. He jumped off the stone and approached us and it was then I recognized him fully, even though I had known instinctively who it was.

"Friend!!!" I shouted.

17

FRIEND'S RETURN

"Nexus. It is good to see you again," Friend said with a definite warmth.

I stood with my mouth open. I hadn't thought I would ever see Friend again. There was something different about him, but I couldn't define it. It was as if the sun had come down and lit this deep small hole, and made it a place of wonderment. The light that came with Friend was so pure that spirit tears came to spirit eyes. Friend was all that I remembered him to be, and more. It was as if my perception had improved and I could see more of him. But I was also painfully aware that I did not yet know all about him.

"Friend. Why are you … I mean … what are you doing down in a place like this?" I asked hesitantly.

"Waiting for you," he replied.

"Yes, but why underground?"

"You told me to hide in a hole somewhere, and this one looked as good as any other."

I slapped myself on the head. I had said that at our parting. I regretted that. I had said that with anger in my heart and I wish I hadn't.

"I'm sorry, I didn't mean to say that."

"Nonsense, of course you did, or else you wouldn't have said it. As for being sorry, that's your own problem. But I am upset with you for being rude."

"I know, I acted like a rat."

"No, I'm not talking about the past, I'm talking about the present. You are being rude by not introducing your companions."

I was taken aback by Friend. He never missed a thing.

"I'm sorry. This is Spider."

Spider did a funny salute and said, "The pleasure I have in finally meeting you is greatly surpassed by how apologetic Nexus seems to have become."

Everyone laughed at that statement.

"Thank you. I like you too." Friend replied.

I was still trying to figure out this exchange of greetings when I noticed the silence and remembered I had more introductions to make, and introduced Bill.

"This is Bill. He is Spider's apprentice."

"Charmed," Bill said.

"Oh yes, and you?" Friend replied.

There was much more laughter, but again I didn't see what was so funny.

"This is my granddaughter Rose," I said.

Rose ran up and hugged Friend then said with tears in her eyes, "I have always wanted to meet you."

Friend looked at her and said nothing. They just stared into each other's eyes and whole volumes of information passed between them. Rose nodded her head then stepped to one side. She stood close to Friend but kept looking at him and smiling at something I could not see.

"This is my granddaughter Mary," I said.

Mary walked up and shook hands. When their hands touched, Mary's eyes lit up. Nothing was said, but Mary had a look of wonder in her eyes, and would not take her eyes off Friend. She returned to where she had originally stood.

I wondered what was going on.

"This is my grandson Daniel," I said.

He sheepishly said, "Hi."

He said this like a shy school boy meeting his first date.

"Hi," Friend replied.

They smiled at each other and Friend nodded his head. Daniel now looked as if he had just received his first kiss.

"These are Bill's sons, James and Matthew," I said.

"It's nice to meet you," they said.

"Nice to meet you," Friend replied.

I looked around at my companions. Something was going on here, and I was determined to find out what.

"I'm sorry, I can't introduce Cat to you. He's busy keeping us safe down here, but I'm sure you'll eventually meet him," I said.

"Don't worry about that. We have important things to discuss, before the end."

I didn't like the ominous sound of that.

"You'll have to tell me Nexus, what is your attraction for doing everything the hard way?"

"What do you mean?" I asked.

"Correct me if I am wrong, but did I not tell you that you could not help your grandchildren?"

"Yes, you did, but I did just rescue three of them."

"Again correct me if I am wrong, but if you had not talked to Rose in the first place, then probably none of them would have died. And yes, you did just take your grandchildren from the committee building. But what do you plan to do from here? If you go back up there, you'll be overwhelmed and all of you will meet the fate that most spirits befall when they go into the committee building. So all you have done, in effect, is delay the inevitable."

"Can't you do something about it?"

"Why should I?" Friend replied.

"Because you're my friend."

Friend laughed, followed quickly by Spider and Bill. Again Friend's laugh had a certain enchanting power. As long as Friend laughed, I felt nothing was wrong. My grandchildren and Bill's sons felt it too, and stood with a look of awe on their faces.

"Nexus, you never cease to amaze me. You are trying to call upon a friendship that you don't even remember. You are only taking my word that I was your friend. How do you know that I am really your friend? Maybe you are greatly indebted to me and the only reason I am here is to collect. So unless you choose to remember me, I think I will just take a wait and see attitude."

Friend hit a sore spot. I wished I knew who Friend was. I had been mildly scolded again for being stupid.

"Well how about you, Spider? Can you think of a way out of here?"

Spider had hardly contained himself while Friend was speaking. But now that I had addressed him, he couldn't control himself and fell to the floor holding his belly, laughing so hard, tears were pouring out of eyes.

When he regained his composure he jumped up and said, "Oh yeah, millions, but none that would help you. But whatever you decide to do, I would hurry, there are some humans on their way to chase Cat away, and then some of those demons will start coming down here. They are not as unfamiliar with the underground as you."

"Bill?" I said hopefully.

Bill smiled and said, "I already told you that I am really only an observer."

He snickered a bit then continued, "So I think that you must try to figure something out."

I turned away from Spider and Bill and looked at Rose. She looked up at something over her left shoulder and smiled, then looked to her right at Friend. Their eyes met for a few seconds and then Rose turned back to me and said, "Grandfather, I love you and I will abide by any decision you make."

She too burst out laughing and the others all joined in.

What was so funny? We were all about to be captured by the committee and God knows what would happen to us, and all these spirits were laughing their heads off. Spider, for effect I guess, laughed so hard that his head actually did fall off. His body reached over, picked his head up and put it back between his shoulders. The others found this so funny that it was a while before I could get anyone to listen to me.

"Friend, would you help me, if I remember who you are?" I asked.

"Maybe. There are no guarantees, but let's just say that it wouldn't hurt."

He smiled, and again a warmth filtered down through my body that reminded me of someone, but who?

"Okay, can I ask some questions to help me determine who you are?"

"You can, but you might find it helpful if I asked you some questions first," Friend replied with another smile.

"Okay, ask away."

Friend cast his eyes on me. His stare felt heavy, like there was a great amount of weight whenever he looked at something. He perused me for a moment then finally said, "So, I don't have to remind you to keep out of other people's business. It is all you can do to concentrate on your own fate, is it not?"

"Okay," I replied. "But are you trying to suggest that I should leave my grandchildren to their own fate? Should I just leave them here now and go? If I wanted to I could go to the sacred cave by traveling through the earth. Maybe I could teach them how to do that as well."

I turned to Spider and asked, "Could you help me teach them?"

Spider smiled at me and said, "The question is not whether I could help you. The question should be asked of your grandchildren as to whether they want to learn how to travel through the earth."

Rose snickered and said, "I'm sorry Grandfather, I really have no interest in learning how to do that. I ..."

She stopped herself from expressing her last thought. I became suspicious again.

"What?" I asked.

"Nothing, just leave it at that Grandfather."

She smiled at me.

I looked back to Friend.

He said, "I don't presume to tell you what to do Nexus, but I do suggest that you finish what you have started. Finish this foolishness with your grandchildren, but do try to avoid giving out advice to just anyone."

"What do you mean?"

"You tried to tell James Hope what he should do."

"Well, you should have seen him, he was pathetic."

"It doesn't matter what someone is going through, ultimately you can not help them. You tried when you were alive, which was useless. It was even more useless when you were dead and tried to help the living."

"Why?"

"It's harder for you to relate. How much do you have in common with the living? Your perspective changes greatly when you're dead."

"Well, what about you? You help me."

"I think we went through this already. I do not help you. I answer your questions, and if you are ready to change, you may. I just exist. I am myself. If you see something in how I exist, then your understanding may improve some aspect of your existence, and then maybe you'll change. That is all someone can do to initiate change."

"Okay. I think I understand."

Friend laughed. "We can only hope."

Spider scratched his head and sang, "Hmmm. Hmmm. Hmmm. I understand. I understand."

Then he did a series of cartwheels out of the room. He didn't come back. I wondered at his exit and where he could be off to now.

"Do not worry about Spider. He has his own agenda," Bill said.

Yes. What was it? What was Bill's? What was Friend's? And who was Friend? I wasn't any closer to that answer.

Friend started the conversation again by asking, "Since becoming involved with the committee, haven't you wondered what it is about? And just how they accomplished anything?"

"Yes, of course those things entered my thoughts."

"Well, do you have any ideas on the subject?" he continued.

"The Chairman is quite mad. I don't know how he has accomplished anything. I mean he seemed smart, but I can not understand anyone who would follow him willingly."

"He's not really mad. And he will accomplish his goal."

I looked at Friend like he was crazy.

"What??!!" I exclaimed.

"Eventually, he will storm the gates of heaven and set himself up as ruler.

"Did you not know that when you are dead you can do whatever you desire."

"But ..."

"But what? You find the Chairman's goal to be unreasonable. Just because it is not your goal does not mean that it has no worth. Eventually the Chairman will run out of energy. Even if he finds methods to replenish himself, the universe will eventually run out, and all will run out with it. When that happens the Chairman will dissipate and his consciousness will return to God. He is part of the whole and the whole will become larger with each additional sum."

"That doesn't make sense," I said confusedly.

"It makes perfect sense. You are limited only by your own imagination. How do you think the rods that the committee members have work?"

"I don't know."

"Of course you do, that's why they work. You tapped into the belief system of the committee. They believe that they can drain the energy of another consciousness, so it appears to work."

"What do you mean appears to work? They hurt you when they touch you with them."

"Pain was an added embellishment that you added. You seem to like things to hurt when applied to you. You're strange that way," Friend said.

"I am not!!"

"You can say what you like, but the evidence says otherwise."

"Okay, let's forget the pain part for a minute, what do you mean that, the rods only appear to work?"

"No one can destroy energy. Energy is eternal. So the energy of consciousness can not be destroyed. It can only be changed. Those whose energy is absorbed by the rods are not gone. They merely are in a different state. They have dissipated and are now with God. Not a horrible fate like you have imagined. Probably the pain you experienced when a rod touched you was your own resistance to joining God."

"I wouldn't resist that," I said meekly.

"Are you sure? You do have a big ego, you know."

Bill and Rose laughed at that statement. Friend just smiled.

I wasn't so sure what Friend was telling me. When I first met him, everything he told me sounded so awe inspiring. This was less so. I had a hard time accepting these latest bits of information.

"Again, you can believe what you want, the limits of your imagination are your only limits," Friend continued. "Just what do you think ascension is? It is a concept that your imagination has given meaning to."

"My friend Christopher Tims said that ascension is moving to a higher vibratory state. And when I saw Paul ascend, it was as if he had just disappeared. Is that what happened to Paul? He just vibrated away?"

"I'm afraid the problem is that there are limits to your imagination and language. So the description of what happened filtered through the limits of your language. The words ascension and vibration have a certain meaning to you. So what you witnessed filtered through those two words to give you meaning for the event. If you were vibrating with Paul, you would have understood because you would have been witness to the experience as Paul perceived it. But instead you were unable to perceive what was happening, so from your perspective Paul just ceased to be. "

"So just what is ascension anyway? As I understand it, ascension's just when ghosts disappear. "

Friend laughed. Again I had a strong feeling that I should know who he was, but I could not be sure who.

"Ascension is not much different than what I have already told you. I merely used concepts that I thought you could understand. Ascension is essentially choosing where you want your consciousness to reside. I called it joining to a higher consciousness. The ultimate ascension is joining with God. You can do it now or you can do it later. The universe is set up so that everything will do that eventually anyway. There is no escape from it. It all depends where you choose to be.

"You can join to a higher or a lower consciousness. Some make it a game, some take it as the most serious goal that there can be. The beauty is that you have free will. Your choices are no better or no worse than anyone else's. They are your choices and your choices alone. "

I took time to digest what Friend was saying. It seemed so simple yet I resisted the concepts. Was it as Cat, Spider and Friend had been saying all along, that I was having a hard time just letting go of my former existence?

Spider rolled into the room. He was holding onto his legs with his arms, making a loop with his body, and he rolled like a hoop. He jumped up and said, "Cat is currently defending the hole against two humans. There are more coming. He won't be able to defend it much longer, using Nexus' time frame. "

"What do you mean, using my time frame? " I asked.

Spider and Friend exchanged glances. I could almost here the words 'would you like to tell him?' and 'no you can do it, he likes you better anyway.'

They both looked at me and Friend spoke, "One thing that you haven't caught on to yet is how time works. You are still trapped by your bodily notion of what time is, even though you did escape that trap for brief periods."

"Is that why time has been behaving strangely?"

"Time doesn't behave strangely. You just have a strange notion of what time is, so when it doesn't behave how you believe it should behave, you call that strange."

"Why is my notion of time strange?"

"That's obvious, because it doesn't explain time."

"Huh?"

"Time is not linear as you believe. Time is a series of events in which all things exist.

"Let's say that there is a quantum moment for time. Each quantum moment is joined to others. The easiest route through time is to jump to the quantum moment next to the moment that you currently occupy. You choose the direction to jump.

"Here is the catch. Each moment is joined to an infinite number of other moments directly next to it. Usually a consciousness is joined to a higher consciousness, and it is the choice of the higher consciousness which determines the path through time. So the individual in that consciousness is usually unaware that there is a choice. This happens because disjointed travel through time is too confusing for a lower consciousness to be able to form thoughts."

I shook my head, not fully comprehending what Friend was saying.

"But any consciousness, at any time, can discover that it can jump. And it does, thus, seeming to opt out of the given time agreement. You can do it now. Cat will only continue to defend the hole as along as you cling to this current time frame."

"Wait, it's all too confusing to me. All I wanted to do was prevent my grandchildren from being destroyed by the committee. And from what you have just told me, it sounds like it doesn't matter."

"It matters as long as it is important to you."

"Okay, but we started this conversation on the premise that if I figure out who you are, you would be able to help me get out of the situation I am in. How has what you have told me helped me get to that point?"

"The information I have told you can be used to get out of your situation, if you could just expand your imagination. But I guess I really told you to prepare you for what I want to ask you now."

Rose started to giggle, then laugh.

She appeared to have her arm around someone, and be whispering to that same unseen someone.

Friend said loudly to me, "Pay attention. Remember I told you about the human consciousness and that there were two sub-consciousness parts, male and female?"

"Yes."

"Well, I want you to imagine an interaction between the two parts, what do you see?"

"I see two parts that don't understand each other," I replied.

"Why is that?"

"I don't know, if I knew that I probably would never had had any trouble with the female sex."

"Okay, here is what I want you to do. Use your imagination. Because there are no words that I can use to describe the interaction between the sexes that you will understand, I will resort to the use of a metaphor.

"Imagine that an interaction in the human consciousness has just occurred. Now at the quantum level of consciousness the event can be quantified as a complete event. Within that complete event are the male and female components. Now here comes the metaphor. Let's suppose that the complete event is the turning on and off of a flashlight. The entire event is the light traveling across a distance and illuminating some object. Now, within that quantum event are the two properties of waves and particles. Males as you remember are the particles, and females are the waves.

"So from the perspective of a particle, the male, he sees that event as straight forward. He traveled from the flashlight to the object on a straight path. Nothing complicated, he just went from point A to point B. Sometimes though, inspiration comes to him and he sees that entire event. He joined to the higher human consciousness and saw that event. Being a male he thinks 'I see the entire event and I can see the male component, therefore by subtracting the male event from the total event, I can see the remainder, which should be the female component.'

"Wrong. That is why most enlightened males think they understand females. They think of the female subconscious as a subtractable sub event of the whole. The only way for some males to understand the female component of an event is to immerse himself in the female consciousness, or the quantum wave component of the beam of light from our flashlight.

"Now for the female to understand the male, it is basically the same. The trap lying in wait for the female however, is that the quantum wave can encompass the whole event. Some females think that they can see the whole event because of this effect. The wave spreads out over the entire beam of light from our flashlight, occupying all the space within the event. It is not the whole event however, because it is missing the male component. Some make the claim that the female consciousness is the entire consciousness, because to the casual observer this appears to be true. But the quantum wave component of the beam of light is not the entire event, because there are quantum particles, representing the male component, traveling through the wave. So even though the wave appears to cover the entire event, it is missing the particles that are illuminating the object at the end of the event.

"So, ultimately the female must distinguish between the female sub-consciousness and the human consciousness, or to use our metaphor again, the wave from our light beam and our entire beam of light. But not many do because the female sub-consciousness is so much more encompassing of an event than the male sub-consciousness that few see the necessity to do so.

"In order for either sub-consciousness to understand the other, the first step is to see the entire consciousness.

"So, most males viewing the entire consciousness fail to make the step to see the female consciousness because their observation is that the female sub-consciousness is just the whole minus the male sub-consciousness. This is because the leap to the whole consciousness was so large for the male ... particles being only a small component of a light beam ... that he doesn't understand the subtle difference between the whole and the female component.

"Most females who make the subtle jump to the whole consciousness ... waves being everywhere within the beam of light ... do seem to understand the male sub-consciousness because they understand the differences between the whole and the female sub-consciousness. It's not that they subtract one from the other, it's that they can easily see what is not the female part and can be one with that other part more readily.

"This is the basic difference between male and females. *Do you understand Nexus*?"

"I think so," I said.

Spider howled with laughter. The rest joined in as well.

He said between laughing spasms, "Nexus ... you are ... one of the best ... at deceiving ... yourself."

I resented that remark.

"Well, I wouldn't want to interfere with your delusions, but I'm getting bored," Spider said after calming down a bit, "Maybe if he would stop ignoring the others who are here, we could bring this to a swifter conclusion."

Spider directed this last remark to Friend, who smiled in agreement.

"What do you mean?" I asked.

"He certainly has trouble understanding what others mean, doesn't he?" said Bill.

"I warned you about that," Spider said to Bill.

Spider looked at me, then looked at something beside Rose, then said, "Perhaps you shouldn't vibrate so fast. In spite of what we have been trying to tell your father, he just doesn't seem to get it."

Father? What was Spider talking about.

"That's better," Spider said.

Slowly I began to see what Spider was talking about. Beside Rose I saw a spirit standing with one arm around her. He gradually came into focus, and I recognized him as my son. Rose's father. I understood now what she had been doing all this time.

Spider said to me, "Nexus, your children are here. They've partially descended for you."

They came running to me and we hugged.

Mary and Daniel came to their mother and they hugged too.

I had tears in my eyes. It had been a long time since I had seen them. I had many questions that I wanted to ask them, but especially my son. How did his quest to find his mother go?

"Hi Dad."

I could barely speak, "Hi."

"I know you are wondering about Mom. I told you I would find her and bring her back. I knew you would come to this place, so we waited for you here."

I waited with silent anticipation at what he would say next.

"Yes, she is here."

I looked all around, but I could not see her. I thought that maybe she was still vibrating too high for me to see. I turned to Spider.

He shook his head. He looked ready to explode with laughter.

"She's right here."

He was pointing, but for some reason I couldn't tell exactly where.

"Here Dad, right here," my son said.

He was pointing at Friend. Friend smiled. I fell into the depths of that smile. I could see it as an event. Within that event there were two components, one male and the other … female.

My wife magically appeared where Friend had once been.

I stood in utter amazement. Friend was my wife?

Spider exploded. He couldn't contain his laughter any longer and it had a contagious effect on the others. Most rolled on the floor with Spider in the utmost state of euphoria.

Nothing could contain them.

I, on the other hand, no longer heard their laughter. I could only see and hear my wife. She smiled at me. I could remember every instance when that smile had been directed at me. How could I be so stupid? No one else had such a smile. That was why I felt so much warmth whenever Friend smiled at me. Friend *was* my wife.

I didn't know how to feel. I had an overriding joy at seeing her again. I felt the loneliness of forty years that tore my heart each time I looked and she wasn't there. I felt the guilt of a father who took his children from their mother.

I wanted to hide, I felt so conspicuous, it hurt.

She took a step closer to me and extended her hand ever so gently.

I looked at her hand for a long time. I had forgotten how beautiful her hands were.

I took her hand in mine and felt the pleasure of her touch once again.

I looked up into her eyes. She looked into mine, and I saw the depths that had always eluded me. I saw the truth. Why I had loved this woman, and why I always loved her. And why I loved her now.

The light within her shone. It was the purest light I had ever experienced.

I embraced her with all my strength.

I cried. Tears from the heart. Tears of joy, sadness and regret. But mostly tears of pure love.

I cried in her arms and she held me and comforted me.

In the background the others had started an impromptu dance.

"I feel ... I feel so foolish," I said

"That's the first thing you can think of to say to me after forty years?" she replied.

"No ... I mean ... I feel like an idiot."

"Well, we always knew that."

She laughed.

"I missed you," I said.

"Well, you're getting closer."

"What can I say? I regret my actions, I was wrong? To say that would mean that all I had done for the past forty years was wrong. Didn't I do a good job raising our grandchildren?"

"You did what you had to do. It doesn't me an that I have to approve. I lived my life the way I chose, as did you. I could only live in the civilized world. I died when it died. But I am not interested in rehashing old arguments. I am more interested in hearing *how much* you missed me."

It was my turn to laugh. I had expected that the next time I met my wife I would be dragged over burning coals. I knew what she wanted to hear.

"I missed you more than the moon, more than the oceans, more than the mountains."

"Uh huh?" she said skeptically.

"I missed you more than the earth beneath my feet."

"That little I see," she said sarcastically.

I picked her up. She was as light as a feather. I swung her around and spiraled her into my body so that our lips met the moment our bodies touched. I kissed her to the applause of the others. Spider broke out into some silly song about a baker who accidentally baked his true love into a pie and the story of his search for her after he died.

"How was that?" I said.

"Adequate," she replied.

It was a game we always played, I retaliated the only way I could, by tickling her.

Having missed it for so long, I enjoyed our game immensely.

My wife sighed, "I'm afraid that we have come to the end though."

"What do you mean? What end? We're just getting started," I said frantically.

"It all has to do with choices. You have made yours, and I have made mine. Now it is time to finish what you have started. You chose a long time ago to create a legacy. You gave our grandchildren a world to live in. Other people's grandchildren died or were never born. You're well on your way to accomplishing your goals."

"On my way?"

"Yes. We have grandchildren and great-grandchildren alive now, but for how long? The planet is becoming increasingly hostile. Soon the level of radiation will prevent human life from existing on this planet."

"How can I correct that?" I asked.

"That's not my problem. I'll leave that to you."

My wife looked hard at me before continuing, "There is one other here with us you should meet."

"Who?" I asked eagerly.

"I think you should ask your daughter to introduce her."

I looked to her and waited.

I heard her say, "Don't be shy. Come join us."

Slowly a small spirit appeared. It was a child. She couldn't have been older than six when she died. She was beautiful. I didn't recognize her, but she did remind me somewhat of Melissa when she was young.

I looked at my daughter inquisitively. I had no idea who she was. My daughter was silent. I looked back to my wife. She had a small scowl on her face. The scowl I knew from experience meant there was something important happening here and I should figure it out soon.

"Hello," I said to the girl.

"Hello," she answered shyly.

Her voice was melodious. For some reason a tear came to each of my eyes. I was reluctant to ask her another question. It was as if I feared to know the answer. After a moment I found my voice and asked cautiously, "What is your name?"

She answered with no hesitation, "Lolita."

She followed her answer with a small giggle.

That simple answer brought me to a complete stop. If I was alive, my heart would have broken. I was shocked. If this was the Lolita I thought it was ...

I looked quickly to my wife. She nodded her head once. I looked at my daughter and she said, "Yes, this is my first grandchild."

I fell to my knees in front of Lolita. Tears were now flowing freely from my eyes.

I quietly said to her, "How?"

"How, what Great-Grandfather?" she said then tilted her head.

"How did you die child?"

"I got sick. I got very hot and fell asleep.

"Then I found myself with Grandmother and Great-Grandmother."

My hands started to tremble. I felt old.

Older than I had ever felt. I reached out to Lolita and put my hands on her shoulders. She smiled at me.

I was devastated. I had devoted my whole life to the birth of this child. The joy that I had felt at being reunited with my family was gone. My life was laid bare before me. I closed my eyes and wept.

I felt her small hand on mine and her gentle voice ask, "What's wrong, Great-Grandfather? My uncle Bobby always told me to tell him why I was crying. He said that it doesn't hurt as much if you share your feelings with someone else."

She looked worried.

But hearing these words from Lolita made me want to laugh. I had used these same words to a crying Bobby when he was about six years old.

I smiled at her. The look of worry that had crept over her young face vanished. She returned my smile. I hugged her and said, "Why … why … why?" quietly over and over again.

"I came to tell you something Great-Grandfather."

I stood up and held Lolita in my arms. I felt youthful again.

"What is it little one?"

She put on a most serious face and said, "The end is near the beginning."

"What?" I asked.

She repeated herself, "The end is near the beginning."

I shook my head and said, "I don't understand."

Lolita became agitated.

"Great-Grandfather, the end is near the beginning!"

I didn't know what she meant, and I couldn't think of anything to say to her.

"Do not fret Lolita, your great-grandfather doesn't understand you because of his dual nature. Part of him understands, so be content, your message was delivered," my wife said to her.

Lolita smiled again. I put her back on the ground, and she hugged her great-grandmother.

"Why is he like that?" Lolita asked my wife.

My wife crouched down in front of her and said, "The part of him that doesn't understand is not here with us fully. That is his choice for some reason. Part of him is in another place. That is why he appears stupid to us. If he chose to be here totally, he would understand fully what you have told him. Does that explain it for you?"

"I think so," she replied.

"Well, I'm glad she understood. Now will someone please explain it to me." I said

A chorus of laughter broke out at my expense. But when the laughter died down no one offered an explanation. I stood perplexed.

Spider stepped forward and said, "Cat needs help. He is greatly outnumbered and will only last a few more minutes."

My wife quickly replied, "We had better be going then."

"Wait," I said.

"No time for any more questions. We will have to talk on the surface."

"But I thought if I figured out who you were my problems would be solved."

My words were not heard, or they were ignored. Everyone started running toward the entrance to the burrow. I stood for a moment, contemplating. What was going on? I wasn't sure, but I knew that the thought of not seeing my wife again was too much for me. Whatever happened I would never leave her again. Also the riddle that Lolita gave me burned in my head. The end is near the beginning?

I ran after the others, but I didn't catch up to them until the entrance.

I was alarmed by what I saw.

18

CHOICES

I saw Cat jumping back and forth over the top of the hole. He was fighting off many opponents. But he steadfastly refused to leave the entrance to the burrow unguarded.

This was what I had expected. What alarmed me was the fact that just before my wife left the entrance to the burrow she burst into a magnificent light. It was as if all her energy was being devoted to the creation of this light. I felt a fear that if she kept on shining as she did she would use up all her energy, and she would fade into nothing. All the energy to sustain her consciousness would be gone. She would cease to exist.

I ran to catch up to everyone. They exited the hole just ahead of me.

I caught up to her and yelled, "What are you doing?"

"Giving you a bit more time," she replied.

"Won't you cease to exist?"

"Yes," she said calmly.

"Stop it." I shouted angrily.

"Well hurry up and make up your mind as to what you are going to do."

I scanned my surroundings. Cat was busy fighting six humans. But now that he no longer had to defend the hole, he had taken the offensive. I was amazed. He had grown to the size of a small lion, and in spite of the fact that he had several wounds that were bleeding profusely, he wasn't having any problem defeating his opponents. One after the other fell after being struck by Cat's claws. Soon there would be no humans left alive.

What was disturbing was the fact that we were surrounded by thousands of committee members, interspersed with hundreds of the tall demons.

They were all standing in a huge circle around us. Those in front were hiding their eyes. The light coming from my wife was painful to them, and they would not approach any closer even though they were being pushed from behind.

"What should I do?" I yelled to my wife.

"Well, if you are asking me what to do, I already told you that I can not help you."

She then smiled wryly and continued, "The problem you've been having up until now is that you haven't been asking the right questions. If you ever asked the right question the right answer would become obvious."

I was extremely upset by my wife's actions. It felt as if she were committing suicide. But contributing to my discomfort was the sight of so many demons so close. Of course, I tried not to let on that that was part of the problem.

My wife looked at me for a moment then started to talk, but not fast enough for me, "You have many choices. All you have to do is think of them."

"Okay. Let me see. We're about to be overrun by the hordes of the committee. I'd already dismissed this choice, but I guess I could join the committee. Do what the chairman wants, and the rest of you could go free."

"Well, it is a choice. The chairman will stop his attacks on you and the grandchildren, and you will have saved them from a horrible fate."

"You're making fun of me aren't you?" I said suspiciously.

But at that moment I had a vision of me shaking hands with the chairman. I joined the committee, and I participated in drills with the committee's army.

The vision continued. We trained for years. Our energy was replenished from other unfortunate spirits. Finally, after many years, the number of spirits in the committee numbered millions. Energy was everywhere.

Many sets of stairs appeared in the field in front of the chairman's home. We ran up these endless stairs until we came to a gate. There was only one spirit in front of the gate. Many committee members fell with the wave of this spirit's hand.

But the hordes that followed overwhelmed this spirit and we poured through the gate.

There was an army on the other side of the gate. The two armies crashed like two mighty waves coming together.

No one could stand in my way. I cut down spirit after spirit. I hacked millions with my sword. I grew weary of the endless battle. There seemed no end to it.

Finally I saw a castle in the distance. It was beautiful. I knew that was where I wanted to go. I led a charge towards the castle, not caring if any followed me. I forgot about the chairman and anything that he wanted. I just wanted to be inside that castle. None would stop me from getting there.

I hacked and hewed my way through bodies to the castle walls. Ladders appeared from the committee members. We scaled the walls. The defense was fierce, but I helped to clear a path on the top of the wall. I saw a second wall inside with towers so beautiful, that I felt pain that I was not touching them. I made my way through a door that led to a tunnel to the second wall. There was but one defender. An enormous toad. Without hesitation I attacked. Nothing was going to prevent me from getting to those towers.

The toad watched my approach. When I was near, it unleashed its enormous tongue and ensnared me in it. I struck at the tongue that now held me. My sword merely bounced off its surface. I watched in horror as the toad opened its huge mouth, the darkness within absolute. Slowly the toad brought its tongue back into its mouth, bringing me with it.

The darkness encompassed my entire vision. I heard a faint cry 'Nexus, Nexus,' coming from some distant point. Suddenly I heard someone shouting, "CLAUDE!!!"

At the sound of my old name I saw the source of the voice.

I was back in front of the buildings that held the committee. The committee members all around. My wife was standing in front of me.

She said, "You're back. You certainly get carried away. I thought you were in a hurry. What do you think of your first choice?"

"It was horrible. No. I will never join the committee."

"I told you not to judge them. They are doing what they are doing. But fine. You have made a choice. Strike number one from the list.

"Can you think of any other choices? Keeping in mind that I will not fight. So if you are to stop my energy from expiring you will have to leave this protective circle and defeat all of the committee before my energy runs out."

"I guess I could choose to fight."

"If that is your choice, I recommend that you make up your mind quick, and get working at it right away. "

I gripped my sword tighter and looked at the horde that was watching my every move.

Again I went into a vision. I saw myself raising my sword and charging into the ranks of the committee. Bill, Rose and the other youngsters ran happily after me. Spider was busy picking up rocks and slinging them over our heads, causing holes to appear among the ranks. Cat and Lolita stayed with my wife. Cat licked his wounds, seeming quite content to watch my gross stupidity, as he would call it. Lolita watched with wide eyes while holding onto my wife's hand.

At first my only opponents were the ordinary spirits of the committee. I dispatched spirit after spirit with each swing of my sword. Bill and Rose were fighting gleefully by my side. The rest formed a loose circle at my rear, preventing us from being overwhelmed. But as the ranks of ordinary spirits were thinning, the demon-like spirits soon began arriving. They were no push over. They were exceedingly quick. I battled my fear as well as these demons.

I swung at the first to arrive. He ducked and jumped at me. I gave way, trying to bring my sword down onto his back. He knocked me over and grabbed me with one of his enormous hands. Fortunately, my sword albeit weakly came down on the demon's back. He exploded into multicolored pyrotechnics. I was singed by the release of energy which was not compatible with mine.

Two more demons leapt at me while I was still on the ground. Again fortune smiled on me, because they got in each other's way. I quickly rolled to one side, wildly slashing back at the spot I just occupied. They both landed on my swords' edge, again causing an explosion of light and sound.

I jumped up to see Bill being held by two of the demons. I lunged and hacked at one of them. He exploded.

I turned and saw Rose in a strength contest with another demon.

James and Matthew had been struck many times by rods, and were fading.

My children, who had swords of their own were shouting in delight. They were fighting like demons themselves. No one seemed to be able to hit my children.

Daniel however, had four demons holding him. One pulled too hard and yanked off one of his arms. I last saw him disappearing beneath a mob of spirits.

Mary was still free, but she had somehow been isolated from the rest of us and was completely surrounded. Only the quick rock throwing of Spider kept her from being overwhelmed. Her mother charged the demons in her direction in an attempt to help her.

I struck at the demons holding Bill and Rose, then dispatched two more before I noticed that the light was fading.

My son made a sudden charge into the crowd and a clear path opened back to my wife. I saw her light fading. The multitudes that had been kept at bay by her light ran forward. Cat jumped at an advancing demon, tearing at his face, and felled him. I lost sight of him as hundreds ran by towards my wife. Her light was almost out when the first demon lunged at her.

Spider threw a rock at this demon, and it exploded. But no more rocks could he spare to help others because he, too, was completely surrounded.

I saw some demons reach my wife. One grabbed Lolita from my wife's arm and Lolita screamed as he ran away with her.

I tried to run towards them. But two large hands grabbed me from behind and held me in a bear hug, pinning my arms. The demon holding and squeezing me held me up above the crowd. I saw the last of my wife's light go out as she was struck by one gatherer's rod.

I screamed, "Nooooo!!!!"

Suddenly I heard a shout in my ear, "CLAUDE!!!"

I was back beside my glowing wife. She was looking at me curiously. I was panting heavily.

"You really do get carried away, don't you?" she said.

I could only nod my head in the affirmative.

"You know, it doesn't really matter what you choose to do. The end result will always be the same," she continued.

I looked at her in disbelief and said, "I really don't care for that option."

"No wait. This is important. You seem to be very attached to an outcome that you think should happen. You're looking for some miracle, where we're all transported to some other location and we all exist happily ever after. I've made my choices already.

"I'm just telling you now that your choice doesn't have to involve what you expect," she said.

I shuddered. After the visionary experience of my first two choices, I had trouble imagining any others.

"Claude, listen, I'm not as attached to the outcome as you are. Don't worry about me. I'm fine. I can make my own decisions with regard to my own fate.

"As for you, in each of your first two choices, your energy would have been dissipated. You're really attached to your human form, that's why you chose the name of Nexus for yourself. But if you lose your form, it is no big deal. The consciousness that is you will cease, but not the energy that was you or was touched by you.

These pieces will spread across the universe and from it new consciousnesses will arise. Each having benefited from being part of you.

"I will love each of these pieces as much as I love you."

The warmth from her smile washed over me.

"Remember, I will not fight. I think it a waste of time because it really doesn't matter. Do you understand?" she said emphatically.

I shook my head, no.

"I guess you don't understand. Oh well, you will just have to think of something else."

"What? What else is there?"

"I already told you. I can't really help you. The answer has to come from you."

"Well, I guess I could try to ascend. I mean, you, Spider and Cat have been telling me all along that it something I should be doing."

I had said this as a sort of joke, because I had no real intention of leaving. I would never leave friends and family in a tight situation like this.

"You could ascend if you want ..." she said.

"I thought you said there was no existing happily ever after."

"I said that there was no choice where we *all* exist happily ever after. I didn't say that *you* couldn't though."

"How could I be happy if I left everyone here, while I left to go to some paradise?"

"How do you know unless you go?" she replied.

Suddenly the sky opened up. Light came pouring down. It felt alive. The touch of it was more pleasurable than my entire existence up until now. One millisecond within its presence was worth more than the sum of my entire existence. The light was overwhelming. I wished nothing more than to go to its source.

I said, "It's beautiful."

My wife replied, "Go if you want."

Spider and Bill shook their heads yes. Rose and my children smiled at me. Cat ignored me. Daniel, Mary, James and Matthew seemed puzzled, as if I had already disappeared.

I started to fly. My will carried me up to the source of that magnificent light. With ever quickening speed I moved towards the light. As I got closer, my perception changed. Time moved more slowly. So in spite of the fact that I was moving at ever increasing speeds, my view of things improved so much that every microsecond felt like an hour.

I looked around. I was covered in a pure white light. I saw others that were also moving towards the light. Their faces were the epitome of joy. They ignored everything around them and stared intently at the light, except for one. He was staring at me. He was slightly ahead of me, looking back, he was beckoning me on.

Paul!!! It was Paul. He smiled when I recognized him.

Paul waited for me. I looked at the source once again. Tears came to my eyes.

Again I looked at those around me. I wished that my friends and family could be here, but especially I felt the absence of my wife. I wanted her to be here. But more than that need I wanted to find the source of the light.

A small part of me wished to be with my wife, but I was powerless to change course. The light drew me like a small pebble being attracted to a large planet. No matter what I wished I would fall into the planet and willingly be incorporated into the larger mass.

I cried now for two reasons. I cried for the sheer joy I felt, but I cried as well for the fact that I would soon be totally lost and never again experience, in the same way, the existence I once had.

It would only be a matter of moments before I would fall into the light source.

I held myself, wrapping my arms about myself, bracing for the imminent collision.

I felt a strange bulge in one of my pockets. I stuck my hand in to find out what it could be and to my surprise, it was a rock. It was black. The blackness of the rock could not be illuminated by the light. I saw in it a rock spirit looking out at me. The rock opened as if it had hinges. The black inside looked inviting. It reminded me of all that I knew.

I was me again. I could forget about the light if I chose. I was still hurtling towards its source. But I concentrated on the black void inside the rock. Either the rock grew or I shrunk. I then found myself inside the rock. I could control where I wanted to be. I wished with all my heart to be back with my wife.

The light was beautiful, but the thought of being there without my wife was too much for me.

I found myself coming out of a black tunnel to a light source. The light came from my wife, and to me that light was just as beautiful as the heavenly light that I experienced. I remembered that the light from my wife would not last forever, not like the eternal light that I knew was all around us.

"I take it you didn't like that choice?" my wife said.

I blinked at her. The memory of the light still filled me.

"No, I liked it, but ... "

"But you are still attached to saving everyone, aren't you?"

Spider laughed, then said, "If you like my rock, keep it, I have plenty more."

I felt my pocket and felt the same bulge. The rock was still there.

Spider laughed some more.

Spider's laugh brought me back. I remembered my situation.

I asked my wife, "I can't think of anything else, can't you help me?"

"No, not really. I guess you're going to run out of time," she replied.

"Time. I wish I could go back and make some changes. Maybe none of this would have happened."

"You didn't listen to me when I explained to you about time, did you? Time is about consciousness. You exist where you choose to be. Choices influence the flow of time. You can go back any time you want."

"Go back? What do you mean?"

"Go back to a time before the bad times, and make different choices. Create a new reality. That way you can save your grandchildren and give them a world to live in."

"Wait a minute. If you haven't forgotten, I'm dead, and besides I'm just one spirit. What possible impact could I have? Wait don't tell me, I could appear before people and say 'I'm on a mission from God,' and then they would jump and save the planet. If I remember correctly, the rest of the world tried to stop the Russian civil war and failed, and what could anybody possibly do to stop the plagues that ravaged the world?"

I realized that I had started to rant and I stopped talking. I was disappointed with my choices up until now.

"Are you finished?" my wife asked.

"Yes, but isn't there another choice?"

"There are many others. In fact there are infinite choices.

"But you're not thinking clearly, and you may not have the vision to see any more."

"Why not?" I asked.

"You're limited by your own imagination. You can only make choices based on what you understand."

"Well, I'm not so sure I understand the last choice."

"Claude, you have the habit of filling in the words for others before they have finished saying what they wanted to say. If you will just listen, I can tell you about your last option."

"Okay, I'm sorry," I said to her.

"Remember what I told you about time?"

"Yes, but I didn't say I fully understood it."

My wife waited for me to stop talking again, then continued, "I told you that you can disjoint yourself from your current time frame and jump back to another."

"How can I do that?"

"Merely concentrate on where your consciousness was, instead of where it is now."

"What?"

"Your existence is not linear. You merely chose to experience it that way. If you so chose, you can concentrate on any part of your existence and be there. Remember, there are an infinite amount of quantum time units beside any moment. The path that you take through time depends on your choices."

"But what good would it do for me to go back? Are you telling me it is possible to change the past? And how can I do anything if I'm dead."

"If you had been listening, you would have heard me saying that there is no past or future, there is only consciousness and where you chose to be. If you go back, to use a concept that you understand, then you will be alive, because you will be concentrating on the part of your existence when you *were* alive."

I had to stop and think for a moment. I was just realizing that I had an opportunity to rewrite my life. I could go back to a time back before the bad times, when I was with my wife and children. I didn't have to leave my wife.

My heart sank with the thought I would probably just die with her. We would have no surviving grandchildren. The existence I already experienced would be for nothing.

"What good would it do?" I said.

"Take all your experience of a full existence back with you. Remember what I told you. Join with the higher human consciousness. Remember that it is the higher human consciousness that determines the path of all human spirits through time. Once you have joined with the human consciousness, speak your message. Explain that if things don't change, this is the future that will unfold. The planet will become hostile to life and the human race will die out.

"Teach others who will listen how to join to the higher consciousness. When enough voices issue the same message, change is possible."

At that moment my wife closed her eyes. Her light began to fade. The committee members surrounding us grumbled and moved forward.

She opened her eyes and the light shone full again.

For some reason tears started to come to my eyes. I looked deep into the eyes of my wife. I moved closer to her and kissed her. She looked at me, but said nothing. Her very essence was disappearing.

I started to panic. I felt a hand on my shoulder. It was Spider.

He said to me, "Well, you've already thought of four choices. Chose one. All of them are fun."

Rose added, "Grandfather, now is the time. You can't delay any longer."

I turned to look at my wife. I would keep my eyes on her from now on, no matter what else happened. She was using all her energy in the production of her light. Talking would take away from that, and her light would go out.

I continued to talk to Spider while looking at her.

"I do not know how to initiate my last option."

"Sure you do," Spider said, "It is an innate ability. Use your imagination."

Lolita, who had been quiet up until now, said, "Great-Grandfather, the end is near the beginning."

At that moment I saw a scene from my past. A door appeared beside me and I could see back to the past. I saw myself lying asleep in a bed. I recognized it as a place I used to live before the bad times. I understood what Lolita was trying to say to me. I smiled at her, and she knew that I now understood.

I looked at the door and then to my wife. I did not want to leave her like this. Nor did I want to leave the others, surrounded by the committee, with no hope of escape.

Bill said, "Be practical Nexus, you only have moments left, make a choice."

Cat added in, "Nexus, therrre is one otherrr choice that nobody mentioned."

"What?" I said.

"Do nothing, that's what yourrr doing rrright now. Is that yourrr choice?"

"No."

"Then it's time to chose," Spider said.

My wife was nothing but a wisp, barely visible. The door to the past was also fading.

I looked at my wife and said, "I love you."

She nodded and smiled at me.

Just before the last of her energy was gone, I leapt through the door to the past.

19

THE PAST

"Claude!! Claude !!"

I opened my eyes. I saw a ceiling. I was lying in the bed I had seen in my vision.

"Claude, when are you getting up? We'll be late. I told you we had to get up early."

I jumped out of bed. I stared at my hands. I was young again. I felt the vigor flow through my live body.

I looked to the source of the voice talking to me. It was her.

"Claude are you okay?" my wife asked.

"Okay?"

I began to laugh like a mad man.

My wife gave me a strange look.

I jumped at her. Picked her up and kissed her passionately.

At first she was confused, then she returned my kiss.

She pushed me away and I let her down.

"It's too late for that, you had your chance last night."

"Last night?"

"Yes, last night. We were just starting to get romantic, *and you fell asleep!*"

I laughed.

She said, "Oh, you find that funny do you?"

I couldn't find words to answer. I just stared at her. I had missed her so, and now here she was.

She looked at me seriously and said, "Are you feeling okay? Did you have a bad dream or something?"

I grinned widely ... yes dream ... a dream of future's past.

"Yes, I had a dream."

I realized that the other place where I was, was here. I was both in the future and here, simultaneously. But the person who I was, couldn't fully comprehend the concept of choosing to place my consciousness wherever I wanted, or that time could not restrict my choice. So the best I could do was to dream about the future, and place my limited dreaming consciousness with my future self. That was why I was so stupid when I was there. I now realize that if I so chose, I could place my entire consciousness with my future self.

But that would be counter-productive at this point. I had come back to change things.

While I had been standing and thinking, my wife moved closer to the bed, picked something up, and said, "What's this rock doing in our bed?"

I muttered quietly, "Spider?!"

My wife said, "What?"

I hugged my wife again and said, "Nothing. It's only a dream."

She looked puzzled.

I laughed then said, "I think I'll have to write it down ... a book."

I stared at a far away, distant point, and heard voices from a probable future.

Then said, "Yes, a book."

Epilogue

It is impossible for me to say whether the events from that night I fell asleep early were a dream, or my experience from the future was real. I do know however, that in my life, when I join to a higher consciousness, I do seem to know more, and I do see the world as if I were older and wiser. And when I lose the connection to a higher consciousness, my world does seem a lot smaller, and I feel as if a part of me is gone.

However, I do not wish to offend anyone who believes that the name of Grandfather needs to be earned, and believe that I have taken the title before my time. Believe me, I can wait. I will relish the time that I have between now and then. And maybe if I earn that title, I will live up to that honor.

The message that I would like to leave to the readers of this book is that there is hope for all of us. Never give up hope. Life is a gift to be appreciated and not wasted. Use every moment as if it were your last.

Also I hope that I have sparked a curiosity in your heart for you to want to find your connection to a higher consciousness. Follow your heart and listen. You, too, will find your path. There are infinite choices out there. All it takes is to start making some of them.

Lastly, I wish to thank you. I appreciated the opportunity to have shared my story with you.